THE MARQUESS' QUEST FOR LOVE

The Strongs of Shadowcrest
Book Six

Alexa Aston

ARE YOU SIGNED UP FOR DRAGONBLADE'S BLOG?

You'll get the latest news and information on exclusive giveaways, exclusive excerpts, coming releases, sales, free books, cover reveals and more.

Check out our complete list of authors, too

No spam, no junk. That's a promise!

Sign Up Here

www.dragonbladepublishing.com

Dearest Reader;

Thank you for your support of a small press. At Dragonblade Publishing, we strive to bring you the highest quality Historical Romance from some of the best authors in the business. Without your support, there is no 'us', so we sincerely hope you adore these stories and find some new favorite authors along the way.

Happy Reading!

CEO, Dragonblade Publishing

Additional Dragonblade books by Author Alexa Aston

The Strongs of Shadowcrest Series
The Duke's Unexpected Love (Book 1)
The Perks of Loving a Viscount (Book 2)
Falling for the Marquess (Book 3)
The Captain and the Duchess (Book 4)
Courtship at Shadowcrest (Book 5)
The Marquess' Quest for Love (Book 6)

Suddenly a Duke Series
Portrait of the Duke (Book 1)
Music for the Duke (Book 2)
Polishing the Duke (Book 3)
Designs on the Duke (Book 4)
Fashioning the Duke (Book 5)
Love Blooms with the Duke (Book 6)
Training the Duke (Book 7)
Investigating the Duke (Book 8)

Second Sons of London Series
Educated By The Earl (Book 1)
Debating With The Duke (Book 2)
Empowered By The Earl (Book 3)
Made for the Marquess (Book 4)
Dubious about the Duke (Book 5)
Valued by the Viscount (Book 6)
Meant for the Marquess (Book 7)

Dukes Done Wrong Series
Discouraging the Duke (Book 1)
Deflecting the Duke (Book 2)
Disrupting the Duke (Book 3)

Delighting the Duke (Book 4)
Destiny with a Duke (Book 5)

Dukes of Distinction Series
Duke of Renown (Book 1)
Duke of Charm (Book 2)
Duke of Disrepute (Book 3)
Duke of Arrogance (Book 4)
Duke of Honor (Book 5)
The Duke That I Want (Book 6)

The St. Clairs Series
Devoted to the Duke (Book 1)
Midnight with the Marquess (Book 2)
Embracing the Earl (Book 3)
Defending the Duke (Book 4)
Suddenly a St. Clair (Book 5)
Starlight Night (Novella)
The Twelve Days of Love (Novella)

Soldiers & Soulmates Series
To Heal an Earl (Book 1)
To Tame a Rogue (Book 2)
To Trust a Duke (Book 3)
To Save a Love (Book 4)
To Win a Widow (Book 5)
Yuletide at Gillingham (Novella)

King's Cousins Series
The Pawn (Book 1)
The Heir (Book 2)
The Bastard (Book 3)

Medieval Runaway Wives
Song of the Heart (Book 1)
A Promise of Tomorrow (Book 2)
Destined for Love (Book 3)

Knights of Honor Series

Word of Honor (Book 1)
Marked by Honor (Book 2)
Code of Honor (Book 3)
Journey to Honor (Book 4)
Heart of Honor (Book 5)
Bold in Honor (Book 6)
Love and Honor (Book 7)
Gift of Honor (Book 8)
Path to Honor (Book 9)
Return to Honor (Book 10)

The Lyon's Den Series
The Lyon's Lady Love

Pirates of Britannia Series
God of the Seas

De Wolfe Pack: The Series
Rise of de Wolfe

The de Wolfes of Esterley Castle
Diana
Derek
Thea

Also from Alexa Aston
The Bridge to Love (Novella)
One Magic Night

PROLOGUE

Bridgefield, Kent—1 September 1803

ON THE MORNING of his birthday, Byron Balfour awoke with a splitting headache, regretting the amount of ale he had drunk at the village tavern last night. He had never been one to drink to excess. Then again, he was now only eight and ten years of age. That was what university was supposedly for. At least, according to his older brother Dawson, who had recently graduated from Cambridge this past spring.

He had not seen Dawson all summer. His brother had gone straight from university to their family's London townhouse, where he joined their parents for the remainder of the Season. Having just completed his education at Eton, Byron had yet to partake in the social scene in town and would not do so until after university.

He would be leaving in two weeks for Cambridge and was excited at the educational opportunities which lay ahead, having always been drawn to subjects such as history and maths. Dawson had insisted that Byron rent the same rooms he had, and the family solicitor had made those arrangements. His brother had written to him, saying he'd left an assortment of books and furniture, along with hints for how to get along with difficult dons. A list also awaited of Dawson's favorite places to dine and which foods he recommended.

Byron idolized Dawson, who was four years his senior. His brother had taught him everything a boy needed to know to become a man. How to ride and hunt. How to fish and swim. Dawson had even taught him how to read. They had shared a bedchamber during their early years, and after they were supposed to be in bed fast asleep, Dawson would either read stories of adventure to Byron or simply make up ones off the top of his head. He wanted nothing more to be than the kind of man his brother was. Caring. Sympathetic. Intelligent. Honorable.

As the older Balfour son, his brother currently held the courtesy title of Earl of Linden and one day would inherit their father's title of Marquess of Bridgewater. Since Byron would not inherit anything, he was destined for a career in the military, as many second sons pursued. While their father had been perfectly willing to buy Byron's commission and ship him off to war upon his graduation from Eton, it was Dawson who insisted that his younger brother receive the same university education he himself had, telling the marquess that it would make Byron a better officer and give him a few years to mature in order that he might be more inspiring to the men he would lead into battle.

As always, Father bowed to his heir apparent's wishes, for which Byron had been grateful. While he had grown up knowing he was meant for the army, to think of taking on that mantle of leadership at such a tender age had frightened him. While he possessed intelligence, combined with common sense, he knew he needed time to continue to mature physically and emotionally. Gratitude had filled him when Dawson fought for those extra years to give him a chance to become the man Byron hoped he could be, as well as the luxury of a university education, before his commission was purchased.

He rang for a servant and requested both hot and cold water, the hot to wash with and the cold to dunk his head into, hoping the headache would abate when he did so. Once dressed and shaved, he made his way downstairs to breakfast, where he found his father dining with Lord Hampton.

Viscount Hampton owned the estate next to Bridgefield, and he and Byron's father had been the best of friends since boyhood, attending both Eton and Cambridge together. Even as adults, they spent much of their time in the country together, as well as at events in town during the Season.

Mama was not fond of Lady Hampton. Byron had once overheard Mama telling a friend that Lady Hampton was the most disagreeable person she had ever encountered. He concurred with his mother. Lady Hampton was extremely unpleasant to be around. She treated servants rudely and was dismissive of many others. Still, the two women were expected to keep company with one another because their husbands were such dear friends. He felt sorry for Mama and supposed she was breakfasting in her room as usual.

"Ah, come in, Byron," his father said. "Lord Hampton has joined us for breakfast this morning."

He went and shook hands with the viscount. "It is always good to see you, my lord."

Taking a seat, he told the footman he would like coffee. While he did not like the taste of the brew, it was much stronger than tea, and he hoped it would help clear the fogginess and help the pounding in his head.

It did not surprise him that his father did not wish Byron a happy birthday. Though he yearned for his parent's love—and would have settled for his respect—the Marquess of Bridgewater had little use for his younger son. All his attention had gone toward Dawson. Byron had never been jealous of his older brother, understanding both their roles within the family. Instead of aspiring to be like his father, he had always wanted to be more like his brother.

He ate in silence, listening to the two men talk about various acquaintances and things that had occurred during the Season. Byron only wished Dawson had come home to Bridgefield when his parents had. Instead, his brother had accepted an invitation to a house party at Season's end. He hoped they would have at least some time to spend together before he left for Cambridge.

Suddenly, Dawson appeared in the breakfast room, immaculately turned out as always, a broad smile on his face.

"Good morning," Dawson said cheerfully. "Especially to you, Lord Hampton. It is good to see you at Bridgefield this morning."

Pleasantries were exchanged as Dawson took his seat and accepted coffee from a footman.

"Did your house party already end?" Byron asked.

"It did," his brother replied. "Two betrothals were announced at its conclusion. I have come to gather that is the sole purpose of holding a house party."

He saw his father and Lord Hampton exchange glances, but neither man spoke.

"What exactly is it that you do at a house party?" he asked, curious, especially since he doubted he would ever be asked to attend one.

"It is an excuse for bringing eligible men together with unwed young ladies, so that they might get to know one another better," his brother said matter-of-factly. "There are walks, rides, and drives through the country. Card play and dancing. Games on the lawn. Many boring nights of the ladies present showing off their musical skills." Dawson grinned. "Or lack of them."

"Are you . . . one of the gentlemen who is now betrothed?" Byron asked, finding it hard to picture his carefree brother ready to take on a wife.

Dawson laughed. "No, little brother. I have no intention of wedding for several years. The party was given by a duke and duchess, however. You will learn once you enter Polite Society's company that one never says no to a duke. Even though I was not in the market for a bride, I did make some good connections, however."

Byron didn't remind his brother that he would not become a part of the *ton* because he was destined for a career in the military.

His brother tucked into his meal, while Byron pushed the food around on his plate, not hungry. He did consume two additional cups of coffee, and the headache began to recede.

Finishing his food, Dawson asked, "Are you up for a ride this morning, Byron? I want to go about the estate and see how things are since I have been away for so long."

He caught the pleased look on his father's face, hearing of his heir's concern regarding Bridgefield. Since his brother would one day be the marquess, it was important for Dawson to take an interest in the tenants at Bridgefield. He couldn't help but wonder exactly what Dawson would do, now that his education had been completed. With their father still alive and well, he was the one responsible for the care of Bridgefield and its tenants. Of course, Father had a steward who actually did most of the work. He decided he would ask Dawson what his role would now be when they were away from the house.

"Of course. Let me go change into my riding clothes. I will meet you at the stables."

Half an hour later, a groom brought out their horses, and both men mounted. Though Byron knew the headache could very well return while being jostled about, he did not care. He enjoyed all time spent in his brother's company.

"Happy birthday, Byron," wished Dawson as they set out. "I hope you are not upset that Father did not acknowledge the day during breakfast."

Though it had stung, he pretended otherwise and asked, "Why would he? He never has before."

"I have already talked with Cook. She is making a cake for you so that we might celebrate. Just the two of us. I will bring the cake and snatch a bottle of Father's best brandy. We can meet up in the stables this evening."

He groaned. "No drinking for me. I actually went into Bridgehampton last night to celebrate with a few of the local lads. I had several drinks. Too many, in fact. My head pounded fiercely when I awoke this morning."

His brother laughed. "The cure for consuming too much alcohol is to drink more."

"I will pass. On the brandy. *Not* the cake."

It touched him that Dawson had not only remembered his birthday, but he had spoken to Cook about it. His parents never had seen the day as call for celebration and never mentioned it, even in passing, while Dawson's date of birth was celebrated each year with fanfare.

They rode for over two hours, walking their horses for the most part so they might talk as they went. He learned a few things about the Season, which his parents attended yearly, but they never mentioned anything about it to him.

"Actually, it can be quite a bit of fun, yet boring at the same time," Dawson noted. "It is pleasant to spend time in the company of your friends, but some of the social affairs can be rather dull. Especially if you are not seeking a bride on the Marriage Mart."

"What is that?" he asked.

"You see, each spring, a group of girls makes what is called their come-out. This debut simply means they are officially entering into Polite Society. Women of our class use the Season to search for husbands. The events include an incredible number of balls. While I enjoy dancing, I had no desire to wed, so I never danced more than once with a woman. If you dance twice with the same one in a single night, it shows you are incredibly interested in her. Hostesses invite gentlemen, such as myself, so that ladies' dance cards might be rounded out. Yes, I danced with a good number of women. I also attended countless card parties, routs, and musicales."

Dawson's eyes lit with mischief. "The fun, though, is getting to spend time with your friends after some of the boring events, which end far earlier than balls do. I would go out with them. We would make our way from one gaming hell to another, gambling and drinking the night away, not returning home until well after dawn broke."

"You *do* that kind of thing regularly?" he asked, not bothering to hide his shock. Byron knew Dawson was no angel, but he found it hard picturing his brother wasting his time with such activities.

"Oh, my naïve little brother. I do far more than that. I bedded a good number of women this Season. Not any of the young girls making their come-outs, of course, but there are always willing wives who are bored with their husbands or pretty widows who are eager to take a tumble with a handsome young buck."

Byron was speechless. For the first time, he was seeing a side of his brother he never had before. Admittedly, he worshipped Dawson and wanted to be just like him. Still, their lives would be very different as adults and the paths they would pursue. After his officer training, he would be off to fight. The war with Bonaparte was dragging on, and he did not think it would be over anytime soon. That meant after university, Byron would be shipped to the Continent and lead soldiers in the fight against the Little Corporal. This talk of the Season and bedding women would have nothing to do with him.

Before he could ask his brother what he would do now at Bridgefield, Dawson asked, "When do you leave for Cambridge?"

"In two weeks. I am glad to be renting the same rooms you did while you were there. I am looking forward to extending my studies."

Dawson chuckled. "You always were the academic between the two of us. University is for more than academics, however, little brother. I have told you that very thing, but you will understand better after you arrive in Cambridge and can see for yourself. These upcoming years are for learning about people. About life. You will certainly need to learn how to drink and wench. You are quite good at maths, so I assume you will have some skill when it comes to gambling."

He was outraged at his brother's words and did not bother to hide it. "This is what you did your entire time at Cambridge?"

Dawson shrugged. "For most of it. Yes, I did enough to get by in order to graduate, but I looked upon those years as time away from Father. Away from the obligations he always preaches to us about. I will certainly take those on when the time comes and meet my responsibilities. After all, I am the heir apparent. I know what is expected of me."

His brother did favor Father physically, being stout and handsome, with blond hair and blue eyes. Byron's looks came from his mother's side of the family, with his hair black as coal and having Mama's gray eyes. He did know his brother would be a dutiful marquess. It just surprised him how Dawson had been so cavalier about his years at university.

He had never been one to judge others, however. Perhaps he, too, might sow a few wild oats during his own Cambridge days. Once he entered the army, however, it would be all business. His father had drilled into his sons how important duty and responsibility were. Byron would be representing both king and country on the battlefield, as well as being responsible for the men serving under him. He would not take such an assignment lightly.

They returned to the stables and handed their reins off to a groom, strolling back to the house.

"What will you do now that you are back at Bridgefield?" he asked, wondering if his brother would settle down now that his university days were behind him.

"With university no longer looming over me, I am certain Father wishes me to take more of an active interest in estate matters. I will be spending time with our steward and learning as much about estate management as I possibly can."

He did not think that would keep Dawson occupied enough, especially since his brother had just come off the social swirl of the Season.

Curious, he asked, "You said you are not looking for a bride. When do you plan to wed?"

Laughing, Dawson punched Byron in the arm playfully. "I will put that off for as long as possible." Then sobering, he added,

"I know what is expected of me. I will keep attuned to the situation. Father seems to be in decent health at this point, so I feel no need to chain myself to one woman. I assume in the next five to ten years, I will take a wife, however. Mama will be more than happy to see grandchildren from me, especially since she will get none from you."

He had never really thought about the fact that he would, most likely, not have any children, nor even wed. The army would be his life. Byron would be as wedded to his career as he would a woman. He supposed he would look upon the men he commanded as his children. True, he had heard the occasional army officer wed, but that was infrequently done, and those wives remained behind in England when officers shipped out for war. Or at least he supposed they did. What woman would wish to live a harsh life with no luxuries, always on the move when the army advanced or retreated?

"Playing uncle to your children will be good enough for me," he told Dawson. "As it is, who can predict the future? I may spend my entire adult life abroad if England cannot contain and defeat Bonaparte."

"You would still be granted leave every now and then, I assume."

Byron doubted it. Once his commission was purchased, the army would own him. War did not cease merely because a man tired of it and wished to take a few weeks to visit his home and family. In some ways, he believed Dawson a bit naïve but did not call him out on it.

They entered the house and were met by their butler.

"His Lordship wishes to see the both of you in his study."

"We will be there shortly, Jarrod," Dawson said easily. "First, we must wash the scent of horse from us. Have water sent up for baths for the both of us."

"Yes, my lord."

That was the difference between being the first and second son. Byron would have gone immediately to their father's study because he had been summoned. Dawson, comfortable in being Lord Linden and the heir to the marquessate, would take his own time before answering the summons.

More than an hour later, he went and knocked on his brother's bedchamber door and was admitted. Keller, their father's valet, was tying Dawson's cravat. He supposed now that Dawson had returned to Bridgefield permanently, he would need his own valet, or possibly share Keller with the marquess.

"I came to see if you were ready."

His brother glanced into the mirror, nodding satisfactorily. "Yes. Shall we go?"

They went to Lord Bridgewater's study, a place Byron only entered upon rare occasions. The room was the marquess' sanctuary. He spent many hours within it, only entertaining Lord Hampton in it, with no other visitors coming here.

Jarrod announced them, and they stepped into the room. Immediately, he noticed the irritation in his father's eyes, which the marquess quickly masked. Byron knew Father would never complain about how long it took them to arrive.

"Have a seat, boys," the marquess said from his seat by the window, indicating the two chairs nearby.

As they did so, Dawson cheekily said, "You know, Father, we are not boys. We are both men."

Father frowned. "You will always be boys to *me*, Linden."

The marquess' tone wiped the smile from his brother's face, and Byron wanted to deflect their father's displeasure.

"We had been out riding, Father," he said quickly. "We did not want to offend you by filling your study with the stench of horse and sweat."

"Very well," the old man said brusquely.

Trying to continue to smooth things over and placate their father, Byron asked, "What would you like to speak to us about today, Father?"

What followed was one of the marquess' lengthy lectures on honor, duty, and family obligations. The Balfour brothers had been subjected to these many times over the years, from the time they could walk. While he had thought Dawson was cut from the exact cloth as Father, Byron now realized his brother rebelled a bit if his behavior at university was to be believed. Still, he knew Dawson would make for an excellent Marquess of Bridgewater when his day came. His brother was intelligent and would settle down and take his responsibilities seriously.

He kept an attentive look on his face while thinking of other things. No conversation was ever expected during these lectures. Instead, his father would ramble for an hour or two before dismissing his sons.

This time, things were different.

Byron sat up slightly when he heard the word *marriage* uttered, especially since it had been a topic he and Dawson had just discussed during their ride together.

He hadn't heard exactly what was said and so looked to his brother, who wore an incredulous look on his face.

"You wish me to *marry* her?" Dawson asked, his voice raised in anger.

Who was the her?

In the blink of an eye, Father sprung to his feet and struck Dawson. The sting of the slap shocked Byron, as did the handprint instantly appearing on his brother's face. No one had ever touched either boy, which made the display of sudden violence so jarring.

As he seated himself again, the look in the marquess' eye turned deadly. "You will never speak to me like that, Linden," he told his older son. "Ever."

The chill in the room could have frozen a lake, and the silence stretched out for some minutes. Byron's gaze dropped to his lap, worried how Dawson would react. His brother, though, kept to his seat and remained quiet.

Finally, Father said, "I have spoken to the both of you about duty and honor for many years. Byron will serve our king and country and be duty-bound to the crown and his men. He must remain honorable in order to maintain the respect of other officers, as well as his soldiers. You, on the other hand, Dawson, are to follow in my footsteps. A marquess is but one step below a duke. You will have the eyes of Polite Society upon you. You will not fail. You will make me proud from my grave."

Father took a deep breath and expelled it. "Lord Hampton is the brother I never had. My chosen family. We have been close for over fifty years. It is our wish to unite our families."

Now, he knew what was going on. Father had told Dawson he was to wed Jacinda Bowles, the viscount's spoiled daughter. While Dawson was a good man, he did have a stubborn streak. Ordering him to wed Jacinda would not sit well.

"I know you have never liked being told what to do," the marquess said, echoing Byron's thoughts. "I also know you *will* do as you are told. Most every marriage that takes place within the *ton* is not the choice of the bride or groom. It is the parents who make their wishes known. In this case, I expect you to wed Jacinda. She is but eleven years of age now, Linden. That gives you a good number of years to enjoy the company of . . . other women."

"Then I have no choice in the matter," Dawson said flatly.

"No. Frankly, the choice was never yours. Lord Hampton and I have spoken of this on numerous occasions. I simply felt it was time to make you privy to our discussions. We have agreed to the dowry and other details of the marriage settlements. In fact, we signed these documents in town before we both traveled down to Kent after the Season."

Byron knew the fact the marriage contracts had already been arranged would irk Dawson to no end. Yet Father was right. Marriages were strictly business arrangements. His brother should have suspected this would be the outcome.

"You did not need my signature on these papers?" Dawson asked, his tone neutral.

"No. Nor did I need your permission," the marquess snapped, his displeasure with his older son still evident. "As I said, the chit will not make her come-out for seven years or so."

"Has she been told?" Dawson demanded.

"She will be told. In time. No sense in it now."

"Why would she even need a Season if she already has an intended husband?" Byron asked.

Father turned to him, baffled, as if he just now realized Byron was in the room.

"Why, the girl will need a bit of town polish on her. All girls make their come-outs. Jacinda will not be an exception. I believe she will be the leading girl in her come-out group. A diamond of the first water. It will be a feather in Linden's cap to wed the beauty of her Season."

"I will do as you request, Father, and honor the contracts which have been signed," Dawson said, sounding as if the choice of bride had been his all along. "Jacinda Bowles will stand out from the other girls who make their come-outs. It is only fair to give her a Season to enjoy and allow our courtship to be played out in front of Polite Society."

It made Byron secretly glad that he would not have to wed a woman of his parents' choice and that he would simply enter the army. He did feel a bit sorry for his brother, though. He would be stuck with Jacinda for the rest of his life, even years before they wed. Even if Dawson found himself attracted to another girl, he would not be allowed to act upon his feelings because of the secret commitment.

"I am glad you came to your senses, Linden," the marquess said, approval in his tone. "We should toast to your betrothal."

Drinking was the last thing Byron wished to do, but he accepted the snifter of brandy his father handed to him.

"To the union of the Balfour and Bowles families," Father said, satisfaction written on his face.

The trio tapped their crystal tumblers against one another's. Byron brought the glass to his lips and winced as he downed the brandy. It burned a trail from his throat to his belly. He hoped he would be able to keep it down.

"We need to tell . . . to tell . . ." Father's voice trailed off as an odd expression crossed his face, something between surprise and bewilderment. Then he dropped the empty snifter and clutched at his chest, clawing at it.

As he dropped to his knees, Dawson calmly said, "Have Jarrod summon the doctor."

Byron ran from the room, shouting for the butler. When Jarrod came around the corner, he sputtered, "Father is ill. Gravely ill. Send for the doctor at once."

He raced back into the study, seeing that his father was now prone. Dawson knelt beside him, loosening Father's cravat.

"The doctor is coming, Father," his brother said reassuringly, his voice almost eerily calm. "You will be fine."

Panic filled the old man's eyes as he struggled to take a breath. Byron took one of Father's hands and held it tightly, seeing the light ebb from the marquess' eyes. Then he stilled, his eyes wide with terror in death.

Dawson reached out and swept his palm over them, closing them. "He's gone, Byron."

"Gone," he echoed, not comprehending the swiftness of the events. "But he was just talking," he insisted. "He was fine."

"I think it must have been his heart. At least, that is what the doctor will say of the suddenness. How he clutched at his chest and then collapsed."

"You . . . are the Marquess of Bridgewater now," Byron said, his voice full of wonder at the power his brother now yielded.

"I am," Dawson said firmly. "I plan to make him proud. I will live up to his expectations. And I will marry that damned chit. Because it is what *he* wanted. The Balfours and Bowles will unite in marriage."

Dawson, the Marquess of Bridgewater, rose and poured more brandy into two snifters and handing one to Byron, who came to his feet, still a bit unsteady, but wanting to support his brother.

Doing his part, their dead father lying at their feet, Byron held his tumbler high. "To the Marquess of Bridgefield."

"Thank you," his brother said, tapping his glass against Byron's, and both men drained the contents.

"I will not force you into the military," Dawson revealed. "You will go only if you wish to do so. I know it is the tradition for second sons to enter the army, but you will always be welcomed here at Bridgefield, Byron."

"Thank you," he said, numbed by what had occurred during the last few minutes.

He would reflect upon Dawson's offer. No, the Marquess of Bridgewater's offer. They would never again be on equal footing as brothers. Bridgewater would wield more power than Byron might ever have imagined.

In that moment, he knew his path forward lay with the army. If he remained at Bridgewater after graduating from Cambridge, he would have no set role. No goals to achieve. Father had constantly lectured them about honor and duty. His would be to his king and country.

Byron would keep this to himself, however. He would only let the marquess know of this decision four years from now.

CHAPTER ONE

London—1 September 1809

CAPTAIN BYRON BALFOUR awoke in a cold sweat, his heart racing, the battle scene of blood and gore still fresh in his mind. He sat up, pushing his fingers through his hair, trying to slow his heart, breathing in and out carefully, as he had taught his men to do when they were terrified.

No, he was no longer Captain Balfour, officer under Wellesley, attacking the French armies under Joseph Bonaparte at Talavera.

He was the Marquess of Bridgewater.

Why the bloody hell had Dawson challenged someone to race their phaetons through Hyde Park, both of them deep into their cups?

Actually, it sounded exactly like his brother. As a boy, Byron had worshipped the ground Dawson trod upon. No one could ride better, run faster, or shoot as well as Dawson Balfour. It was only when their father passed, six years ago to this day, did Byron begin to glimpse the true Dawson. He supposed he had hints of his brother's character along the way. He hadn't judged his brother for not being as academically oriented as he himself was. Dawson had said and done all the right things after their father collapsed and died. He had even encouraged Byron to continue with his plans to go to Cambridge, telling him there was no sense in him staying at Bridgefield to mourn a man who had cared little for him.

Eager to pursue his studies, Byron had left Kent, glad he could escape. It was at Cambridge that he shone. The dons had tried to convince him to become an academic himself, but he had in his head—and heart—that he was meant to serve his country. Dawson had purchased Byron's commission for him, sending him off to war. His brother had written to him several times a year, but the letters were usually ones he wrote when drinking. The text rambled. Most often, the missives were sent from London, instead of Bridgefield. In his heart, Byron knew his brother was neglecting Bridgefield and its tenants and only hoped the steward exercised full control. The pedestal he had placed Dawson upon when Byron could barely walk had toppled, showing Dawson was not the best of men. Certainly not the one their father had envisioned taking over at Bridgefield.

Yet Byron had not been prepared for that role. It was one he did not want and never would have wished for. He had found a home in the army, his fellow officers his brothers-in-arms, his men ones to be encouraged, praised, and pushed onto the battlefield.

Today, he turned four and twenty—and felt another score older than he was. He also felt adrift. He had only spent two years in the army, with no thought of ever doing anything else. Now, he carried his new title like an albatross about his neck. He could hear echoes of phrases his father had spoken over the years and only hoped he would be able to manage his new responsibilities well.

Climbing from the bed, he washed with the water the inn-keeper's wife had brought the night before, wishing it were warm so that shaving was not so difficult. He donned his captain's uniform, knowing he would soon give it up for clothes more appropriate to his station. The thought of so many prying eyes on him made Byron ill. At least he had just missed the Season and all the social swirl surrounding it, and would not be forced to move amongst Polite Society straightaway.

His immediate concern was Bridgefield. He would learn more of the status of things when he visited with Mr. Pilsbury, the Balfour solicitor, this morning. Then he would check on the London townhouse and make haste to Kent.

Going downstairs, he stopped for breakfast, forcing himself to eat. The food lay as a lump in his belly. Byron told himself to shake off his gloom and worry. He could not change anything which had occurred up to this point. It was what happened beyond today which mattered most. If Bridgefield had been neglected, as he believed, then he would put things right. He had always possessed a thirst for knowledge, and there would certainly be much to learn in the weeks and months which lay ahead. It might not be as bad as he suspected.

At least, that's what he told himself.

After breakfasting, he sat sipping a second cup of tea. The tea served in the army had been too weak for his tastes. The coffee had proved even worse. Byron had never acquired a taste for the brew at any rate. He removed Pilsbury's letter from his pocket and read through it several times, mulling over the contents.

The solicitor had briefly written of what he termed an *accident*, saying that Lord Bridgewater, who had been fond of racing, had challenged a friend to a phaeton race in Hyde Park. Byron read between the lines, Pilsbury intimating that the marquess had been drunk without directly coming out and stating that to be the case. At any rate, both men had crashed, with his brother perishing immediately and the other man dying the next day.

Pilsbury had told Byron the wisest action was to sell out as quickly and return to England as soon as possible, asking that the new marquess visit Pilsbury's London office to receive an overview of the estate. That meeting would occur this morning.

He returned to his room for the small knapsack which carried an extra shirt, a comb, and his shaving equipment. Men in service of the king traveled lightly, and Byron was no exception. He held all his earthly possessions in his hand, at least the ones Captain Byron Balfour had owned. He had no idea what he had inherited with his title.

When he had arrived in London last night around seven o'clock, he had chosen not to go to the family's townhouse. It was located in Mayfair, and Byron had only been there twice. He wasn't even certain he could locate it on his own. Instead, he had chosen to take a room for the night at an inn which was close to Pilsbury's office. Because of that, he now set out on foot to see the solicitor.

Using the address on the letter he had received, he soon located his destination and entered, going to a desk where a clerk sat. Using his height and tone which oozed authority, Byron said, "I need to speak with Mr. Pilsbury at his earliest convenience."

The clerk sat up a bit. "Do you have an appointment, Captain?" he asked, obviously recognizing Byron's rank from his uniform.

"No, I have just arrived from the continent." He swallowed, and for the first time uttered the words which would forever define him. "I am the Marquess of Bridgefield."

Immediately, the clerk shot to his feet. "Yes, my lord. Please, wait here a moment. I will let Mr. Pilsbury know you have arrived."

Faster than a Frenchman retreating from one of Wellington's attacks, the clerk was off. Returning less than a minute later, he said, a bit out of breath, "If you will follow me, my lord. Mr. Pilsbury will see you at once."

Byron did so, moving along a corridor and entering the door the clerk indicated.

Already, the solicitor was on his feet, bowing to his client. "Lord Bridgewater, it was good of you to come. Please, have a seat. Might I offer you some tea?"

"No, thank you. I would rather get down to business, Mr. Pilsbury."

"Yes, of course." He nodded, and the clerk shut the door.

Both men took a seat on either side of the desk, and the solicitor reached for a stack of documents.

"I have quite a bit of information to share with you, my lord."

"Before that, tell me of my brother's death," he said. "The unvarnished truth."

Pilsbury winced. "I believe I wrote to you that—"

"I know what you wrote," Byron said impatiently. "*I* am now the Marquess of Bridgewater. You have no loyalties to my brother or father. Only to me," he stated. "And I expect to hear the entire truth regarding what took place."

With that, the sordid tale unfolded. Much as he had believed, his brother had been inebriated, as had the other fellow. Both horses had to be put down, as well.

"Who did Bridgewater decide to race? I suppose I will need to go and offer my condolences to the family."

The solicitor's eyes widened. "You do not know, my lord?"

Impatience filled him. "How was I to know? I have been fighting in Portugal and Spain. I only know what you wrote to me of, Pilsbury."

The older man's face flushed. "You are correct, my lord. I . . . I am not quite certain how to tell you this."

"Spit it out!" he roared, tired of the man dancing around the facts.

"Lord Hampton," sputtered the solicitor. "It was Lord Hampton who also perished in the accident."

Byron stilled, his thoughts racing, trying to comprehend what he had just heard. "Our neighbor? My father's closest friend?"

Pilsbury nodded. Byron sat, stunned by this news.

Finally he found his voice. "Why would Lord Hampton accept such a challenge from my brother?"

Meekly, the solicitor said, "Lord Bridgewater—that is, your father—often issued these types of challenges to his closest friend. In fact, all of London watched with interest when your father and Lord Hampton placed bets with one another. They were known for their antics. Your brother simply took up the mantle once he took on the title. He and Lord Hampton became close friends. They drank and gambled together."

Pilsbury hesitated, and Byron believed the solicitor wanted to add *rutted together* to that list.

"At any rate," the solicitor continued, "it was not unusual for them to make a bet with one another. Both were interested in horseflesh and gambled at the drop of a hat. It might have even been Lord Hampton who challenged Lord Bridgewater to the race. That is a possibility."

Clearing his throat, he said, "I will need to pay a call on Lady Hampton to express my condolences. And the new Lord Hampton."

He thought a moment, deciding Cedric Bowles must have turned one and twenty recently. Most likely. Cedric had still been in university.

"There is no Lady Hampton, my lord," he was informed. "Lady Hampton passed away last winter. From what I gather, Lord Hampton celebrated rather than mourned her death."

Byron shook his head. At least his mother would be relieved she no longer had to spend time in the woman's company.

Then it struck him. Dawson was to have wed Jacinda Bowles. The marriage settlements had been drawn up years ago. Jacinda had lost not only her father—but her future husband.

"Let me go over everything with you, my lord," Mr. Pilsbury said. "We have much ground to cover."

He decided to let the question of the betrothal lie for now.

Two hours later, he had an accurate vision of his financial worth. Obviously, Bridgefield was the crown jewel, but he had a few other scattered properties and several investments in various companies which earned him more than a tidy sum.

"I apologize that it is not more, my lord," Pilsbury told him. "The previous Lord Bridgewater had several gambling debts at his death. Those markers were called in, and I was forced to pay them."

"You did the right thing," he assured the solicitor. "I will tell you now that you will see no gaming debts accrue with me. Yes, I enjoy the occasional card game, but I do not have my brother's fascination nor his addiction to gambling."

"The state of your affairs is quite solid, my lord. Your investments have been wise and are paying excellent dividends. The tenants at Bridgefield bring in a healthy sum each year."

He decided now was the time to address the matter of his brother's marriage.

"What of the marriage settlements signed by Lord Hampton and my father? I know this was several years ago and that my brother was committed to marrying Miss Jacinda Bowles."

"That contract would be null and void, my lord, with the death of the marquess," the solicitor shared.

"Do you know if Miss Bowles was ever informed of the betrothal?"

"I am unaware of that, my lord. I can look and see which solicitor represented Lord Hampton when we wrote the contracts and contact him. He might know. Or you could speak with the new Lord Hampton when you call upon him and see. Why?"

"It was my father's wish that the Balfour and Bowles families come together."

Pilsbury frowned. "Surely, you realize you are under no obligation to do so. Both men are dead. And Miss Bowles may not even have learned of the arrangement."

"True."

But his father had always instilled the ideas of duty and family obligations into him. Byron believed it would be the right thing to do if he stepped in for his brother and wed Jacinda. The thought left him with a poor taste in his mouth. She had been a spoiled, selfish child. He doubted under her mother's hand that she had changed much. Still, he wanted to do the right thing. He would need to visit with Lord Hampton and settle matters.

"If that is everything," he said, rising.

Pilsbury winced. "Actually, there is another matter which

must be addressed, my lord."

Byron took his seat again. "What is causing such a pained expression, Pilsbury? You have already told me of the gaming debts you have paid off on my brother's behalf. Does he owe his tailor? Or his wine merchant? Has he purchased horses from Tattersall's and neglected to pay those bills?"

"No, my lord. This involves . . . a very . . . delicate matter."

Awareness filled him. "Did Lord Bridgewater have a mistress? Am I to pay her off, as well?"

"Not exactly. The situation is more . . . complicated than that."

"Just say what needs to be said, Pilsbury. I need this to be over and done. I wish to get to Bridgefield as soon as possible and take up my duties there."

"It is Miss Truman. Forgive me. I mean Mrs. Smithson."

He let out a long sigh. "Tell me. Tell me now, so that I might rectify anything neglected by my brother."

"Oh, Lord Bridgewater did take care of them."

"Them?"

Pilsbury turned beet red. "Mrs. Smithson has a daughter. Amity. The girl is five now."

The story came rushing from the solicitor once he mentioned the girl. Apparently, Miss Verity Truman, daughter of a viscount, was compromised by Dawson. When she found she was with child, the marquess informed her they could not wed because he was already betrothed. Miss Truman refused to go away from the prying eyes of Polite Society and have the baby, then give it up, which caused her father to disown her. The viscount put out the word that his daughter had died of a fever.

Fortunately, Bridgewater had done the best he could. He had purchased a small house for Miss Truman in St. John's Wood. The child, Amity, had been born there, and the marquess paid for the handful of servants required to run the household and tend to its occupants.

"Lord Bridgewater pays Miss Truman, who goes by the name

Mrs. Smithson, a yearly sum. The allowance covers the salaries for the staff and any maintenance required on the house, as well as any necessities." The solicitor paused. "You are under no obligation to continue this arrangement, however, my lord."

How could he *not* continue the payments? His brother had gotten a lady of good birth with child, one who had been ostracized by her family to the point of them pretending she no longer existed. If he did not keep up the payments, this woman and Byron's niece would be out on the streets.

"Keep the payments in place," he said crisply. "Have you informed Mrs. Smithson of Lord Bridgewater's death?"

"Not directly, my lord. She may have seen the death notice in the newspapers, however, if she reads them."

He rubbed his eyes wearily. "I have so much to handle. Was the marquess still seeing Mrs. Smithson?"

"No, my lord. In fact, he never laid eyes upon his daughter. Once he discovered Miss Truman was with child, he cut all contact with her. Everything has gone through me, from then on, until now."

"Then we shall keep to that arrangement," he told Pilsbury. "I may or may not decide to meet this woman and her daughter. For now, though, I have more pressing matters which require my attention."

Byron hadn't a clue how he was going to be a marquess, much less deal with everything that came with it. For now, meeting the woman Bridgewater ruined was asking for more than he was willing to give. He would not turn his back on the two, however. They were innocent in this. He had discovered he had more money than Midas. He would never miss what it took to keep a roof over their heads and clothes on their backs.

"Do you think they have ample funds?" he asked.

"What Lord Bridgewater provides to the pair is . . . adequate."

That meant Mrs. Smithson had to scrimp.

"Double it," he said. "They will benefit from you doing so."

Pilsbury shook his head in wonder. "You are a most generous man, my lord."

It was merely the right thing to do. To try and correct one of the many wrongs perpetrated by his brother. Hearing of this woman and the child she had borne hammered the final nail into Dawson's coffin. The beloved brother he had adored had feet of clay in the end.

Byron determined to be the best Marquess of Bridgewater the family had ever seen.

CHAPTER TWO

Lake District, England—1 September 1810

A S THE CARRIAGE rolled along, Lady Mirella Strong looked out at the scenic landscape of the Lake District, still marveling that she had been given this opportunity to visit the area.

She glanced to her aunt Matty, who had been responsible for suggesting the trip to Mirella and Effie, her younger sister. Aunt Matty, who was their father's sister, had never wed. She treated Mirella, her sisters, and cousins as her own children. Mama had raised all six of them with Aunt Matty's assistance, and the older woman was one of Mirella's favorite people in the world.

It was odd being away from Shadowcrest. Her family was rapidly changing, thanks to the recent marriages within it. Her brother James, absent for many years, suddenly resurfaced. His tale of being kidnapped from the London docks while he was visiting Strong Shipping, their family business, had been quite remarkable. Even more remarkable, James had fallen in love with Sophie Grant, a widow who defied all of Polite Society's unwritten rules and ran Neptune Shipping, Strong Shipping's biggest competitor. Sophie would give birth to their first child at the end of this month, so the traveling Strongs would need to return in time for that event.

Mirella had always been close to all the girls in her family, but her older sisters, twins, had both wed a short time ago. Pippa was now on an extended honeymoon, voyaging around the world with her husband, who had been a sea captain and was now Viscount Hopewell. Georgie had just made her come-out this past spring and had wed a former army captain in June. August had returned from war to take up the title of Marquess of Edgethorne, and the pair were summering in Scotland at Dalmara, one of August's properties. They, too, would be returning to Kent in the near future.

Most remarkable of all was that Mirella's mother, the widowed Duchess of Seaton, had found love with James' closest friend. Drake Andrews had been a ship's captain for Neptune Shipping, but with his marriage last month to Mama, the captain had given up his seafaring ways and had taken up the reins of Neptune Shipping, managing the company for Sophie. That was, without a doubt, the biggest change in Mirella's life because she had a stepfather who adored her, her sisters, and her cousins. Mama had made a typical *ton* marriage as a young lady, her parents selecting her husband for her. Mama had become the second wife to the Duke of Seaton, who was eager for sons. Instead, Mama had given the duke four daughters, as well as taking in the newborn twins of Seaton's brother, who had no interest in raising girls after his wife died birthing them. Lyric and Allegra, though her cousins, were more like sisters to her.

Mirella herself should have made her own come-out alongside Georgie this past spring. Unfortunately, she had slipped on a patch of wet grass while they were walking in Hyde Park shortly before the Season began, falling and breaking her forearm and elbow. If there was anything in this world Mirella enjoyed, it was dancing. The doctor had forbid her from doing so because of the clunky plaster cast she had to wear while her bones knitted together again. Because of that, she had decided to delay her come-out until next April.

She knew she was the reason why they were touring the Lake

District now. Mama and Sophie had decided to help introduce Allegra and Lyric into society. The twins had refused to make their debuts because of convoluted reasons, but both were still eager to find the love match the other Strongs had recently made. Mama had planned a lovely house party in their honor, and it was now taking place at Shadowcrest. Since Mirella had yet to make her own come-out, she had felt odd. It would be awkward attending the party under those circumstances, so Aunt Matty had come up with the perfect solution—a visit to the Lake District, which included stopping to see Lady Benton, Aunt Matty's friend since childhood. Her aunt was a yearly visitor to Benbrook, home to Lord and Lady Benton.

Naturally, her younger sister Effie had been invited to come along. Also accompanying them was Effie's governess, Miss Feathers. The four women traveled in luxury. James had provided his roomiest and most elegant ducal carriage for their journey. He had insisted they take it, since he and Sophie would be at Shadowcrest for the entire house party they hosted.

"Every time I think the landscape cannot grow prettier, it simply outdoes itself," declared Effie. "Thank you again, Aunt Matty, for bringing us to the Lake District."

Her aunt smiled. "I was more than happy to do so, girls. I have been coming here regularly to visit Flora since shortly after she and Lord Benton were wed. She has been my dearest friend for many decades."

Although Aunt Matty was two years past her sixtieth birthday and her hair was white as snow, she still was quite a beauty. Her face was barely lined and her cornflower blue eyes, a trait of the Strongs, stood out.

"What has been your favorite place we have visited so far?" asked Miss Feathers.

Mirella enjoyed Miss Feathers' company. The governess had been with the family over six years and had served as governess to all the girls in the family. While Miss Feathers still tutored Effie in subjects such as French and history and comportment, Miss

Feathers had become a dear friend to all the Strong women. Mirella was glad Aunt Matty had included Miss Feathers on this journey.

"That would be hard to answer," Effie said. "The lakes alone are gorgeous, but seeing the mountains simply takes my breath away." She turned to Mirella. "What do you think has been your favorite place?"

"I have been taken with this northwest area of England, the same as you," she replied. "I did, however, especially enjoy seeing Windermere. I know it is the largest of the lakes in this region. The town of Windermere was also a delight."

"I couldn't agree more," Miss Feathers said. "Windermere has also been my favorite stop of our journey. And getting to tour Wren Park. That was a most beautiful home."

Touring homes of members of Polite Society was something unique to the Lake District, Mirella had discovered. Once they agreed to travel with Aunt Matty to the region, her aunt had given them each a copy of Thomas West's *A Guide to the Lakes*. First published in 1778, the book detailed the Lake District, stating it was more than comparable to areas in places such as Germany and Switzerland, where many gentlemen took their Grand Tours. Because of the Jesuit priest's guidebook, more young gentlemen—and later other visitors—began making their way to see the Lake District for themselves. It had become tradition for travelers to stop by the grand country estates located in this region and ask to take a tour of the house and its grounds. This especially occurred during the summer months, when most of the owners of these homes were in town at the Season.

So far, they had stopped twice, with housekeepers giving them a tour of the huge family homes. Despite both houses being most impressive, Mirella thought Shadowcrest was even more beautiful than the homes they had seen on this journey. She realized that one day, when she wed, Shadowcrest would no longer be her home. Excitement filled her as she thought about next year's Season and how she hoped to find her husband during it. James had told both Georgie and her before the start of the previous Season that they should not be in a rush to wed. If they did not find the man they wished to spend the rest of their lives with, they were not to compromise or settle in any way. He had emphasized his home would always be their home, for as long as they wished for it to be.

She had appreciated that. Though James was the son of the Duke of Seaton's first wife, James never referred to Mirella and her sisters as being his half-sisters. From the time he came home, James had made it known that they were true siblings.

"Oh, we are close to Grasmere now," her aunt said, excitement in her voice. "I truly believe you will find it to be the most beautiful of all places in the Lake District. After all, Wordsworth resided in Grasmere and wrote about its scenic beauty."

Poetry was something that had been new to Mirella. While Miss Feathers had given the girls a through education, teaching them grammar and composition, maths, and history, she allowed them to also pursue topics they were interested in. For her part, Mirella was inspired by music. She spent at least two hours a day at her pianoforte. Both she and Georgie were the most accomplished musicians in the Strong family. Because of the time she had devoted to her music, she had not spent any time reading poetry.

It changed leading up to this trip. Besides giving Effie and her the popular guidebook describing the Lake District, Aunt Matty had presented both girls with a copy of Mr. Wordsworth's collected poems, telling them which particular ones had been inspired by Wordsworth's living in Grasmere. Mirella had grown to love several of them, especially an ode that was fresh and arresting and another poem about daffodils in the forest.

"Do you think we will be able to see where Mr. Wordsworth lives?" she asked.

Aunt Matty said, "Actually, he lived at a place called Dove Cottage until two years ago. it turned out to be too small for his growing family, and he has since moved away from Grasmere. I did hear the last time I came and visited Flora that a fellow writer of his acquaintance has taken up the lease, however. I am certain we can at least stroll by Dove Cottage if not see inside it."

"Oh, I would like that, Aunt," Effie said enthusiastically. "I have come to enjoy Mr. Wordsworth's poetry very much. Miss Feathers has spent time with me, going over some of the poems line-by-line, and helping to enlighten me as to their meaning."

The governess smiled indulgently. "I am glad his poetry has come to your attention, girls. Especially now that you will be seeing the very places which inspired such creativity. Why, you might wish to try your own hand at writing poetry."

Effie laughed at the thought. "That is not something I will be attempting, Miss Feathers. You know once we are back at Shadowcrest, I will be out and about on the land again every day once our lessons are done."

Her sister stroked the cat sitting in her lap as she spoke. Effie was mad for animals and rescued strays left and right. Daffodil, the cat who had come along with them, was Effie's favorite. She had insisted she could not leave Daffy behind at Shadowcrest because they both would be heartbroken. Her sister frequently went about Shadowcrest wearing breeches, visiting tenants along with Caleb, Allegra and Lyric's brother, who served as the Shadowcrest steward.

Mirella had also spent quite a bit of time with her cousin since Caleb had come to live and work at Shadowcrest. She knew one day when she had wed, she and her husband would be responsible for their own country estate and its tenants and staff. Because of that, Mirella wanted to know as much about estate management as possible. While she knew it would be more the role of her husband to deal with the land and tenants while she was in charge of their household, she was naturally curious and interested in many things. Caleb had explained to her about various crops and how they were grown and harvested. Her cousin had also interested Mirella in various livestock at Shadowcrest, and she had learned about the raising of them and their sale at market. She wanted to be the best mistress of the house she came to live in and call her own, as well as supporting her husband in all his endeavors.

Why, she might fall in love with someone who owned property in the Lake District.

The thought inspired her for a moment, thinking how lovely it would be to awaken amidst such beauty in nature. Then again, she would be so very far from others in her family. As part of her widow's settlement, Mama had been awarded a small manor house called Crestridge, less than ten miles from Shadowcrest. While her mother and the captain would live in town a good part of the year, thanks to his role at Neptune Shipping, they would sometimes be in the country, both at Crestridge and Shadowcrest.

Pippa's husband Seth owned the country estate next to Shadowcrest. Hopewood and Shadowcrest shared a lake between the two estates, and so Pippa would always be close by. Though not in Kent, August and Georgie would reside at Edgefield, which was only a couple of hours' carriage ride away in Surrey. Mirella did not wish to choose a husband based upon where his country seat stood, but it would be nice to be near her sisters and mother.

That got her to thinking about the house party taking place at Shadowcrest. She wondered if Lyric and Allegra would come out of it betrothed. If so, she wondered where their husbands might own property.

She pushed all those thoughts aside as she caught sight of the lake. Grasmere Lake was stunning. The River Rothay flowed into the lake, which was surrounded by fells and mountains. She could not wait to explore it, hopefully by horseback and on foot.

"The town of Grasmere is but a mile from this lake," Aunt Matty shared. "We will be passing by it on the way to Benbrook."

"How far is Benbrook from Grasmere?" asked Miss Feathers.

"Oh, I would say a good three miles or so," Aunt Matty guessed.

The women fell silent, drinking in the beauty of the lake and its surrounding area. They did pass the town of Grasmere, and Mirella would be eager to explore it since they would be staying with Lord and Lady Benton for the next week before their return to Kent. She hoped to be outdoors quite a bit of their time, soaking up the beauty of Grasmere.

They arrived at Benbrook, a truly lovely estate, what Aunt Matty called her second home. Her aunt was the first to be handed out of the carriage, and Mirella heard her aunt's squeal of delight as she caught sight of her lifelong friend. The two embraced, with an older gentleman looking on. She assumed him to be Lord Benton.

Effie slipped Daffy into a straw basket, closing the lid, and a footman handed the three of them down. They went to meet their hosts.

"We are delighted to have you come to stay with us," Lord Benton said, introducing himself and his wife. "Matty is quite special to both of us. In fact, she was the one who introduced us that Season. After these many years, I look upon her as both sister and friend."

"It is so good to finally meet you in person," Lady Benton told them. "Matty has spoken of all of you for so many years."

She thought it a bit odd that the couple never attended the Season. Then again, the busy slate of social activities did not appeal to everyone. Especially knowing now how gorgeous the Lake District was, Mirella thought that she might even find it hard to leave this landscape for the crowds and smells of London.

"Come inside," Lady Benton encouraged. "I have had my housekeeper place Lady Mirella and Lady Effie together. That is what Matty requested."

"We are used to sharing a bedchamber, my lady," Mirella said. "Thank you for your hospitality."

"I will have hot water sent up to you all. Tea will be served on the terrace in an hour. It is simply too nice a day to stay inside for it."

They were taken to their bedchambers, and a maid unpacked

Mirella and Effie's trunks for them, while another brought the hot water. They washed and changed their gowns, making their way downstairs and out to the terrace with the assistance of a maid who brought them through the large French doors which opened onto the terrace. Lord and Lady Benton were already seated outside, along with Aunt Matty and Miss Feathers.

She was happy Miss Feathers was being treated well. Some would have made a distinction with her being a governess, but Miss Feathers had been given a bedchamber across the hall from Effie and her. It struck Mirella that the governess would complete her service to the Strong family in less than two years. Effie would make her come-out the year after Mirella, and then Miss Feathers' work at Shadowcrest would be done. She wondered if Miss Feathers would be willing to take on a new generation of children since it was certain there would be babies coming from all the newlyweds. She would take Miss Feathers aside and ask about her plans. Not now, but down the road.

Taking a seat, Mirella said, "Our bedchamber is so light and airy, Lady Benton. And the fresh flowers were simply beautiful."

"Our mother enjoys arranging flowers," Effie said. "She would also have appreciated the arrangement."

"Thank you, my dears," the countess said. "We are fortunate to get a good deal of rain, so the flowers never go thirsty." She paused. "There you are, my boy. Come and join us."

She looked up and saw a man approaching. Not just any man, but one who was rather tall. His clothing was elegantly cut, showing off broad shoulders and muscular legs. His hair was black as a raven's, and he had the most unusual shade of eye color, a deep gray. Mirella had never seen anyone with eyes such a distinct color.

Rising, as did the others, she prepared to be introduced to him, her heart slamming against her ribs. She had never had such a physical reaction to a man before.

He moved toward them, confidence in his stride, but he appeared much too dour for her taste. His jaw was tightly set, and he looked as if might pain him if he were asked to smile.

Reaching them, he bowed. "Good afternoon, Lady Mathilda. It is nice to see you again."

"Aunt Matty, my lord. I have told you that you have leave to address me as thus."

The man nodded brusquely. "Yes. Aunt Matty. Of course."

"May I introduce my traveling companions to you?" her aunt said. "These are my nieces, Lady Mirella Strong and Lady Euphemia Strong. And our family's governess, Miss Feathers. Ladies, this is the Marquess of Bridgewater, nephew to Lady Benton."

He glanced to her first, and Mirella's heart skipped a beat. "Lady Mirella," he said perfunctorily, taking her hand briefly but not kissing it as she expected.

The marquess did the same with Effie and then merely bowed to Miss Feathers.

"Take a seat, everyone," the countess said. "The teacarts have arrived."

Mirella wondered how she was going to swallow anything and keep it down.

CHAPTER THREE

BYRON MADE HIS way to the drawing room for tea after having spent the entire day closeted with Benbrook's steward. He would only be in the Lake District a week, and already two of those days had passed.

He appreciated the invitation from his aunt and uncle to visit them. They had been loving and supportive of him his entire life, and he had always looked forward to their rare visits to Bridgefield. The couple had wanted him to come and visit before now, but he had spent the last year immersed in learning all he could about being the Marquess of Bridgewater and his obligations to his tenants and estates. Besides Bridgefield, he also owned two smaller properties and had visited them on separate occasions.

While he thought his own steward competent and had learned much from the man, Franklin was getting on in years and had let his employer know that he would be retiring in the near future. Because of that, Byron had wanted to meet with Uncle Hugh's steward at Benbrook, asking questions of him and seeing what he might learn.

Today had been enlightening. He realized now that he might wish to replace his own steward sooner, rather than later. It seemed Franklin was mired in the past and not quite up to date on newer farming methods.

Looking forward to finally spending time with his aunt and uncle the rest of the afternoon and evening, Byron headed to the drawing room for tea, only to be stopped by Mills. The butler reminded him that tea would be served on the terrace this afternoon and that Lord and Lady Benson's guests had arrived.

As he approached the open French doors, he heard laughter, and it struck him. Mills had said *guests*. Plural.

He recalled Aunt Flora writing to him, extending the invitation to visit, which Byron had gladly accepted. When he confirmed the dates she wished him to come and arrived this week, she mentioned her close friend Lady Mathilda would also be visiting during a portion of his stay. Byron had actually met the woman years ago and found her to be quite delightful. Though reluctant to be sharing his visit with another guest, he had hoped her presence would not interfere too much with his own time with Aunt Flora and Uncle Hugh. Hearing now that others accompanied Lady Mathilda, Byron wished he would have had advance warning. He would have declined the invitation and suggested another time for him to come to Benbrook.

He paused, listening a moment. Yes, there were definitely others present besides Lady Mathilda. It soured his mood. He would simply have to make the best of things. He didn't want to cut his visit to Benbrook short, but most likely, he would do so now. He could use replacing his steward as the excuse.

Stepping through the French doors, he caught sight of the four guests. Lady Mathilda had not changed much, although it had been a good decade since they had met. Three young ladies accompanied her. One was quite pretty but dressed in a manner that suggested she was a companion or governess. The other two might be some of the nieces Lady Mathilda had spoken so fondly of.

The pretty blond was so young that he guessed she would not be making her come-out for another couple of years.

It was the other one who drew Byron's attention, though.

She had the most beautiful shade of auburn hair, with bits of red, gold, and brown all spun together, the sun striking it so that her hair seemed to catch fire. For a moment, he longed to unpin it and run his fingers through the silky locks, a thought which had never occurred to him upon spying any woman.

It shocked him to his core.

He moved toward them, seeing as he drew near that the two young women also possessed the same cornflower blue eyes Lady Mathilda did. It was a striking color and added to the beauty of all three women.

Byron greeted Lady Mathilda first, since they had a previous acquaintance, and she insisted he call her Aunt Matty, as she had upon their first meeting. He agreed, and she introduced the two young ladies, who were, as he had guessed, her nieces. The other woman was the family governess. He greeted each individually, taking Lady Effie and Lady Mirella's hands briefly—and managed to maintain a neutral expression when he touched Lady Mirella. The auburn-haired beauty moved something within him.

Something he had never felt—and could not afford to explore.

"Take a seat, everyone," Aunt Flora said. "The teacarts have arrived."

They did as requested, and Byron listed quietly as the conversation centered around where the four had been touring since they left Kent. He added nothing to the conversation until Lady Mathilda mentioned their time in Windermere and how much they had enjoyed it.

"I see," he said brusquely, not really wanting to converse with her or any of them.

He caught Uncle Hugh frowning at him, and he told the group, "Today is Bridgewater's birthday. It is one of the reasons we wished for him to come and visit us now. He is alone at Bridgefield, and we wanted him to be around family for his birthday."

"Happy birthday, my lord," all the women echoed in unison.

Lady Effie asked, "Which birthday are you celebrating, my lord?"

Byron thought it a rather personal question and that the girl was quite impertinent. Still, these were guests of his aunt and uncle and so he said, "I am five and twenty today, my lady."

The girl then asked, "How long have you held your title, my lord?"

"A little over a year," he said crisply, not elaborating, wishing the attention would turn away from him.

Lady Mirella caught his eye and smiled at him, which took his breath away. He had never had such a physical reaction to a woman, and it troubled him greatly.

"You know, my lord, it is quite all right for you to participate in this conversation at teatime," she teased. "We may be four talkative women, but I promise that we do not bite."

He felt himself flush, uncomfortable under her scrutiny.

"I would love to see your gardens, Lady Benson," Lady Mirella continued. "Since I have finished my tea—and Lord Bridgewater has barely touched his—perhaps he would not mind showing them to me."

It was the last thing Byron wanted to do, being alone with this woman, but he realized his behavior had already bordered on churlish.

Looking to his aunt, he said, "I would be happy to show Lady Mirella the gardens, Aunt Flora, with your permission."

"Of course, Bridgewater," she responded, smiling indulgently at him. "We will see the two of you later. Enjoy."

He watched as Lady Mirella dabbed a napkin to her lips, causing him to wonder what it would be like to kiss her. Quickly, he vanquished the improper thought and brushed his own cloth against his mouth, setting it aside and rising.

"The gardens are this way, my lady."

They left the group and walked the length of the terrace, to where the stairs lead down to the ground. He took two steps and paused, realizing she was not following him. Turning, he looked up at her and saw the quizzical expression on her face.

Gently, she said, "My lord, the usual behavior is to offer your arm to a lady, especially when stairs are involved."

He cringed inwardly, realizing his mistake.

Climbing up the steps, he said, "My apologies, my lady. I have been buried in the country for the past year, with no one but servants surrounding me. I am out of practice being around civilized company."

With that, he extended his arm, and she placed her fingers lightly upon his sleeve.

The spark which raced through Byron was unlike anything he had ever known. It startled him that he had so strong a physical reaction to such a slight touch. Deliberately, he did not meet her gaze and instead guided her down the steps. He knew since they were taking a turn around the gardens that he should continue to allow her to hold his arm.

It might undo him, however, and so he let his arm drop when they reached the grass. Let her think him boorish. He would never see her after he left Benbrook.

Or would he?

Thinking better of the situation, he said, "Perhaps you might be more comfortable tucking your hand through my arm, my lady. It will be easier to guide you along the garden path if you do so."

"And your arm won't get nearly as tired that way," she said.

He caught her lips twitching in amusement. Again, a rush of desire rippled through him, and Byron decided being alone with her was dangerous. He would show her the gardens and then make certain he spent no more time with her unless others happened to also be present.

They stepped into the gardens and talked of various flowers. That is, Lady Mirella spoke. Byron merely listened. Partway through the gardens, they came upon a bench, and he asked if she would care to rest for a few minutes. She agreed, and they both took a seat upon it.

"You seem to know quite a bit about flowers," he pointed out.

She laughed, the sound both musical and seductive. "That is thanks to my cousin. Lyric is the gardener in the Strong family. I suppose after growing up with her, she has passed along some of her knowledge about plants and flowers to me, and I did not even realize it."

"You grew up with your cousin at Shadowcrest?"

She nodded. "Yes, there were four of us who are sisters. Effie is my youngest sister, while Georgie and Pippa are my older ones. They are twins. My cousins Lyric and Allegra are also twins, and they were born on the same day my sisters were. My aunt, whom I never knew, died giving birth to them."

Lady Mirella frowned slightly, and he wanted to kiss away the small crease that formed above the bridge of her nose.

"Let me just say that my uncle is one who is not fond of girls. He had two sons already and decided not to have much at all to do with his newborn daughters. After a time, it was decided they would come and live at Shadowcrest. Mama was eager to take in Allegra and Lyric, and she is the one who raised them as her own, so they are more as sisters to me than cousins. Aunt Matty also had a hand in raising the six of us, and she is one of my favorite people in the world."

"Is that why you and your sister accompanied her to Benbrook?" he asked.

"It actually was Aunt Matty's idea for us to come and experience the Lake District for ourselves. She has spoken of it—and your aunt and uncle—often and fondly, and she wished for us to see the area for ourselves. Pippa and Georgie both wed during this past year, and they are honeymooning with their husbands now. Mama and Sophie decided to give a house party in Lyric and Allegra's honor. I did not think it appropriate for me to be present during it since I have yet to make my own come-out."

"Why is that?" he asked, being drawn in not only by her beauty but also by their conversation.

"The twins were to have made their come-outs this past spring but did not. It was a family matter, which I would prefer not to discuss, my lord, but they are eager to make a love match as others in my family have. They allowed Mama and Sophie to hold this house party for them after the Season ended."

"Who might this Sophie be?"

"Oh, she is my brother James' wife. James is the Duke of Seaton, and Sophie is his duchess." She laughed again. "I have thrown quite a few names at you, Lord Bridgewater. I suppose I will need to test you at the end of our stroll to see how well you have been listening to me."

Those cornflower blue eyes sparkled, drawing Byron in.

"But enough about me, my lord. Tell me about yourself."

He deflected her question. "When are you to make your come-out, my lady?"

"I will be doing so next Season," she revealed.

His heart sank. He had planned to attend next Season because it would be the debut for Jacinda Bowles.

And Byron intended to offer for his neighbor at the end of it.

"Will I see you at the next Season, Lord Bridgewater? I know your aunt and uncle do not frequent it. I do not recall Georgie mentioning your name this past year."

"That is because I did not go to town for it," he told her. "Lady Effie asked how long I had held my title. I was a soldier, Lady Mirella. A captain in His Majesty's army."

"You were a second son," she observed.

"I was," he confirmed. "My brother gained his title soon after he graduated from Cambridge." Knowing he couldn't admit the entire truth to this woman, he said, "My brother was in a carriage accident." It was not quite a lie, but neither was it the entire truth.

Sympathy filled her face. "And you lost him. You lost your identity, as well."

"That is an interesting remark," he said. "What do you mean?"

"I suppose you were pushed aside most of your life, my lord.

That your parents—your father especially—focused on his heir apparent. You entered the army, fully knowing it would be your career. Then you were ripped from all you knew and told to return to England, so that you might take on the title of the Marquess of Bridgewater. While I am certain you were an excellent army officer, you probably have floundered a bit, trying to find your way regarding the responsibilities of the title you now hold, all while mourning your brother."

She was not only beautiful. She was intuitive and intelligent. But he wanted to clear up one thing.

"I did not mourn my brother as much as I thought I would. He was not the man I had believed him to be," Byron admitted, thinking about Mrs. Smithson and her daughter.

Concern filled her eyes. "How so, my lord?"

He took a deep breath and slowly expelled it. "I will admit freely that I worshipped Dawson. He was the best of brothers, and we spent our childhoods together as the closest of friends. He taught me all I knew, from how to swim to how to fire a weapon accurately. I am a better rider and hunter because of the lessons he imparted."

Hesitating a moment, he decided to plunge ahead. "But Dawson became someone I truly did not recognize after he went away to university. When he took his title, he continued in a lifestyle which I did not approve of."

She placed a hand gently on his arm. "You cannot judge him so harshly, my lord. Your brother did what all young men do, sowing a few wild oats during his university days. Having the title thrust upon him at so young an age had to be difficult for him. Most young men in their twenties are gadding about town, enjoying life and their freedom from responsibilities. Your brother had to assume his obligations earlier than most. It takes longer for men to mature than women, I believe."

"You are being most kind, Lady Mirella. Perhaps I am being too hard on Dawson. I think of the idealized version of him, the one I idolized, and he was not that man at the end of his life. The carriage accident I spoke of was no accident at all. I was trying to make it seem something it was not. My brother was deep in his cups and challenged our neighbor to race against him in Hyde Park. Both men crashed their phaetons into one another. Dawson's death was instant, while Lord Hampton passed away the next day."

He raked a hand through his hair. "My father and Lord Hampton were friends from boyhood. His estate and ours abut one another. The fact that Dawson was responsible for his own death, much less Lord Hampton's, was a bitter pill for me to swallow."

Lady Mirella squeezed his arm gently in reassurance. "And you had to deal with the mixed feelings within you regarding both their deaths, as well as the death of your career. I am certain it was difficult to leave behind the friends you had made in the army and the men you led in battle. It must also be very hard to put aside your disappointment in your brother."

She removed her hand from his arm and placed it in her lap again. Byron squelched the urge to claim it again.

"You are most astute, my lady. It had never struck me that I was mourning for the career I lost. Yes, I was a decent officer. I thought I had found my place in the world, and it was very difficult to leave behind what I had committed heart and soul to. Especially because I knew nothing about being a marquess."

He brightened. "But I am learning. I spent the entire past year at Bridgefield and my other two estates, learning all that I could from my steward and others. While I was happy to accept Aunt Flora's invitation to come and visit her and Uncle Hugh, I will admit that I also wanted to view Benbrook with new eyes. How it functions. I was with the Benbrook steward the entire day, pumping him for information."

She smiled, and that smile tugged on his heartstrings.

"You will be a remarkable marquess, my lord. I know it in my bones. I do not want to boast, but feel free to ask me questions about estate management. My cousin Caleb is the Shadowcrest steward, and I have done my own share of asking him how Shadowcrest is run. I would be happy to share any information I possess with you."

He frowned. "Why would you have done so?"

"One day, I hope to wed. My husband and I will be responsible for all that happens on our country estate. While the bulk of its management will lie with my husband and our steward, I thought it important to learn all I can so that I would be able to understand those duties and help in any way I could."

Byron could not think of a single woman of his acquaintance who would have taken the time to do what Lady Mirella had done. He believed most women in Polite Society had no idea what was involved in running an estate. But the woman seated next to him apparently did because she thought it would be important to one day share that load with her husband.

He yearned to get to know her better. To talk with her. Kiss her. See if they were suited for a life together. Yet the shadow of his father loomed over the both of them, and Byron felt the pressing responsibility of seeing his father's wishes of uniting the Balfour and Bowles families come to fruition. Yes, he was mightily attracted to Lady Mirella.

But his future lay with Jacinda Bowles.

Rising, he said, "Shall we return to the house, Lady Mirella?"

A shadow flickered across her face, the emotion unreadable to him, but he sensed her disappointment. He hid his own as he offered his arm to her. They returned to the house.

"Thank you for showing me the gardens, my lord," she said. "I will see you this evening at dinner."

Byron watched her walk away, feeling a piece of him go with her. He cursed under his breath, wishing he didn't feel the strong pull of obligation which his father had instilled in him.

Because in another life, he believed he might have found love with Lady Mirella Strong.

CHAPTER FOUR

MIRELLA PARTED FROM Lord Bridgewater but knew she was not ready yet to go back to her bedchamber. While she loved Effie a great deal, her youngest sister could be overtalkative at times, and Mirella needed time to herself now to think. She doubted anyone would be in the drawing room and made her way there, relieved to find it empty. She went to the far end of the room and took a seat, gazing out the window upon the very gardens she had just strolled in with Lord Bridgewater.

He intrigued her. He infuriated her.

The marquess was an enigma. When he had first appeared upon the terrace, she had picked up on the fact that he was unhappy they were there. Mama had always said that Mirella was excellent at reading the moods of others, and she wondered why he would be upset seeing the Bentons had guests. He had been standoffish, not entering the conversation during teatime, until forced to do so. That was why she had asked to stroll in the gardens with him. She wanted to bluntly ask why he was so resentful of their presence.

No, she could not lie to herself. It wasn't the only reason she had wished to take a turn with Lord Bridgewater. The man was incredibly attractive. His height alone was impressive, but his muscular frame appealed to her greatly. Those gray eyes of his drew her in. She wanted to get to know him better. The expression *still waters run deep* came to mind, and she thought it accurately described Lord Bridgewater. Curiosity filled her, and Mirella wanted to know what was behind the serious façade of the marquess.

Not having made her come-out, she had been around very few men of Polite Society, so she did not know if the attraction she felt to the marquess was unique—or if it happened often between men and women. Something told her that the spark evident between her and the marquess was unusual.

Mirella had always been a happy, optimistic person, yet at the same time, she was quite practical. She was eager to make her come-out and find a husband. Until recently, she had not thought to love that husband. Her own parents' marriage was proof that two individuals could co-exist in a marriage and have little to do with one another. She had thought simply to find a gentleman who interested her, one whom she believed to be honest and reliable, two traits important to her.

Then her family had been struck with arrows of love from Cupid's bow.

She had seen Pippa, tomboy that she was, grow girlish, swooning over Viscount Hopewell. Georgie, too, had fallen head over heels for Lord Edgethorne. The marquess was terribly scarred from battle—even missing one eye—and yet Georgie had loved August from the start.

James and Sophie were also a shining example of the power of love, bringing together the rivals of England's two biggest shipping empires, uniting them in marriage. Even her mother, making a new start with Captain Andrews, had finally found what other Strongs had.

Because of what she had witnessed, seeing the incredible transformations in the lives of her loved ones, Mirella had known it must be a love match for her—or nothing at all. In a way, she had almost been relieved when she had been unable to participate in the last Season. It gave her more time to learn about herself, as well as additional time to decide that a love match was most important to her.

She had caught the various couples in the family kissing, so she understood part of love did deal with the physical. Already, she felt a strong pull toward Lord Bridgewater.

The marquess seemed her opposite, however. Closed off from others. Incredibly sober. He also had no family around him to help support him, whereas she had Strongs coming out the seams who loved her and wanted the best for her.

How on earth was she supposed to pursue him?

She had believed it was the role of a gentleman to show interest in a lady first, but now she wasn't so certain. Had Pippa and Georgie told the men they were attracted to of their interest? How did James and Sophie or Mama and the captain come to be? Suddenly, Mirella had too many questions and absolutely no answers.

Her heart told her that there was a strong possibility Lord Bridgewater could be meant for her but that he would never speak up. Would he consider her too brazen if she made known her interest in him?

Mirella decided her best course of action would be to get to know the marquess during this visit to Benbrook. She knew from watching other Strongs that love involved more than the physical and emotional connections. Her Strong relatives had also formed a bond of friendship with their future spouses. Perhaps that was the way to proceed. Mirella didn't know if men and women in Polite Society forged friendships with one another, but she intended to extend an offer of friendship to Lord Bridgewater and try to get to know him as well as she could during the next week.

She hoped that he would be attending the Season next spring, and she could pick up the threads of their friendship when they became reacquainted at the various social affairs. She believed it might give her an advantage over other ladies he might meet while in town. It would also test her feelings for the marquess, being separated throughout the autumn and winter months. If they came together next spring and she still harbored feelings for him, Mirella would know then that the marquess was the one for her.

She only hoped he would feel the same toward her.

Her fingers practically itched to play. She had not done so since they had left Kent. They had been staying at inns, with no pianofortes in sight, but there was one in this room, and Mirella went to it. She had done enough thinking. It was time to lose herself now in music, which had always been her passion, salvation, and comfort.

Sitting, she placed her fingers on the keyboard, taking a moment to decide which composer she wished to play. Then her fingers began to dance along the keys, and the music took her over.

When she finished playing the piece, she sensed she was not alone. Turning, Mirella saw that Aunt Matty had slipped into the drawing room. Rising, she joined her aunt on the settee.

"Every time I hear you play, Mirella, it is such a treat. Your talent is immense. I almost wish you could play professionally."

She laughed. "That will never come to pass, Aunt. I will always keep up with my music, however, even when I wed someday."

"How did your stroll with Lord Bridgewater go?"

She sensed her cheeks heating and said, "The Benbrook gardens are quite lovely. You will have to go through them with me. Lyric would have been so proud because I pointed out several different varieties of flowers and plants to the marquess. He seemed unfamiliar with gardens."

"I am not asking about the gardens, Mirella. I am asking about how you feel about Lord Bridgewater," Aunt Matty said, her gaze intense.

Her aunt knew her all too well. "I do not have a great deal of experience with men," she began. "That is what my come-out will be for. I will say, however, that I am greatly intrigued by Lord Bridgewater."

"You feel something about him, don't you?" her aunt pressed. "Something almost indescribable. Probably hard to put into words since, as you said, you do not have much experience."

"How did you know, Aunt Matty?" she marveled.

"I saw the way he looked at you," her aunt said matter-of-factly. "From the time he took your hand upon being introduced, I could tell something had passed between the two of you. He was rather cold to us, though. Flora even apologized for his brusqueness after the two of you left us."

"He is not the kind of man I thought I would be attracted to," she admitted. "In all honesty, I believed I would be drawn to someone jovial and outgoing. A man who was friendly to all. Instead of being open, Lord Bridgewater seems closed off from others."

Aunt Matty looked at her knowingly. "And yet you are still drawn to him."

"He is struggling, Aunt Matty. He took on his title a year ago and was hopelessly unprepared for it. From what I gather, he received little to no attention from his parents."

A knowing light filled her aunt's eyes. "Yes, that is quite common amongst the *ton*, the heir apparent receiving all the attention, while other sons—and even daughters—are ignored."

"It is worse than that," she revealed. "Bridgewater idolized his older brother. Apparently, they were very close during their childhood. Then this brother gained the title and seemed to turn a bit . . . wild. While the current Lord Bridgewater is all about honor and duty, thanks to his army experience, I think he found his brother lacking in his role as the Marquess of Bridgewater."

Aunt Matty nodded. "It is hard when you have such a high opinion of someone you love whom you are close to, and then you discover how they have disappointed you and others. Hugh told me that his nephew has always been on the serious side, even as a child. That he and Flora did their best to try and give the boy a bit of attention since he received so little from his parents. Hugh said that the marquess has spent a good bit of time with the

Benbrook steward during this visit, trying to learn from him so he could take back new ideas to his own estate."

"Yes, I know Lord Bridgewater is trying his best to learn about estate management. I offered to help him if I could. You know how both Effie and I have spent a great deal of time with Caleb, and most likely, we know more than the usual person about the scope of an estate and how it is run."

"Are you going to pursue a friendship with Lord Bridgewater while we are here?"

"That was my very idea. There is something between us. Something unnamed pulls me toward him. I thought if I could be open and get to know him some during this visit, a foundation of friendship might be forged. I would like to think that it might help come next Season when I make my come-out and he is present. If I am a friendly face, he may turn to me. If in the coming months my feelings toward him change, then it would still be nice to see him next Season."

Aunt Matty looked at her knowingly. "I think the spark you have felt will only grow in magnitude."

She looked at her aunt a long moment. "You know what you are speaking of, don't you, Aunt Matty?"

It surprised her when tears misted the older woman's eyes, and Mirella reached out and took her aunt's hand.

"Can you tell me about it? I have never thought to ask you about your youth. Why you never wed. I know you made your come-out. As a duke's daughter, it would have been expected of you."

"Yes, I made my debut into Polite Society many years ago, the same year Flora did. She met Hugh—and I met the love of my life."

"How did I not know this?" she asked.

"Flora and Hugh know about it because they were present and saw the events unfold." Aunt Matty patted their joined hands. "The only other person I have ever spoken to of this was Pippa recently, when she had questions about her and Seth."

"Would you be willing to share your story with me?" Mirella asked quietly. "If it is too upsetting, though, we need never speak of it again."

"No, perhaps it is time I told you. I am close to all six of you girls, Mirella, but I have always felt a special bond with you."

A dreamy expression filled Aunt Matty's face, and Mirella eagerly anticipated what her aunt would tell her.

"I came to town all those years ago with stars in my eyes, ready to make my match. After all, as you pointed out, I was a duke's daughter. I would most likely have my pick of the eligible bachelors at the Season. I was quite the beauty back then, and my dowry was substantial. I entered the Season with high hopes of finding a husband from a good family, one who would give me plenty of children to love."

Aunt Matty swallowed. "From the first, I was quite popular, my programme filled at each ball. While I found many of the gentlemen present amusing and handsome, only one stole my heart."

Perplexed, she asked, "Why did you not wed this man?"

"Sadly, he was leaving England. He was the second son of an earl, and his family had purchased a commission for him in the army. He was to be a lieutenant and would leave for his officer's training mid-way through the Season. His mother thought it would be good for him to share in the company of other young people before he left and have a bit of fun. After his training was complete, he had already been told his group would be shipped out to North America. This was at a time when the colonies still were a part of the British empire."

Her aunt sighed. "Oh, how I loved him, Mirella. His kisses took me to places I could never have dreamed of. His touch was simply magical."

Aunt Matty paused. "But he told me that he could not offer for me. That it would be inappropriate for an army lieutenant to wed a duke's daughter. And even if we did marry, we would be more than three thousand miles apart while he went to fight in what became known as Pontiac's Rebellion. I begged him not to go. To change his mind. To stay in England with me. I told him how much I loved him. That I would always love him—and only him."

Her aunt shook her head sadly, and Mirella's heart ached for her loved one.

"He would not utter words of love to me and give me hope, which I will admit pained me. He told me the commission had been purchased, and his family expected him to do his duty to England. We parted with one last kiss, and I never saw him again."

She found her own eyes welling with tears. "Oh, Aunt Matty. I had no idea that you had loved a man so deeply."

"I still love him to this day," her aunt admitted. "I tried not to. I did another couple of Seasons with the intention of finding myself a husband. But no one appealed to me after having known my lieutenant."

"Do you know what became of him, Aunt Matty? Did he rise through the ranks?"

"He died of his battle wounds, only a few months after he arrived on the war front," her aunt said, shocking Mirella. "I received a letter from one of his fellow officers. My beloved was dying, too weak to write, but he begged his friend to write to me in his place. In the letter, he told me how much he loved me and how hard it had been to walk away from a life with me. That his last thoughts would be of me."

By now, tears fell down her aunt's cheeks, and Aunt Matty pulled a handkerchief from her sleeve, wiping them away.

"I knew in my heart that I could never love another as I had loved him. I decided I would devote myself to my family instead. It would not have been fair to wed when my heart and soul would always belong to someone else."

Aunt Matty cupped Mirella's cheek. "From the moment we laid eyes upon one another, I felt a connection with him, much as you have experienced with Lord Bridgewater. I think your plan sound, my darling. Get to know this man further during the next few days. Let the months go by and see if your feelings ebb or if they grow stronger with his absence. Next Season, you can reacquaint yourself with him, as well as meet a good number of other eligible bachelors. Your heart will tell you what you need to know."

Mirella wrapped her arms about Aunt Matty, hugging her tightly.

"Thank you for sharing your story with me. For always being here for me."

Aunt Matty brushed the tears from Mirella's cheeks. "Come. We should return to our bedchambers and prepare ourselves for dinner. Flora will be sending up hot water for our baths, knowing we have been traveling and would enjoy soaking for a good, long while."

She returned to her room, where Effie was already bathing. Her sister was chatty as usual, not noticing how quiet Mirella was.

She would take her aunt's advice. Hopefully, her heart would speak loudly enough so that Mirella could hear it—and act accordingly.

CHAPTER FIVE

"Move aside," Byron barked at his valet. "I can tie my own bloody cravat."

"Yes, my lord," Keller said meekly, stepping back.

Gritting his teeth, he tied the cravat once and did such a terrible job that he started over. Again, a second time, the result was dismal.

"My temper got the best of me," he told the servant. "Would you have a go at it, Keller?"

"Of course, my lord," the valet said eagerly, returning to stand in front of Byron and effortlessly tying the cravat. "That should do, my lord."

Glancing in the mirror, he saw the knot was perfect and added, "I have been out of sorts, Keller. I did not mean for you to suffer the ill effects of my sour mood."

"Anything else you require, my lord?" the valet asked, seemingly unsure how he was supposed to respond to what Byron revealed.

"No. That will be all until later this evening. Go have your supper. Take a walk about the grounds. Enjoy the countryside. The sun will not set until eight o'clock or so. I won't require you for another hour or two after that."

He watched the valet leave the bedchamber, angry at himself

for snapping at the servant. Byron had been out of sorts ever since he discovered his aunt and uncle's guests at tea. No, that had merely annoyed him. It was the stroll through the gardens with Lady Mirella that had him so vexed. And it wasn't the lady herself which had him disgruntled.

It was the knowing he could not pursue her.

During his years in the military, he had been too busy killing French soldiers and trying to protect his men to think about women. Marriage had not been a choice for him, and he had willingly accepted that. When Dawson's reckless actions caused his death and Lord Hampton's, however, Byron accepted a new reality, one which included providing an heir to the title. Since his father had arranged for Dawson's betrothal to Jacinda Bowles, Byron now felt obligated to see that new arrangements be made and that he would stand in for Dawson as Jacinda's new intended, uniting their families as their fathers had wished.

His own solicitor had explained to him that the marriage contracts were null and void with the death of Dawson Balfour. They had been written before his brother assumed the title. It might have been a slightly trickier situation if they had merely named the Marquess of Bridgewater as the groom, but that had not been the case, according to Mr. Pilsbury.

Still, duty and obligations had been so ingrained into Byron by his father that he told himself that he would honor the previously written marriage settlements and wed Jacinda himself.

He just hadn't told the bride. Or her brother.

Last year, when Byron had arrived back at Bridgefield, he had paid a call on the new Lord Hampton. Cedric had been fresh out of Cambridge, having graduated less than a month before the fatal race took place. The viscount was a couple of years younger than Byron and though they were neighbors and their fathers close, no friendship existed between them. He thought both Cedric and Jacinda too much like the annoying Lady Hampton. In his opinion, both siblings were snobbish and dull.

Still, he had done his duty and gone to see them. He had met with Cedric in what had been Lord Hampton's study. Though now an adult, Cedric still had the air of a lost little boy, in part because he still looked so young and immature, as if he were barely old enough to shave. He had addressed Cedric as Lord Hampton, but even Byron could see the new viscount was in a daze, and not simply because his father had died suddenly. Hampton admitted to Byron how overwhelmed he was at having to immediately take on so many responsibilities. He had whined about how unfair life was and how he was supposed to be in town, drinking and wenching and gambling with his friends for several years, not stuck in the country trying to figure out how to read ledgers and deal with surly tenants, things he had absolutely no interest in.

Byron had murmured a few sympathetic words and then left as quickly as he could. He did not share with Hampton his idea of offering for Jacinda. Though he was still committed to that plan of action, he held back, not informing either of the Bowles siblings what would unfold during Jacinda's come-out Season. He thought it best to merely reacquaint himself with her at the start of the Season and then court her accordingly. It wouldn't be fair at her tender age to draw up the new marriage contracts and then inform her of the betrothal.

In time, he would take Lord Hampton into his confidence and believed the new viscount would be glad to have his sister off his hands. Though Jacinda had not made an appearance during Byron's visit, Hampton had lamented what a handful his sister had become and how he would gladly place her on the Marriage Mart when the time came for her to make her debut.

He did know his neighbors had gone to town this past spring, thanks to overhearing talk amongst his servants. Apparently, Jacinda had demanded to go to town with her brother during the Season and not be left in the country, threatening that she would elope to Gretna Green with a groom if Hampton did not take her with him. More gossip had spread from town to the country, with Byron again overhearing his servants talk about how wild the new Lord Hampton was and how his gambling debts were growing. While Byron did not believe Hampton would be able to touch Jacinda's dowry, his behavior was certainly one of concern.

Next spring, he would make certain to dance with Jacinda and send her flowers. Even make morning calls to show his interest in her. He dreaded having to waste his time doing such things, but she would be expecting it. If she were as disagreeable as her brother had been, she might not have as many suitors as she wished. Then again, she was quite the beauty. Most men would look past her behavior and accept her dowry and hope their children favored her more than them.

Because of this situation, Byron could not show any interest in Lady Mirella Strong. Unfortunately, Lady Mirella was everything he would have wanted in a wife if he were selecting one on his own. She held herself with grace and had a maturity about her which few her age possessed. She seemed witty and intelligent, and she had not been afraid to speak up around him.

Then there were his physical reactions to her. His heart speeding up. The faint fluttering in his chest. Excitement? Desire? He neither knew nor cared. All he was certain of was that she was the loveliest creature he had ever encountered, full of life and spirit, and he must avoid her at all costs. He wanted to cut short his visit with Aunt Flora and Uncle Hugh, but they never attended the Season. If he left now, he did not know for certain when he would see them again. Therefore, Byron decided to remain at Benbrook, despite Lady Mirella's presence and those of her traveling party. He would be pleasant to them, but he would avoid being alone with her at all costs.

Because if he did find himself alone with her, Byron was certain he would kiss her.

And that could prove to be disastrous.

Knowing he could no longer delay making an appearance, he ventured to the drawing room. It was the habit of his aunt and uncle to meet there for a drink before dinner, and they had done so the past two nights of his visit. Of course, the mood would now change with four other guests in attendance. Byron assumed Miss Feathers would also dine with them since she had taken tea with the group this afternoon. Aunt Flora had never been one to stand on ceremony, and so she would treat the governess as any other guest.

He entered the drawing room and forced himself not to search for Lady Mirella. He spied his uncle talking with Lady Effie and Miss Feathers and went to join them.

"Good evening. I hope you are unpacked and settled in at Benbrook," he said, trying to be affable.

Lady Effie cocked a brow at him. "You are being friendly now, my lord? You were a bit unsociable this afternoon."

Byron couldn't help but laugh. The girl didn't censor her thoughts in the slightest.

"What is so funny?" she demanded, looking to her governess.

Miss Feathers smiled indulgently and then turned to him. "My lord, you must be warned that Lady Effie speaks her mind. She does not disguise her feelings in any way."

The lady in question sniffed haughtily. "Well, I do not see why I should pretend about anything. Lord Bridgewater was downright disagreeable this afternoon. I am merely pleased that he has chosen to be pleasant this evening." She looked at him earnestly. "I do hope you will remain this way, my lord. Before, you appeared quite sullen. Perhaps it was walking in the gardens with Mirella that helped improve your mood. Mirella can brighten anyone's day, even if they are in the darkest of moods."

"Did I hear my name?"

Lady Mirella joined them, and Byron felt his skin prickle. The tingling sensation was quite pleasant. He took in the powder blue evening gown she wore, noting her hair simply dressed, swept away from her face. The hairstyle only enhanced her natural beauty.

"I was just telling Lord Bridgewater how he seems to be in a much better mood than he was previously," Lady Effie said. "I credited you with the improvement in his conduct."

"I am sorry if I was rude this afternoon, Lady Effie," he apologized. "I promise to be on my best behavior during the rest of your visit."

"See?" the young lady said, looking at her governess. "It is perfectly fine to let someone know their behavior has offended you."

Miss Feathers blushed. "Restraint, my lady. It is wise to practice it."

Lady Effie smiled triumphantly at Byron. "Miss Feathers believes me to be too outspoken at times. Mama, as well. But James, my brother, says I am like a colt running free and that I should not be broken by Polite Society's many rules."

"To fit into Polite Society, though, it would be good if you learned to curb your tongue, Effie," her sister cautioned. "Exercising a bit of self-control never hurt anyone. It will also keep you from treading upon others' feelings."

"Well, I find you to be quite delightful, my lady," Byron said, sticking up for the young woman.

"Thank you, my lord. And as far as Polite Society goes, I am not certain I even wish to be a part of it."

He had never heard such a remark uttered before and couldn't help but ask, "Why not?"

"I think there are too many rules to adhere to," Lady Effie explained. "Silly rules, at that. And I am not one for dressing up in fancy gowns and parading about. To be honest, most of the time, I would rather be around animals rather than people. I even brought my cat with me on our journey. Daffy, which is short for Daffodil."

Byron looked from one sister to the other. "It is hard to imagine you are sisters because you are so different from one another."

Even though he found the youngest Strong sister's attitude unique, he was still taken with Lady Mirella.

"We do not favor one another physically," Lady Mirella agreed. "My auburn hair comes from my paternal grandmother, while Effie's blond hair is from her maternal grandmother. The rest of our siblings and cousins all have dark hair."

"But we all possess the Strong eyes," Lady Effie pointed out. "Just like Aunt Matty and our father."

"The shade is most becoming to you both," Byron said gallantly.

They were summoned into dinner, and he did his best to be friendly and not aloof. Surprisingly, he enjoyed the meal more than any he had eaten in a long time, thanks to the addition of their guests. Mills even brought out a birthday cake Cook had made for him, and the group became quite merry eating it.

After dinner, Aunt Flora suggested they return to the drawing room. He and Uncle Hugh skipped having a cigar and opted to bring their snifters of brandy with them. Byron took a seat beside Lady Mathilda, in part because he had not spoken with her this evening, but more so because it meant he did not have to sit with Lady Mirella.

"Lady Mirella, you simply must play the pianoforte for us," his aunt declared. "Matty has spoken with great pride over the years of the musical talent you and Lady Georgina possess."

"I would be happy to do so, my lady," Lady Mirella said, rising from her seat and sitting at the pianoforte.

The moment she moved her hands to perch above the keys, Byron sat up. While he had thought her a charming, intelligent woman, she now looked like a queen, confidence brimming through her. Then she struck the first few notes of a piece, her fingers flying across the keyboard in a blur. He sat, fascinated, his jaw falling open in wonder. She played Beethoven as Byron had never heard the composer's works played before. He had listened to others perform on the pianoforte before, both men and women.

None held the talent Lady Mirella displayed.

When she finished, everyone applauded her efforts, Byron most of all.

"My niece is certainly talented," Lady Mathilda remarked to

him. "She has practiced daily from the time she was a small girl. Why, I believe the only time she has been away from it has been on our way to the Lake District."

"Play something else, my lady," Uncle Hugh encouraged. "I am most fond of the pianoforte. I played as a young boy but did not keep it up after I went to university."

"What would you care to hear, my lord?" Lady Mirella asked.

Uncle Hugh asked for Schubert, saying he had a particular fondness for the composer.

Lady Mirella smiled, and Byron's heart melted. "Oh, I have always enjoyed playing Schubert's compositions, my lord. His work moves me greatly."

She placed her hands on the keyboard again, still for a moment, and then she dived into the music. Again, Byron had never heard such remarkable playing in his life and wondered what other talents Mirella Strong possessed.

When she finished, Uncle Hugh went to the pianoforte to speak with her, and Lady Mathilda turned to him.

"What do you think of my niece, Lord Bridgewater?" the old woman asked.

"She has a rare talent, my lady. I am astounded at her playing."

Lady Mathilda smiled. "Mirella possesses many talents, my lord. Her beauty is but a small part of her. I like to think she is beautiful both inside and out."

Lady Mirella began playing again, and this time, Byron recognized the work of Mozart. He sat, entranced, watching her fingers and then her face. When she finished playing, he was certain of one thing, one terrible, frightening thing.

He had not only fallen in love with the way Lady Mirella Strong played the pianoforte.

He had fallen in love with her.

CHAPTER SIX

MIRELLA AWOKE TO Effie's sneezing. She turned toward her sister and saw Effie's red nose and swollen eyes.

"Oh, no! Are you ill?"

Effie nodded, misery on her face. "I woke up a few hours ago and have tried to stay quiet so that you might be able to get enough rest. It is one of those nasty summer head colds. I felt something coming on last night at dinner and was hoping I was wrong."

She rang for a servant and asked for hot water and extra handkerchiefs. Effie wasn't hungry, so Mirella merely requested hot tea be sent up, with honey.

The tea arrived, and Effie was able to drink two cups of it while a maid helped Mirella dress for the day. She did her own hair, pulling it back in the chignon she favored.

"I am going down to breakfast and will tell Aunt Matty and Lady Benton that you are under the weather, then I will be back up to sit with you."

Effie blew her nose loudly, shaking her head. "No, Mirella. There is no reason for you to be cooped up all day, just to watch me while I rest in bed. Besides, Daffy can keep me company." Her sister stroked the cat, who was curled against her side.

Plans had been made the previous evening for Lord Bridgewater to take her, Effie, and Miss Feathers riding around Grasmere Lake, and Mirella said, "I do not wish to ride without you."

"You know me. I usually get over a cold in a day. Two at most," Effie reminded her. "There is no sense for you and Miss Feathers not to ride out with Lord Bridgewater and see some of the area."

She looked at her sister doubtfully, and Effie's jaw set. Of all the Strongs, Effie was the most stubborn. When her mind was made up, there was no changing it.

"I am determined you will not stay, Mirella. Go and enjoy yourself. Miss Feathers, too."

"I will go to breakfast and inform the others, then I will come and check on you," she promised. "If you are worse, I will stay behind."

When she reached the breakfast room, Mirella saw she was the last to arrive.

"Forgive my tardiness, but Effie is ill."

"I hope it is not anything too serious," Aunt Matty said, concerned.

"It is merely a summer cold. As Effie herself said, she usually recovers fairly quickly. She reminded me of that very thing when I offered to stay with her today. Naturally, she refused me. Obviously, she will not be able to go riding with us, however. She will need to spend the day in bed."

Miss Feathers said, "I will volunteer to stay home with Effie. I can sit and read while she is resting in bed and even catch up on my letter writing. There is no sense for you not to see the lake and the surrounding area, Lady Mirella."

She bit her lip, thinking if the governess stayed behind, it would be only her and Lord Bridgewater on the excursion.

"That sounds like a wonderful compromise," Lady Benton said. "Bridgewater, you can show Lady Mirella Grasmere Lake. I would also suggest stopping in the village for some gingerbread," she told her nephew. Turning to Mirella, the countess added,

"Grasmere is known for its gingerbread. You simply must try it."

"Gingerbread is a particular favorite of Effie's," she said. "Though she doesn't have much of an appetite now, she might perk up a bit if I do return with a treasured sweet."

"Then it is settled," declared Lord Benton. "I hope Lady Mirella will enjoy her tour of the area. Be sure to stop by St. Oswald's, Bridgewater. The old church is fascinating."

"I will," the marquess said, avoiding looking at her.

She knew he was aware of the physical reaction she had had to him because she believed he, too, felt it, the same as she had. It worried her to be alone with him, but then again, they would be on their horses, riding around the lake and into the village. Surely, nothing untoward might happen on such an outing.

At least, Mirella hoped that would be the case.

They finished the meal, and Lord Bridgewater said, "Would it be convenient to leave now, my lady?"

"If you could give me half an hour, my lord. I wish to check on Effie again, and I will need to change into my riding habit."

"Then meet me in the foyer. We can go down to the stables together."

She excused herself and returned to the shared bedchamber. Her sister dozed in the bed, Daffy snuggled against her, and Mirella decided not to ring for a maid to assist her, thinking it might disturb Effie. Quietly, she changed from her gown into her riding habit, choosing a hat she believed to be rather smart with her ensemble.

As she prepared to leave the room, Effie stirred. Mirella went to the bed, and her sister looked up.

"Good. You are going riding, after all. Take in all the sights for me so that you might show them to me in a few days."

"Miss Feathers has said she wishes to stay with you, Effie. She insisted." Mirella smiled. "And she wore that stern, governess look. I simply could not tell her no."

Effie laughed—and sneezed three times.

"We will take you both out once you are feeling better," she assured her sister, bending and kissing Effie's brow. "Now, get some rest."

As she exited the bedchamber, Miss Feathers was coming down the corridor, carrying a book with her. Mirella told the governess that Effie had had a restless night and would most likely sleep most of the morning.

"Do not worry about your sister, my lady. If Lady Effie needs anything, I will be there to help her."

"Thank you for staying with her. I appreciate it."

Miss Feathers smiled brightly. "No sense in you having to miss out on the tour of the area just because your sister is ailing."

She took her leave and went down the staircase, finding Lord Bridgewater waiting at the bottom of it for her. Just one look at the marquess, and her heart began thumping wildly against her ribs. Even her belly seemed to erupt with a bevy of butterflies fluttering madly.

"How is Lady Effie?" he asked as they went out the front door and headed to the stables.

"Her head is stuffy. She is blowing her nose quite a bit. She did not sleep well last night and will try to catch up on her rest today. Effie is rarely ill, but she always bounces back quickly. You will have to play tour guide again and take her and Miss Feathers around the lake and village if you are willing to do so."

"She is a bright, inquisitive girl, isn't she?"

"She is," Mirella agreed. "Effie is the most loveable of all the Strongs. I hope you will forgive her impertinence."

"I did not mind it. I found her quite refreshing. Although I have never attended the Season before, I truly believe she will have to learn to watch what she says around members of the *ton*."

"Effie will make her come-out not this coming Season but the next," Mirella informed the marquess. "That gives her a little more time in which to mature." She chuckled. "Knowing Effie, she will continue to say what she thinks, not caring what Polite Society makes of her."

Lord Bridgewater frowned. "The girl will have to understand

that in order to acquire a husband, she cannot be too outspoken."

His words rankled her. "Effie will be Effie. That is all there is to it, my lord. If there is a gentleman who disapproves of her forthright manner, then he is not the man for her. Besides, she is the daughter of a duke and sister to another one. No doubt, Effie will have a large line of suitors wishing to woo her."

"The same could be said of you, Lady Mirella," the marquess noted.

"Frankly, my lord, I do not worry about the number of suitors who will try to court me. I am looking for two things in a husband."

Curiosity filled his face. "And what might those two things be?"

"The first is, I wish for a man of good character. The gentleman I wed will need to be honorable and truthful. He must value family. Family is extremely important to me. I have the support of a large, loving one, and I cannot imagine wedding a man who does not cherish family as I do."

"And the second thing?" he asked.

As the stables came into sight, she said, "You will probably think me most foolish, but I am seeking a love match."

"Love?" he barked out, startling her.

"Yes, my lord," she said assertively. "I will wed a man whom I love, one who loves me, as well. This generation of Strongs is known for making love matches, and I will settle for nothing less."

She stole a glance at him and saw his jaw set. Immediately, she wondered if this man would be capable of love. He already had been cast aside in his family, an afterthought to his brother. The marquess might not understand the true importance of family, much less have an idea how to give and receive love.

These thoughts captioned Mirella as far as thinking of Lord Bridgewater as husband material went. While there might be a physical attraction between them, that would not be enough for a successful marriage, in her mind. She would have to temper her feelings—and reactions—toward him.

A groom met them. "Going for a ride today, my lord? It's a fine one for doing so."

"Yes, we are," Lord Bridgewater replied. Turning to her, he asked, "What kind of rider are you, my lady?"

She looked at the groom. "I was brought up in the saddle. I can ride any mount that you provide to me. I prefer mares because I think they have a better temperament, but I will leave the choice up to you, Sir."

"Very well, my lady," the groom said. "Apollo for you, my lord?"

The marquess nodded, and the groom left them to go and saddle their horses. Conversation between them ceased, with Lord Bridgewater striding off, hands behind his back, fingers locked, as he surveyed the land, his back to her.

Mirella decided her attraction to this man was a terrible idea. He barely seemed capable of decent conversation, much less open to the idea of love. She came to the conclusion that it was good she felt a pull toward him, though. She might feel an attraction to other men during the Season, but she could not let that dominate her thoughts, much less cloud her judgment. While she still believed desiring her spouse would be important, she wanted to build a solid foundation, alternating stones of friendship with love and respect.

The groom appeared, leading one horse, a large black that looked to be at least seventeen hands. She figured it must be Apollo, meant for Lord Bridgewater.

Another groom followed with a chestnut beauty. He brought the horse to her and said, "This is Lady, my lady. She has a sweet temperament, but she can also fly like the wind if you ask her to do so."

Mirella stroked the horse's nose. "It sounds as if we were meant for one another, Lady. I think we will have a perfectly wonderful ride together."

She looked around for a mounting block and did not spy one.

Before she could ask the groom for a hand up, Lord Bridgewater came toward her, saying, "I will assist you into the saddle, Lady Mirella."

Suddenly, his hands captured her small waist, almost spanning it, and he lifted her with ease into the saddle. Mirella caught a whiff of bergamot, thanks to his nearness, and her heart raced, the feel of his hands still on her even after he had released her. She swallowed, taking up her reins, stroking Lady's neck, trying to calm herself before the ride began. Horses were sensitive to the moods of their riders, and Mirella did not want to get off on the wrong foot with Lady.

In the meantime, Lord Bridgewater mounted his horse and said, "Follow me."

He broke into a canter, and she nudged Lady's flanks. The horse responded, and they quickly caught up to the marquess, riding beside him.

"We will ride to the lake first," he told her.

That was the last conversation between them for the next few miles. As they rode, she took in the landscape surrounding them, finding it moving, very much like the guidebook described.

They reached Lake Grasmere, and he brought his horse to a stop. Mirella did the same, and they both stared out across the water and up to the fells and mountains which surrounded the picturesque valley.

"No wonder Mr. Wordsworth chose to live here. I believe he may be right when he said of Grasmere, 'The most loveliest spot that man hath found.'"

"You read Wordsworth's poetry?"

"I will admit that I had not read much poetry at all until we were destined to visit the Lake District. Aunt Matty gave both Effie and me Mr. West's guidebook, along with a volume of Mr. Wordsworth's poetry. I have found his poems to be quite stirring. Miss Feathers read some of them with us, pointed out why the poet's work is so outstanding."

He nodded brusquely. "Then you should also tackle Coleridge," he suggested. "Samuel Taylor Coleridge is a close friend of Wordsworth's. They wrote a collection together which you might enjoy. It is called *Lyrical Ballads*."

"You sound very familiar with both their works."

His face grew boyish as he said, "I might have been a career soldier, but at heart, I have always been an academic. I enjoy literature, poetry, in particular. Knowing the two men wrote of the area where Aunt Flora and Uncle Hugh resided gave their poems even more meaning to me."

"Which of Mr. Wordsworth's poems is your favorite?" she asked, wanting to gain more insight into the marquess.

He grew thoughtful. "From his earlier works? *Tintern Abbey*. From his time in Grasmere? Perhaps *Ode: Intimations of Immortality*. And what of you, Lady Mirella? Do you have a favorite?"

"I, too, enjoy that ode quite a bit, but I am most fond of *I Wandered Lonely as a Cloud*."

"Let us continue on our way," he said abruptly. "I need to take you to see *The Lion and the Lamb* and *Old Lady at the Organ*."

The quick change of topics puzzled her. "Good heavens, what are those?"

He smiled for the first time, and new, wonderful sensations ran through Mirella, ones which she tried to fight.

And lost.

"It is that peak over there."

She looked to where he pointed and frowned. "I am not quite certain I see either thing you referred to."

His smile widened, further melting her heart, breaking down the walls of resistance she had put up. Those walls had not had time to set, though, and the marquess' smile was magical, tearing the stones from the imaginary wall with ease.

"Because we are not in the correct position to observe those profiles. If we travel to one side, you will see the two animals lying together. When we venture to the other side, we get an entirely different view, and it actually does look like an old woman playing an organ."

She laughed. "I will play the role of Doubting Thomas and not believe in those nicknames until I can see for myself. So, lead the way, my lord."

His brows knit together. "You are not too tired, my lady? I thought we would need to rest a bit longer before we continued on."

Mirella laughed. "I am used to being in the saddle for hours at a time at Shadowcrest," she informed him. "Take me to the old woman first. We will save the animals for last."

He wheeled his horse, and she followed him, curious about the nicknames she assumed locals had given the peak.

And despite wanting to tamp down her attraction to him, Mirella found her curiosity growing about this gruff, poetry-loving marquess.

CHAPTER SEVEN

"My goodness!" Lady Mirella declared. "It really *does* look like a lion hovering protectively over a lamb."

"You sound surprised," Byron said to her. "I told you Helm Crag had these two profiles."

She looked at him dubiously. "You also said the first one we saw looked like an old lady at the organ."

He shrugged nonchalantly. "I told you that is what the locals call it. The fact you could not conjure her and her instrument? Well, that is lack of imagination on your part," he teased.

She swatted at him playfully, stirring his blood. He reminded himself to hold back. He wasn't supposed to be enjoying this time alone with her. Byron had mapped out his future—and it did not include a place for Lady Mirella Strong in it.

Still, she had been wonderful company on this ride. She was effervescent and enthusiastic about life, easy to be with. Slowly, he saw how she was drawing him out, and he liked the person he was when he was with her.

They chatted about the rock formation a moment, and then he spontaneously asked, "Would you care to go to the top of Helm Crag in order to take in the view? It is not a difficult climb up the fell, as other paths in the Lake District can be. Then again, I know it is not what most ladies would be interested in doing."

She smiled at him, and it was like the brilliance of the sun consumed him.

"I am not some wilting flower, Lord Bridgewater. At heart, I am a country girl. While I may not be the tomboy that Pippa and Effie are, I am comfortable walking and riding great distances. You do not have to treat me as if I am a fragile hothouse flower who might die if challenged to climb a hill." She held out her arms. "Besides, it is the perfect day for a walk."

Then she looked about. "Perhaps we might tether our horses over there."

"Yes. Splendid idea," he said, dismounting from Apollo.

Byron went to her, reaching up and clasping her waist, bringing her to the ground. He caught a floral scent on her skin and wished he could bury his nose against her long, slender neck.

They attached their reins to a nearby bush, with Lady Mirella stroking her mount, saying, "We will not be gone long at all, Lady. I promise you fresh water and a large bucket of oats when we return to Benbrook."

She then leaned in and pressed a kiss to the horse's nose, her actions bewildering him.

They began the walk up Helm Crag, and the conversation flowed smoothly between them. Byron could not remember the last time he had enjoyed himself so much in anyone's company.

When they reached a spot familiar to him, he stopped. "That is the rock Dorothy Wordsworth, sister to the poet, used to perch upon. She would write down the poems that her brother dictated as he moved about, drinking in nature."

"Truly? I must sit upon it."

Lady Mirella sat upon the rock, placing her palms flat on it behind her, tilting her face up to the sun. Byron thought her even more beautiful than when they had first met and attributed it to knowing more about the kind of person she was.

She opened her eyes and smiled mischievously. "I would record whatever poems you spouted, my lord, but I am afraid I have neither pencil nor paper with me today."

He laughed easily. "Then we must come back another time when we are both more prepared."

They continued moving up the fell, the sunshine strong for the early September day. For once, no threat of rain was in sight. Byron had gotten used to the unusually heavy amount of rainfall that occurred in the Lake District.

"Oh, how I wish I had been able to bring my paints with me," she declared.

"You paint?"

She laughed, a rich sound that he was quickly becoming addicted to.

"I most certainly do, my lord. While I admit to spending hours at my pianoforte, I also have a bit of an artistic bent. I have been painting landscapes for several years now, and I am only venturing into the world of portraits. I did not want to bring my paints with us, knowing we would only be in the Lake District for about ten days, traveling from one destination to another. I did not want us to be tied to any one place for too long while I painted it and the others merely sat and watched me do so."

Jacinda would not have cared if she kept others waiting. Byron knew the girl to be selfish. He chastised himself inwardly, telling himself not to continue comparing these two women. His mind was made up. He would do his duty to his father and create the family the old man had wanted established between the Balfours and the Bowles.

"Effie will definitely want to walk to the top of this fell," Lady Mirella continued. She grinned. "She will regret not having brought her breeches on this trip, though."

"Lady Effie wears . . . *breeches?*" he asked, appalled at the thought that instantly came to him. It was not Lady Effie in breeches he visualized. It was Lady Mirella. He pictured how easy it would be to stroke her rounded bottom if she wore a tight pair of breeches, as well as admire the outline of her shapely legs in them.

Mentally shaking off that thought, he said, "I am surprised

that your father allowed your sister to wear men's clothing."

She snorted. "His Grace did not pay a bit of attention to the six of us. Girls held no interest for him."

"Then I am surprised your mother did not try and rein in Lady Effie."

An exasperated noise came from Lady Mirella. "You sound as if you are judging my mother very harshly, my lord, and that is the last thing I will tolerate from anyone. Mama did her best to support all of us, no matter what endeavor we chose to pursue. Yes, Pippa and Effie were always the tomboys of the family, the more adventurous of the six girls, but Mama is—and always will be—supportive of whatever we do."

She paused and then giggled, a sound which delighted him. "Besides, you have met Effie. Do you believe that anyone could tell such a headstrong young girl what to do—or not do?"

She laughed, and Byron joined in that laughter, not recalling the last time he had laughed. It felt so freeing, as if he hadn't a care in the world.

Growing serious, she gazed upon him and said, "You should smile—and laugh—more often, Lord Bridgewater. It suits you."

He felt heat flush his cheeks and could not believe he was blushing at what she said.

Was she flirting with him?

They reached a set of stone stairs, which were a bit steep, and he offered his hand, saying, "Let me help you up this staircase. I do not wish for you to slip under my watch."

She laughed merrily. "I do not wish to slip and fall either. After having done so in Hyde Park on wet grass and having to wear that cast for a couple of months, I hope never to break a bone again."

Placing her hand in his, he clasped it. Warmth rushed through him. It was the oddest of sensations, partly physical pleasure, and yet emotional in nature, as well. Holding Lady Mirella Strong's hand seemed the most natural thing for him to do. Regret filled him because he would have given the world to pursue a relationship with her. She had grown up in a large, loving family, with many siblings and cousins surrounding her. Her idea of family was one Byron wished he might create for himself.

The children he and Jacinda would have, however, would be very different from these Strongs. He intended to become fully involved in his children's lives, but his heart told him he would never become friends with Jacinda, much less think to love her.

They reached the top of the stone staircase, yet he kept his hand around hers, even entwining their fingers now. Blood rushed to his ears, the whoosh so loud and pounding that he hoped she would not speak because he would never hear a word she said.

With a few more paces, they stood at the top of Helm Crag and paused, gazing out across the landscape. He heard Lady Mirella's quick intake of breath as she studied the spectacular view from the summit.

This was the longest she had been quiet this morning, and he reveled in the silence and her presence by his side. Byron believed he could die happy at this moment, being in her company and holding her hand.

Finally, she quietly said, "If anyone ever doubted God's presence, he would merely have to come and stand at this spot and take in this magnificent view."

He heard the awe in her tone.

"No wonder Mr. Wordsworth made his home for a time in Grasmere. To think he stood at the very place we stand now is almost beyond my comprehension. His talent is immense because his words capture so much of the beauty of the Lake District, Grasmere, in particular."

She closed her eyes and breathed in and out. Byron watched her do so, and the need to kiss her filled him.

Opening her eyes, she gazed out at the land again. "I am trying to commit it all to memory so that I might paint it when we return to Kent. I find myself agreeing completely with Aunt

Matty. That there is no place lovelier in all of England than here."

Once more, she closed her eyes, frowning slightly, and he knew she was trying to capture the sight before her in her mind's eye. He studied her face, lovelier than any view they would see today, and decided he could not go on until he had kissed her.

Their fingers were still joined, so with his free hand, his placed his palm against her cheek, cradling it. Before she could react, Byron bent, his lips grazing hers.

Touching the magic that was Mirella.

He brushed his lips softly against hers, gently because he doubted she had ever been kissed before. She did not stiffen, however, nor did she protest his actions. Slowly, he gave her a full kiss on the lips, a tender one, one which he would treasure for a lifetime.

Reluctantly, he broke the contact between them, his mouth still hovering above hers, not wishing to part from this woman.

Suddenly, her free hand grasped his nape and pulled him down again to her. Their lips collided. Hunger for this woman filled him. Byron decided if this were to be the only time they would ever be alone together—the only kiss his memory would ever hold—then it should be a proper one.

He released her fingers, his arm going about her, pulling her to him. Her soft, rounded breasts pressed against his chest as he kissed her hungrily. One kiss bled into another. They became increasingly harder, as need rippled through him. She did not object in the slightest, her fingers now playing with the hair at his nape, sending delightful tingles through him.

Byron thought of the old phrase, *in for a penny, in for a pound,* and decided to change the nature of the kiss. He broke it and ran his tongue along her full, bottom lip. Again, she voiced no objection, and so he used the tip of his tongue to coax open her mouth. Then his tongue plunged inside, and he began feasting upon the nectar within. He drank his fill of her, leisurely exploring her. Her reaction was timid at first, then her confidence grew, and she began to answer his kiss, becoming bolder. Their tongues began to war with one another, and he tilted her head, deepening the kiss, gaining domination over her. She made soft, mewling noises in the back of her throat, causing his cock to respond.

That was when Byron finally came to his senses.

Breaking the kiss, he looked down upon her. She opened her eyes, and though she appeared slightly dazed, he could also see satisfaction in them.

He couldn't help himself. He kissed her again, hard, one last time.

Then he broke the kiss for good and studied her. Their breathing was more excited than from the journey they had made to the top of Helm Crag. She gazed upon him, not saying a word.

"I am sorry I took such liberties, my lady," he apologized, releasing her.

Her jaw dropped. Then disappointment filled her eyes. "You just ruined the most beautiful moment of my life with your banal apology, my lord."

The words left Byron speechless. He had merely wished to apologize for his rash behavior, but she looked at if he had wounded her deeply.

"My advice to you in the future when you are kissing a woman? Do not make her feel as if she is the most desirable creature in the world, only to tear her down with an insulting apology."

Lady Mirella turned quickly from him and began to descend the path. Byron followed meekly, thoroughly chastised, regret filling him. Regret for apologizing for what had been the most meaningful moment in his life, as well. And yet even more regret because it would never be possible to be with this woman, one who was as beautiful inside as she was outwardly.

Even when they reached the stone staircase, she did not acknowledge his presence nor seek to take his hand. She managed to get down the steps quite nicely on her own, and he thought her an interesting dichotomy of the grace and beauty favored by the *ton* and yet the country girl she had spoken of being.

They returned to their horses, Lady Mirella stroking her mount and telling the horse how much she had missed her. Byron had never spoken to a horse as it if it were a person, and he found the practice odd—but intriguing.

"Let me assist you," he said, finally breaking the silence between them.

She gave him a withering look but did not protest when he raised her into the saddle.

He, too, mounted Apollo and then asked, "Would you like to go into the village now, my lady?"

"No," she said crisply. "I am done with our time together, my lord. I wish to return to Benbrook immediately."

Her sharp tone caused an ache within him. He wanted to continue spending today with her—the only day alone they would ever have—and hated for things to end between them on such a sour note.

Then an idea came to him. "What of Lady Effie's gingerbread? Grasmere is known for baking this sweet. I thought you mentioned it might be something your sister would appreciate. I am certain you would do anything to cheer her up."

Byron saw that he had played the correct card. That family would always trump any individual feeling Lady Mirella might possess.

"Very well. We will ride to the village and buy Effie some gingerbread. Then we will return to Benbrook."

"While we are in the village, we can also stop by St. Oswald's, as Uncle Hugh suggested. Dove Cottage, where Wordsworth and his family lived, is nearby. Surely, you would like to take in those two places?" he tempted.

He waited a long moment before her reply came. "Very well. You may show me these two places, as well, my lord. That way I can discuss them with Lord Benton."

Happy to claim even a small victory, Byron turned his horse and headed toward the Dove Cottage.

CHAPTER EIGHT

MIRELLA HELD ON to the fury she felt because it kept her from thinking about Lord Bridgewater's heavenly kisses. At this moment, it was more important to dislike the man thoroughly. She was now certain that she did not want to become involved with him. He was not in any way the type of man she was looking for in a husband.

Even if his kisses sent her into the stars.

No, she would not reflect on those kisses. At least not now, with him riding just ahead of her. She needed to pay attention to where she was going. While Lady was an extremely gentle mount, Mirella knew that a skilled rider never let her concentration flag, especially when riding a new horse in an unfamiliar place. When she was in bed tonight, she would open up the memories. Perhaps having a bit of distance as she reflected upon what had just occurred would help her understand her conflicting feelings.

Lord Bridgewater was not for her. Ever.

Again, she was grateful that he had kissed her. She had been eager for her first kiss, seeing how her married relatives seemed to engage in kissing all the time. Mirella hadn't the slightest clue what to do, but she knew enough to allow the marquess to take the lead. His experience in kissing was obvious, and she had learned the lessons he showed her. It was to her benefit that the kisses had been of different varieties. That way, when she eventually did kiss other men, she would have a better idea what was going on and how to compare their kisses to Lord Bridgewater's.

"Absolutely not," she muttered under her breath.

She could not allow herself to compare his kiss to other gentlemen's. It would be unfair to her other suitors.

Because Mirella suspected not only was Lord Bridgewater's kiss superior to any she might receive in the future, it would make him seem the only likely candidate for her hand. And she did not want that. She wanted an optimistic, happy husband, one who appreciated family, not the sober, reserved marquess. Yes, he was quite handsome and had a lofty title and could kiss like the devil himself, but that could not influence her decision regarding her future.

Mirella only prayed that any other man she kissed might make her feel half as special and desirable as Lord Bridgewater had. Of course, he had spoiled everything for her with his insipid apology. Just thinking about that apology got her stirred her up again. Yes, better to keep to her anger and disappointment in him than become starry-eyed over a man who was most unsuited for her.

They rode for about three miles, bypassing the village. She kept quiet, not bothering now to engage him in conversation. The time for drawing him out was over and done. Lord Bridgewater would get little from her, only a polite smile without any kind of discussion over any topic.

Grasmere Lake came into sight, and he led them to a two-storied cottage of white stone. It had several windows, which would let in an abundance of natural light.

They remained on their horses as she studied the place where a genius had once worked.

Finally, the marquess said, "Many buildings in the Lake District are made of stone which comes from the surrounding area.

Those white walls are limestone, which helps to keep the damp out. This area receives more rain than any region in England, so that is important when building a home here."

He pointed up. "The roof's tiles are slate, another product mined in this region. Even the chimneys have arrangements of slate about them to prevent smoke from blowing back down them into the house. I have not been inside Dove Cottage, but Aunt Flora and Uncle Hugh have. She said the downstairs floors are all made of slate. Though they did not go upstairs, Wordsworth's study was located there, in order to give him a better view of the gardens and landscape while he penned his poems."

"I wish we could see the gardens," she said longingly. "Miss Feathers told us that Mr. Wordsworth and his sister Dorothy created them from local plants and that the gardens were a place of solitude and tranquility for him. Aunt Matty mentioned that he composed many of his poems sitting in them during the ten years he lived here."

"The current tenant is Thomas De Quincey, a friend of Wordsworth and a fellow writer, though I do not believe he writes poetry. Shall we go and knock upon his door and see if he would allow us inside?"

"No," she said firmly. "If he is a writer, he deserves to write in peace and not be pestered by the likes of us." She gazed at the cottage. "But thank you for bringing me to see it."

"You are welcome," he replied, taking up his reins and turning Apollo.

This time, Mirella brought Lady into step next to him, regretting her churlish behavior before. Just because he had hurt her feelings dreadfully did not mean she should retaliate in any manner. She would be the gracious, kind woman Mama had raised. Lord Bridgewater would find no fault with her or her behavior during the limited time they would be together at Benbrook.

They entered the village of Grasmere and rode to the center of it, where St. Oswald's Church stood, its tall tower rising high into the sky. She noted the roughcast stone and slate roof. The churchyard stood next to it, and Mirella wondered if Mr. Wordsworth might one day return to Grasmere and spend the rest of eternity here in the place he loved.

"The church is named in honor of St. Oswald," Lord Bridgewater shared. "He was a Christian king of Northumberland in the seventh century and is said to have preached on the site where the church was built. Part of the current building dates from the fourteenth century. Would you care to go inside?"

"I would," she said, eager to soak in the history of the structure.

He helped her dismount, and Mirella tried to calm the rush that ran through her at his touch.

After they tethered their horses, they walked to the front doors, and Lord Bridgewater said, "The tower, the porch, and the south wall are all that is left of the original church. St. Oswald's is unique in that it still celebrates with a rushbearing festival."

She frowned. "I am not familiar with that term, my lord."

"It dates back to the custom from the medieval era, when rushes would be strewn about the earthen floor. The purpose was twofold. The rushes provided warmth and also added a layer of cleanliness. Many churches kept up the custom until the turn of this century. It is dying out now, but not in Grasmere."

"You are a font of knowledge," she remarked.

He shrugged. "I told you that I am an academic at heart. History has always been fascinating to me, and Uncle Hugh shares in that interest. Actually, four churches have been built where the current one now stands. Come, we can enter at the South Door. It is one of the three entrances and has always served as the main door for worshippers."

They entered the building, and it took a moment for her eyes to adjust after the bright sunshine from outside. He explained about the construction of the nave and pointed out the nave windows, giving her the history of each, and then leading them to the chancel, where the altar stood.

"See the stone head above the chancel?" he asked. "That supposedly dates from 1250 AD."

He allowed her to wander about, taking in the architecture, before leading her outside again.

"The tower, from what the locals believe, was built from boulders carted from the riverbed of the nearby Rothay River. The walls are up to four feet thick. Come look at the chest."

He led her to the base of the tower and said, "This is the old Parish Chest from the mid-sixteen hundreds. Inside it, they kept the registers and warden accounts. Obviously, those have been relocated indoors now, but they left the old chest as a reminder of the past."

Mirella was very moved by her visit to the church. "Thank you for bringing me here, my lord. I apologize for my abrupt behavior earlier. I would not have wanted to miss an opportunity to see this."

His gray eyes pinned her. "I hurt you with what I said. You have no need to apologize, my lady."

The air between them became charged. Mirella knew she must break the spell—or she would fling herself into his arms and kiss him again.

"We should locate a bakery so that we might purchase the gingerbread for Effie," she said, brushing past him and heading back to where they had left their horses.

She wished he did not have to help her mount Lady, but she accepted it, trying to ignore the way his touch caused the blood to sing in her veins.

"There is an inn nearby. We have been gone a long time. Perhaps we could stop there first and get something to eat and drink before we head back to Benbrook."

Her belly gurgled in response to his suggestion, and Mirella couldn't help but laugh. The marquess joined in, and she felt a burden lifted from her. While she would not consider him as a husband, she might want to keep him as a friend.

"Lead the way, my lord," she said cheerfully.

The inn was only a quarter-mile from the church. At two in the afternoon, no patrons were in sight in its supper room.

Lord Bridgewater greeted the proprietor and told him, "We have been to the top of Helm Crag and have worked up both an appetite and a thirst."

"Ah," said the bespectacled innkeeper. "Did you spy the lion and the lamb it watches over, my lady?"

"I did," she replied. "I found them quite easy to make out. On the other hand, that old woman and her organ had me nonplussed," she admitted.

He gave her a smile. "My wife says the same thing. She can easily make out the first, but she believes it to be a joke, calling the other profile anything at all. She tells me it's merely a pile of rocks and nothing more. Come, have a seat. I will bring you something refreshing to drink. We still have a hearty stew left, along with fresh bread."

"Yes, please, bring us both," she said.

The food and drink appeared quickly, and Mirella found herself opening up to the marquess about life at Shadowcrest. She told him of James becoming the duke and the changes he was making to the estate under Cousin Caleb's direction.

"I would like to see Shadowcrest," he told her. "You describe things well, my lady. Perhaps it is your painter's eye which helps me to see it so clearly."

"Where is your country seat, my lord? I believe I heard the name was Bridgefield?"

"Yes, Bridgefield is northeast of Maidstone."

"Why, we are also in Kent. Shadowcrest is southwest of Maidstone. We are practically neighbors, Lord Bridgewater."

Mirella couldn't help but think of how it would be nice to wed a man whose property would be close to her family's home, but she could not choose a husband based upon his estate's proximity to Shadowcrest.

Especially Lord Bridgewater. She had already deemed him unfit as a husband. Well, at least not *her* husband.

They finished their meal, and he said, "This was the respite I needed. Thank you for agreeing to spend a bit more time with me, my lady. I hope our falling out will not be permanent."

Gazing at him, she said, "I have forgotten what we even quarreled about."

But she had not forgotten those drugging kisses.

The marquess paid the innkeeper for their meal, and Mirella said, "We would like to purchase some gingerbread. Might you recommend where we could do so?"

He directed them to a bakery about half a mile away, and when they entered, the sweet smells of gingerbread mingled with the yeast of fresh bread. They wound up purchasing a large box filled to the brim with gingerbread, as well as three loaves of the bread which they hoped would be served at dinner this evening.

Lord Bridgewater attached the sack of goods to the horn of his saddle and turned, helping her to mount Lady. She decided this would be the final time he touched her because each time he did, she pined for more. She was glad they had met because she now understood she could be attracted to a man—even enjoy his kisses—but find he would not make a good husband for her. It was something she would keep in mind going into next Season.

He swung up on Apollo, and they returned to Benbrook, where a groom took their horses.

"Oh, Lady must get an extra ration of oats," she warned the groom. "I promised them to her. She was lovely to ride." Mirella stroked the horse's neck, resting her cheek on it. "You are a lady through and through," she told the horse.

As they returned to the house, Lord Bridgewater asked, "Do you always converse with your horse as if it were a person?"

She laughed. "It is a habit I picked up from my sister. Effie adores animals and is always bringing home strays and wounded ones, nursing them back to health. She is in the habit of conversing with them, especially her cat. She brought Daffy with us on this trip."

He frowned. "I have not seen a cat."

"That is because Daffy has been exiled to our bedchamber," she explained. "Apparently, your cook is allergic to the fur of cats, so Daffy has spent her time at Benbrook indoors and away from the kitchens. But as to your question, I do think talking to your horse is important. Especially if you are new to one another, as Lady and I were today. Establishing a bond of trust between rider and horse is important."

"I suppose I will have to try it sometime," he said.

As they entered the house, Mirella thought perhaps the Marquess of Bridgewater wasn't quite so bad, after all.

CHAPTER NINE

MILLS GREETED THEM as they stepped into the foyer, and Byron requested hot water for baths be sent up to both their bedchambers. Lady Mirella left to check on her sister, and Byron asked the butler where his uncle was.

"In his study, my lord," Mills replied.

"Have the first round of hot water sent to Lady Mirella's bedchamber," he instructed. "I need to speak to my uncle, and then I will take time to bathe."

"Very good, my lord," the butler said.

Byron went to see Uncle Hugh, pausing outside the door and taking a deep breath before knocking.

"Come," he heard through the door, and Byron entered the room, closing the door behind him.

"Ah, Bridgewater," his uncle said. "Have you returned from your outing with Lady Mirella? We missed you at tea. Your aunt was ready to send out a search party for the two of you."

Taking a seat, he said, "It was a rather full day. I took Lady Mirella to see all the sights around Grasmere, and we even walked up to the top of Helm Crag to take in the views since this is her first trip to the Lake District."

Uncle Hugh gave him a knowing smile. "And did you enjoy the lady's company? Lady Mirella is like a breath of fresh air. So lovely and spirited."

"I believe she enjoyed our tour quite a bit," he replied.

His uncle's penetrating gaze made him uncomfortable. "That wasn't what I asked, Bridgewater."

He sighed. "Can I not be Byron when we are alone, Uncle Hugh? Do you know not a single person has called me by my given name in years? In the army, I was always Lieutenant and then Captain or Captain Balfour most of the time, and Balfour to officers I was particularly close to. Then I received the news from Pilsbury which changed the entire trajectory of my life. From the moment I met with him, I have been Bridgewater or my lord. Even Mama calls me Bridgewater—in private.

"I miss being Byron, even if it is only you and Aunt Flora who calls me by my name. I feel I have become a title. That the person I am is slowly disappearing, and he will never be seen again."

Sympathy filled Uncle Hugh's eyes. "I well understand that, Byron. When I assumed my own title, I doubt I heard my Christian name for years. Even once your aunt and I wed, she called me Benton for the longest time. Finally, I told her we were partners in life, and I wished for her to call me Hugh when we were alone." He smiled. "She has done so ever since."

His uncle shifted in his chair. "I see nothing but unhappiness in your eyes, Byron. You are a marquess now. Why are you so miserable? You are no longer on a battlefield, having to kill men who are strangers to you. I would think claiming your title and its wealth would be quite pleasant after all which you have been through."

"I will be leaving Benbrook tomorrow," he revealed, an ache filling him.

"What? So soon? Flora will be so disappointed." Uncle Hugh paused, studying Byron carefully. "Does Lady Mirella have something to do with this decision?"

"She has everything to do with it." Byron took a deep breath and slowly exhaled. "I am quite attracted to her, Uncle, but she cannot be a part of my future. I already know who my wife will be."

Confusion clouded his uncle's eyes. "You are betrothed? Why have you kept this from us? When is the wedding? Flora will wish us to be there."

He raked both hands through his hair. "I am not betrothed. Yet. The bride is the same one Father chose for Dawson."

A knowing look crossed his uncle's face. "The Bowles girl. Yes, Bridgewater was close with her father. The two of them were inseparable. He told me of the wedding settlements he and Lord Hampton had drawn up." Uncle Hugh frowned. "But that was for Dawson. Not you, Byron."

"I feel the need to honor my father's wishes and join our families as he planned to be done. Jacinda will make her come-out next spring, Uncle. I plan to offer for her at that time."

"Do you have special feelings for this girl?"

He shook his head. "I have not seen her in years. I did visit with her brother, the new Lord Hampton, after I returned from the war and learned from my solicitor that it was Hampton who had been racing with Dawson."

"Your brother always had a reckless streak," Uncle Hugh noted. "As did your father. That was one of the reasons he got along so well with Hampton. They were peas in a pod in that respect. But that does not mean you must step in and wed the chit, Byron. You are under no obligation to do so. Your solicitor should have made that clear to you. The contracts called for Dawson to wed the girl. Not you."

Stubbornness filled him. "It is what Father wanted. It is what I want."

Uncle Hugh shook his head sadly. "You are chasing after a ghost, Byron. Your father cared little for you when he was alive. He certainly does not care what you do from his grave."

Resolve filled him. "Nevertheless, it was his wish for our two families to join together. The marriage contracts for Jacinda to wed Dawson were signed even before Father's passing. I intend to make Jacinda my wife."

"But you just admitted that you have not even seen her in years. You may not even like her, much less want to wed her," his uncle protested.

Byron already knew he would not like Jacinda. He hadn't liked the child she was, self-centered and rude, and he doubted she had changed in the years since he'd last seen her, especially being raised under Lady Hampton's supervision. Still, he believed it important to follow through on what had been expected of Dawson. As the new Marquess of Bridgewater, Byron wanted to live up to the title and its responsibilities. That included the marriage which should have taken place between his brother and Jacinda. She would still be wedding the Marquess of Bridgewater, just not the one previously intended for her.

"My mind is made up, Uncle Hugh," he said stiffly. "I will attend the upcoming Season and press my suit with Miss Bowles. I will also speak to her brother before the Season begins and assume I will have his support in this endeavor."

He did not mention how Lord Hampton already was having a difficult time controlling his sister. Byron thought that might work in his favor, offering to take Jacinda off Hampton's hands.

Playing devil's advocate, his uncle asked, "What if she won't have you, Byron? What if some other young swain catches her fancy? While you are more handsome than your brother and have far more intelligence and kindness than he ever possessed, the Bowles girl might find someone else more appealing."

"She will do as her brother says," he said dismissively. "Women are under the care of their parents or guardians, as is the case with Miss Bowles, Uncle. While she may entertain various suitors, she will do as she is told."

At least, Byron hoped Jacinda would. From what Lord Hampton had said, his sister was headstrong and close to uncontrollable. He decided to let the Season begin and see the number of suitors Jacinda drew. He would approach her brother at the right time and make his offer. With Hampton's supposed gambling debts growing, Byron might even offer to waive the bridal dowry due him in order to tempt Hampton into entering the negotiations.

"You shared you were leaving *because* of Lady Mirella," Uncle Hugh said. "Do you care to elaborate?"

He refused to tell his uncle that he had lost his heart to the auburn-haired beauty and merely said, "She is a distraction. Admittedly, a beautiful one. I do not need that. My future is set."

Uncle Hugh steepled his fingers on the desk. "So, you are saying you will not stay for the rest of your visit because it might give Lady Mirella hope that something could blossom between you." He paused. "Or it already has taken on life—and you do not wish to hurt her?"

He swallowed painfully. "The latter," he admitted. "I need to end things before they start. Or rather, before they continue."

His uncle studied him carefully. "She will be wounded by your leaving."

"Yes. I know that," he said, his own hurt growing within him. "She will make her come-out next spring, however. You see how she is, Uncle Hugh. A beautiful, bright light. Lady Mirella will easily attract a good number of men."

The thought made him nauseous.

"Is she like Matty?" his uncle asked. "Seeking a love match?"

The question startled him. "Why, yes. She shared that she intended to have one or not wed. She told me that Strongs wed for love, which has included her brother, the duke, as well as her mother and two older sisters." Byron paused. "I did not think Lady Mathilda had ever wed. Was it because she did not find love?"

Sadness crossed Uncle Hugh's face. "No, she found it. The gentleman who owned her heart left to take up his commission, though. He was killed in the American colonies. Matty tried her best to give other men a chance, but her heart was never hers to give again because it belonged to her lieutenant."

"Well, Lady Mirella does not love me," he said flatly, ignoring the fact that *he* loved *her*. "She will easily attract a good number of suitors next Season. I am certain she will make the love match she seeks."

"It will be hard for you to see her with other men, won't it?" his uncle asked softly.

"Yes," he hissed. "It is why I must depart from Benbrook," Byron insisted. "If I could, I would leave now and not even come to dinner this evening."

He stood abruptly. "Yes, I think that best, Uncle Hugh. I will have my valet pack and will leave at once."

"Without even a goodbye to your aunt?" Uncle Hugh asked, frowning.

"Of course not," he insisted. "I will bathe and dress and then speak with Aunt Flora."

"You won't get far," his uncle pointed out. "It is already late in the day, and you shouldn't travel in the dark, Byron."

"I will stay at the inn in Grasmere. Then leave from there first thing in the morning."

Uncle Hugh rose and offered Byron his hand. "You know Flora and I have always supported you in whatever you did, Byron. We will continue to do so. You having a title does not change what is between us. I do believe you are making a mistake, though, in insisting upon wedding your neighbor. Especially when it is apparent that you have strong feelings where Lady Mirella is concerned."

He tried to pull away, but Uncle Hugh held fast to Byron's hand. "Do not sign any marriage contracts with Lord Hampton just yet. Please. Go to the Season. Reacquaint yourself with the Bowles chit. Meet other young, eligible ladies, as well. Even spend a bit of time with Lady Mirella. If she'll allow that."

Byron doubted she would. He had already seen her temper flare. By leaving Benbrook now, he would not be in her good graces.

"Only then, once a few weeks have passed, should you consider if the plan you have for your future is sound. You may meet someone else you would rather spend the rest of your life with."

Gazing deeply into Byron's eyes, Uncle Hugh said, "Marriage is a lifetime commitment, Byron. You want to spend those decades with someone you like. Someone you respect. Hopefully, someone you might grow to love."

In his heart, he knew Jacinda would not be that kind of wife. They would have a typical *ton* marriage, with her providing him with an heir, while he gave her a title and a considerable amount of wealth and status. Still, he knew his uncle meant well.

"Very well, Uncle Hugh. I will make no sudden commitments at the beginning of the Season," he promised. "I will wait and see if Jacinda is the right woman to become my marchioness."

"Good," his uncle said, finally releasing Byron's hand. "I am glad to hear of it."

"This is goodbye," he said to the older man, his arms going about his uncle. "Thank you for always being supportive of me."

"Go and get that bath," his uncle teased. "You still smell like the sweat of your climb and the scent of your horse. I will tell Flora you wish to see her in an hour. Go to her sitting room. We can say that you have received word from Bridgewater and that you must return to attend to an urgent matter."

"Very well."

Byron left his uncle's study and found Mills, asking the butler to tell the stables to ready his horse and carriage for his return home. Clever servant that he was, Mills never flinched, much less inquired why Byron might be leaving Benbrook when the sun would set in two hours.

Returning to his bedchamber, he rang for Keller. When the valet arrived, Byron announced, "We are leaving at once. Pack quickly."

"Now, my lord?" the servant asked, clearly confused. "But it—"

"Make haste, Keller."

"Yes, my lord," the valet replied.

A knock sounded at his door, and he answered it, seeing

several servants with jugs of water in hand and two footmen bearing a bathing tub.

"Come in," he said. "Prepare the bath."

He watched as they rested the tub on the ground and proceeded to pour the steaming water into it. Another servant appeared with soap and a bath sheet.

"Leave," he told them, stripping off his clothes and sinking into the hot water.

For a few minutes, Byron merely rested his nape on the edge of the tub, enjoying the heat of the water. Keller offered to bathe him, but he told the valet to stick with the packing. He scrubbed himself clean and by then, Keller said he was finished. The valet rinsed Byron as he stood and then wrapped the bath sheet about him.

"Go and pack your own things, Keller," he told the valet. "I can dress myself." He paused, smiling ruefully. "Except for the cravat. I will save it for you to tie."

The corners of Keller's mouth turned up. "Very well, my lord. I won't be long."

By the time he had dressed and combed his hair, the valet was back.

"Your carriage is waiting out front, my lord," Keller informed him. "I have asked for two footmen to come for your trunk."

"See that they collect it, and wait for me at the carriage. I must say goodbye to my aunt."

He left the bedchamber and went straight to his aunt's sitting room, noting she was already dressed for dinner. His uncle was also present, and he knew the lie they had concocted had been told.

Aunt Flora threw her arms about him. "Oh, I wish you could stay longer, Bridgewater. You only just got here."

"Perhaps you might come and see Mama and me at Bridgefield," he suggested. "You have not been there in some time. Mama would like that. You know she would have come to see you here, but she cannot abide being in a carriage for that long a trip."

Aunt Flora released him, mopping her eyes with the handkerchief her husband passed to her. "When she was a child, she did get sick when riding in one. I am amazed she can make it to town from Bridgefield."

"It is only because she has the driver stop frequently," he said. "Even then, she tells me that she is often sick on the side of the road."

"We will come to you then for Christmas," Aunt Flora said. "Hugh and I will wish to see what you have done on the estate. Your brother did not spend much time there once he became the marquess. A great deal of his time was spent in town, I gather."

Byron heard the disapproval in her voice.

"I have some marvelous ideas to use at Bridgefield, thanks to speaking with your steward," he said. "Mr. Franklin is getting on up in years, and he is wishing to retire. I plan to hire a new steward and implement some of the things which are being done at Benbrook at Bridgefield."

"Then we look forward to seeing you for the holiday," his aunt said, kissing his cheek.

"We will also see more of you in the future," Uncle Hugh declared, a broad smile on his face.

"How so?" Byron asked.

"Since you have shared with me that you are looking for a bride on the Marriage Mart, we have decided to attend the Season next spring."

The announcement floored him. "But . . . you never come to town."

"We are making an exception," Aunt Flora said. "I love your mother dearly. She is like my own child since our mother died giving birth to her. I raised your mama, Byron, and I know how opinionated she can be. I do not want her to push you into a marriage. Hugh and I will come to town and help temper her opinions. We want you to be happy in your choice of a bride."

Uncle Hugh continued smiling, and he believed the old man

thought to keep Byron from becoming betrothed to Jacinda Bowles.

He smiled. "It will be lovely having the both of you in town," he lied. "Since you have no residence in London, I insist that you stay with Mama and me."

While he would like seeing more of his aunt and uncle, his mind was set. Byron would wed Jacinda—and they would not have to delay the ceremony because the two people he loved most would already be in London.

They left the sitting room, and he swore under his breath when he saw Lady Mirella and Miss Feathers coming toward them. Both women were dressed for dinner.

"Ah, you are in time to say farewell to Bridgewater," Uncle Hugh told the pair.

Byron forced himself to meet Lady Mirella's gaze. "I have been called back to Bridgefield by my mother," he explained. "An urgent matter has arisen. One which only I can deal with."

As he spoke, Lady Mathilda joined them. "Oh, we are so sorry to see you leave, my lord. I am certain we will meet again during the Season, however."

"Yes, Aunt Matty, we most likely will," he said, using the name she had requested, hoping that would soften the blow of his departure. "You must give my apologies to Lady Effie, as well," he continued. "I hope she is doing better."

"Much better, my lord," Miss Feathers said. "Though she will be disappointed you will not be able to play tour guide for her. Lady Mirella was telling us all you saw today."

"Lady Mirella has an excellent memory. She will be able to take the both of you to see the same places we saw today," he replied, once again making himself look her in the eye. "It was a pleasure escorting you about Grasmere today, my lady."

He saw the knowing look in her eyes. She knew he was running away from her—but she was too much a lady to call him out on it.

"If you care to visit Shadowcrest, as we discussed, you are

welcome anytime, Lord Bridgewater," she said politely. "Caleb would be happy to show you about the place and discuss estate management with you."

"Oh, that would be wonderful, my lord," Lady Mathilda said. "We would welcome you to Shadowcrest. You could bring your mother with you when you visit."

Byron would not be taking Mama anywhere with him, least of all Shadowcrest.

"Thank you for the invitation. I must be going, however. It was lovely meeting you all. Please give Lady Effie my best."

He bowed and retreated to where his carriage awaited. The entire group followed him outside. Climbing into the carriage, he looked out the window and waved. Everyone waved back at him, but Byron's gaze went to Lady Mirella. She mouthed one word which he had no trouble deciphering.

Coward.

CHAPTER TEN

March—Shadowcrest

AFTER BREAKFAST, MIRELLA went to the music room in order to practice her pianoforte. She had returned from a week-long visit to Georgie and August yesterday afternoon, and she was eager to get back to playing.

It had been wonderful to spend time with her older sister, who would not be attending the upcoming Season. Georgie was heavy with child and would give birth in mid-April. August was looking forward to the birth of their first child and had confided to Mirella that he hoped the babe would be a girl who favored her mother. She had teased her brother-in-law that it could very well be a boy, and August had said he would be happy no matter what the gender of the child was.

Mirella had found that refreshing. Most titled gentlemen only focused on having sons. Her own father and Uncle Adolphus were the best examples of that philosophy She knew, however, that August and Georgie's babe would be loved. That was all that mattered.

Mama had made her own announcement to the family recently. She and the captain were also expecting a babe, which would come in September. Mirella had been thrilled for her mother, seeing how she basked in the love of her second husband. Mama had assured Mirella that she would be attending events with her daughter during the Season despite her condition, helping to launch Mirella into Polite Society. It would also be the captain's first time to attend social events given by the *ton*, and she knew Mama was ready to show off her handsome husband.

Because her mother was increasing, Mirella suspected Mama might only attend events for the first two months or so before staying home to rest. Mirella would have the escort of James and Sophie for the remainder of the Season, however. Mama would also be staying in town because of the captain's work at Neptune Shipping. The couple lived in the Seaton townhouse at James' insistence. The captain had jokingly told Mirella that while he was a proud man, he was no fool, and he did not mind living in his best friend's large, ducal townhouse. The former sea captain, though, did pay rent to James for the rooms he and Mama shared in the east wing. Mirella understood that he did have his pride.

She thought it would be the best of both worlds. She would still see Mama and the captain on a daily basis during the Season, and she would also have James and Sophie with her at social affairs.

They had finally received a letter from Pippa, which revealed she and Seth were now parents to Adam, who had been born last October. Pippa listed the places they had yet to see and wrote that she believed they would return to England sometime this coming July or August. Mama had immediately planned once the Season ended to hold a house party for family at Shadowcrest, so that everyone might be able to spend adequate time with Pippa and Seth and meet the new addition to the family.

Once they had returned from the Lake District, Mirella had been pleased to learn that both her cousins had become engaged during the course of the house party given in their honor. Less than a week after she, Effie, Aunt Matty, and Miss Feathers had arrived at Shadowcrest, a double wedding took place in the chapel on the estate. It was wonderful seeing how happy Allegra was with Sterling, the Earl of Carroll, and the same was true about Lyric and Silas, Viscount Blankenship. Sterling's country seat was in East Sussex, while Silas' was located in Essex. That made it convenient since both estates were only a few hours' journey by carriage from Shadowcrest.

Though she had thought she would have the company of her cousins when she made her come-out this Season, both twins were now increasing and would not be coming to town. They would each be six months along by the time the Season began, and both husbands had insisted they wanted to protect their wives and the health of the babes, so they would remain in the country during the social whirl of spring and summer.

Mirella believed Lyric might be carrying twins. Already, her cousin's belly was much larger than Allegra's. It would not surprise anyone in the family if that were the case since Lyric was a twin herself, along with her father and Georgie and Pippa.

The thought of so many babes arriving in their family warmed her heart, and she looked forward to the time when she, too, would give birth to her own children. Even now, she enjoyed spending hours with little George, who had been born at the end of last September, and was now Marquess of Alinwood, the heir apparent to the Duke of Seaton.

Seating herself at her pianoforte, Mirella began to play, finding her focus drifting as she did so. She kept at it, however, practicing for an hour before she gave up. This had been the case ever since she had returned from Grasmere.

And she blamed Lord Bridgewater for being the distraction.

She tried her best not to think of the marquess, especially after he turned tail and abruptly left Benbrook. She had stared at him as his carriage pulled away, mouthing the word *coward* to him. Mirella knew he had understood what she said to him.

Why, after six months, did the man still continue to invade her thoughts? She had already decided he was not the one for her before he even left Benbrook, despite the powerful pull she felt toward him. Just because he kissed deliciously did not mean he was meant for her. She had hoped they might become friends, however, but after he rushed away from Benbrook, she had lost all respect for him.

He had only come up in conversation a few times, mostly after their return from the Lake District. They had stayed another three days with Lord and Lady Benton after Bridgewater's departure, with Mirella taking Effie and Miss Feathers on the same tour which she had gone on with the marquess. Effie had recovered from her cold quickly, immensely enjoying the scenic landscape they viewed.

Aunt Matty had taken Mirella aside only once and asked her how she felt about Lord Bridgewater. She had replied honestly, telling her aunt that while she was physically attracted to him, she did not believe he held the values dear that she did. Because of that, she could not see a future with him. Aunt Matty had let the matter drop after that, never mentioning the marquess' name again.

But Mirella knew she would encounter Lord Bridgewater during the upcoming Season. It was inevitable. Lady Benton had mentioned how her nephew would be attending the Season for the first time since his arrival in England. What had surprised them all was when Lord Benton had shared that for the first time in decades, he and his countess would also attend. Lady Benton had confided that they believed her nephew would be perusing the Marriage Mart, and they wanted to help guide him in his choice of a marchioness.

Of course, Aunt Matty had been delighted that her oldest, dearest friend would be in town during the entire Season. Aunt Matty always looked forward to the events in London, and then she had usually traveled to Grasmere once the Season concluded, in order to visit with the Bentons at Benbrook.

Her aunt had told Mirella that because Lady Benton would be present during the Season, she might postpone her annual trip to Grasmere. What was left unsaid was that Aunt Matty thought Mirella might wed at Season's end, and Aunt Matty would want to be present at the wedding.

She did not know how she might respond seeing Lord Bridgewater after what had passed between them. Despite wishing to banish all thoughts of him, every night in bed, she fell asleep thinking about him and those incredible kisses they had shared at the top of Helm Crag.

What Mirella did know was that she would never kiss him again. The Season would give her the opportunity to be introduced to other eligible bachelors, and she hoped she would find one who kissed even better than Lord Bridgewater. One who would be open to loving her as much as she loved him.

Deciding she needed some George time, Mirella went upstairs to the nursery. She got down on the floor and encouraged her nephew in his crawling, her heart melting at his sweet smile. Already, George had two tiny teeth in the center of his bottom row. When he smiled at her, it gave him an impish appearance.

"It is time for the wet nurse to feed Lord Alinwood," the nursery governess told her.

"Give me five more minutes with him," she pleaded, scooping up the babe and sitting with him cradled in her arms.

Mirella sang a lullaby to him, thinking what a wonderful singing voice Silas had and how her brother-in-law would no doubt sing to the babe—or babes—Lyric produced.

Her song completed, she kissed George's brow and rose, handing him to the wet nurse.

Though she was restless and yearned for a walk, it had been raining since shortly after her arrival yesterday afternoon. She glanced out a window and saw the downpour continued, with no sign of letting up. She had hoped to get in a final walk about Shadowcrest before she left for town tomorrow morning. James and Sophie would accompany her to London, bringing George along with them. Mirella would be having a few new gowns made up for her debut. She had already tried on the ones Madame Dumas had sewn for her aborted come-out last Season, and they all fit beautifully. She still needed several more made up, however. It would be nice to return to town again so that she could spend time with Mama and the captain. James and Sophie would remain in London until Season's end, both devoting time to their separate shipping lines now before the social activities commenced.

She decided to go and see if Caleb might be available. Usually, her cousin was out on the land in his role as steward to Shadowcrest, but the rain most likely had kept him housebound. Mirella went to his office, and he smiled warmly as she entered it.

"Just the person I wished to see," he told her.

Taking a seat, she said, "I am leaving in the morning for town, and I was hoping to visit some with you today."

He reached for a page resting on his desk and said, "I received a letter this morning. It is from someone you are acquainted with."

Her pulse jumped in her throat. Without having to be told, Mirella knew it came from Lord Bridgewater.

Caleb's next words confirmed her suspicions. "It is from the Marquess of Bridgewater. He mentioned having met you at Grasmere at his aunt and uncle's estate there."

"Yes," she said evenly. "He had been an army captain and had come into his title. Lord Bridgewater told me he was having to learn about estate management and had spent a good deal of time with his uncle's steward at Benbrook during his visit. I casually mentioned that he might wish to visit Shadowcrest, as well, in order to meet with you and learn a bit more."

Her cousin smiled. "That is exactly what his note to me said. Lord Bridgewater wrote that his steward would be retiring after next autumn's harvest, and he was looking for guidance in hiring a new one. He also mentioned that you told him how well run Shadowcrest was."

"Well, it is," she said, laughing. "Just because you are my cousin does not mean that I brag on you for that alone. You have helped Shadowcrest to thrive, Caleb. If you are willing for the marquess to visit and learn something from you, I would encourage you to invite him to do so."

Mirella was grateful that she would be gone and not have to be in the same house as Lord Bridgewater.

"I just wanted to speak with you before I replied to his letter," Caleb said. "I will tell him that he is welcome to come. I know James will not mind. You know how he leaves the running of the estate to me so that he can focus his attention on Strong Shipping."

Her cousin paused. "I am only sorry that you will not also be here to visit with Lord Bridgewater."

"It cannot be helped," she said brightly. "James wishes to leave in the morning. He and Sophie have business to conduct, and Sophie also needs to have several new gowns made up for the Season. I will be doing the same and visiting with Mama as much as I can. Now that she spends most of her time in town, I miss seeing her on a daily basis."

She rose. "I will leave you to write to Lord Bridgewater. I assume he will try and come to Shadowcrest before the Season begins. He is expected to attend, according to his aunt and uncle. Lady Benton said the marquess will be taking a bride."

Caleb beamed at her. "He could not ask for a better wife than you, Cousin."

The hot blush heated her cheeks. "Oh, no, Caleb. I am not interested in the marquess. While I believe you will get along with him quite well, I already know the two of us will not suit."

Her cousin looked at her questioningly, but Mirella did not elaborate.

"I am off to pack. Will you be at tea this afternoon? Or perhaps dinner?"

"If the rain lets up, I will not make it to tea," he shared. "And I am meeting a friend in the village this evening for dinner."

"Then be sure to come to breakfast tomorrow so I can see you again before we depart."

"I will," he promised.

Mirella exited the office and returned to her bedchamber,

where a maid was in the midst of packing Mirella's things. Effie arrived, and the two sisters talked about the different gowns Mirella hoped for Madame Dumas to create for her.

"Are you certain you do not wish to come to town?" she asked her sister.

"Definitely not," Effie replied. "First of all, you will be too busy going to events and having dozens of gentlemen call upon you to spend any time with me. Besides, I am calling this summer my Summer of Freedom. It is the last time I will have full run of Shadowcrest without having to think about gowns or husbands or making my own come-out."

She wondered what her sister's debut would be like since Effie despised wearing gowns and hated small talk.

"I know it is more than a year away, but you will give yourself the chance of finding a husband, won't you?" Mirella asked.

Effie shrugged. "I have promised Mama and the captain that I will attend the Season next spring. Whether or not I find anyone interesting—much less wish to wed them—remains to be seen. Why, with all the babies coming in the family, I may be our generation's Aunt Matty and simply flit from one household to another, spoiling all my nieces and nephews."

She wished she could share with Effie that Aunt Matty had found a man she wished to wed—and that she still loved him decades later. That Aunt Matty would have been thrilled to have wed her lieutenant and given birth to his children. Instead, she had made a conscious choice not to wed and had become the foundation of the Strong family, someone they all leaned upon and went to in good times and bad.

Whether or not marriage lay in Effie's future would prove interesting. It would take a very special man to make her sister happy.

Mirella prayed that she would be fortunate enough to find her own soulmate in the Season which lay ahead.

CHAPTER ELEVEN

BYRON WENT THROUGH the morning post Paulson had delivered. In it, he found a note from Caleb Strong. The Shadowcrest steward had enclosed a brochure about crop rotation. He glanced at it and set it aside for later, wanting to read the letter instead.

Dear Lord Bridgewater —

I hope this finds you well. I decided to send this letter to your address in town since I know the Season will be starting soon, and you had mentioned you would travel to London for it.

Again, I want to tell you how much I enjoyed your visit to Shadowcrest. Hopefully, I will one day be able to come and see you at Bridgefield. I would enjoy seeing your estate, as well as the new ways you are implementing the farming techniques we discussed.

I have wondered if you have made any progress in your search for a new steward and hope that is the case.

Please extend greetings to my family for me when you see them. I have written of your visit to His Grace, and he is eager to meet you. Both he and Her Grace have been busy with their two shipping companies, but they will ease back on the reins and allow others to manage a bit more so that they might enjoy the full slate of social affairs during the Season.

If you will remember, my cousin Mirella will be making her come-out this spring. I hope you might show her a bit of kindness and claim a dance with her. Do me a favor and dance a number with her for me. Mirella is the best dancer in the Strong family, and we have taken many a turn on the dance floor at the local assemblies held in the nearby village.

My best to you and your family.

Sincerely,
Caleb Strong

He folded the letter, happy to have heard from the Shadowcrest steward. Not only had he learned a good deal from Strong during his week-long visit to Shadowcrest, but Byron had also forged a friendship with the man. He had come close to confiding to Strong about the child Dawson had sired but held back at the last minute, not wanting to be that candid.

Placing the letter atop the brochure, he handed it to a footman, asking that he take it to the study.

Then he looked to Mama. "Do you have any plans today?"

"I have a fitting at the modiste's," she replied. "Madame Dumas has been quite busy this Season."

"Are all your gowns ready?"

"A good number are," Mama said. "I will still need to return for those still being sewn. I need to schedule another fitting for next week."

He idly wondered what Lady Mirella would wear to tomorrow night's opening ball.

"Are you daydreaming, Bridgewater?"

Byron started. "What?"

"I asked you a question, but you seemed somewhere else," Mama complained.

He and his mother were still trying to forge a new relationship. Though he had been the Marquess of Bridgewater for a good while now, things were still uneasy between them. It seemed Mama even favored the memory of Dawson over the living Byron.

Aunt Flora cleared her throat, giving her sister a look that had Mama gazing meekly at her toast. His aunt and uncle had come to town, as promised, and he was happy they had accepted his offer to stay at his townhouse since they had no place of their own in London. He had told Uncle Hugh it would be ridiculous to rent a house when he had more than enough room for them all.

Byron noticed Aunt Flora still gazing at Mama, who now played with her eggs, spreading them across the plate and then sliding them back together again. Their relationship was more one of a mother to a sister than two sisters. Aunt Flora was more than a dozen years older and had taken on the role of mother to her younger sister when their mother died in childbirth. He couldn't help but wonder about Mama never traveling to Grasmere to see Aunt Flora and Uncle Hugh. She blamed it on the great distance between there and Bridgefield and how she would get sick in the carriage. She hadn't experienced any nausea on the way to town, however, as she had always claimed she did. He wondered if she had used feeling ill when in a coach as an excuse not to have to go to Grasmere.

"And do either of you have plans?" he asked his aunt and uncle.

"I am visiting a friend today," Aunt Flora said. "She is sending her carriage for me this morning."

"I am going to Tattersall's with a friend of mine in an hour," Uncle Hugh said. "He is in the market for a new set of carriage horses and wants my opinion."

Glad that his entire family would be busy, Byron decided he would not put off the inevitable any longer.

Today, he would go and meet Mrs. Smithson and her daughter.

As arranged, Pilsbury had continued to fund the household, doubling the money sent, as Byron had requested. He knew it wasn't necessary to meet the woman whom Dawson had impregnated, but he believed he owed it to her, if only to apologize for his brother's actions. Then again, her child *was* his niece. He couldn't help but be a bit curious about the girl. Did she favor Dawson or her mother more?

He decided he would make the one visit—and that would determine if he ever returned or merely continued funding their needs.

"I will be in my study if anyone has need of me," he said, rising and leaving the breakfast room.

Byron stayed there for a good hour, reading the material Caleb Strong had sent, and going through the stack of invitations which his mother had responded to for them. He could not believe the sheer volume of events which he would be attending. He had made certain not to call upon Lord Hampton and his sister, wanting to wait and reacquaint himself with Jacinda Bowles beginning tomorrow night.

Since his mother had taken the carriage to her modiste's appointment, he left the square and walked two blocks, finding an available hansom cab. He gave the cabby Mrs. Smithson's address in St. John's Wood, and the driver gave Byron a knowing look. He had learned from Pilsbury that the area, while nice, was heavily populated by mistresses of men in Polite Society. This cabby must assume that Byron was off to pay a call upon his mistress. The thought was laughable.

Especially because the only woman he wished to call upon was Lady Mirella Strong.

He viewed the opening ball tomorrow night with equal dread and anticipation. Though he was eager to finally see Lady Mirella after so many months, he doubted she wished to see him, especially the way things had ended between them at Benbrook. Still, he would do as his new friend instructed and try to find a way to place his name on her dance programme.

Byron had had to take dance lessons himself with a woman in Bridgehampton, the nearby town named for his family and Lord Hampton's. He would never have thought to do so until his mother mentioned something about him dancing, telling him if he were looking for a bride this Season, she simply must be a wonderful dancer, because it told quite a bit about a woman.

Since his own mother had never seen to any dance instruction for him, Byron had gone into Bridgehampton after speaking with his butler in confidence. Jarrod had given him a name, and he had approached the woman, asking for private instruction. She had willingly tutored him in numerous dances, all for a hefty price. It had paid off, though. He knew he would be comfortable on the dance floor when he partnered with others from Polite Society, surprised that he had a natural skill for dancing

The hansom cab began to slow, and he looked about him, seeing the neighborhood was composed of neat, cozy houses. The vehicle came to a stop, and Byron paid the driver.

"Shall I wait, my lord, or will you be a while?"

He did not like the insinuations in the man's tone and decided to put no more coin into this driver's pockets.

"No, thank you," he said, moving up the pavement to the door. He waited for the cabby to drive off before knocking.

His knock was answered moments later by a short, stout man dressed in a butler's uniform.

"May I help you, my lord?" he asked, eyeing Byron with interest.

"I do not have an appointment, but I would like to see Mrs. Smithson." He paused. "Tell her it is the Marquess of Bridgewater calling."

The butler's eyes went wide. "Yes, my lord. Please, come in."

He was shown to a small parlor, and the butler left. Before he returned, a woman entered.

"Good morning, my lord. I am Mrs. Bell, housekeeper to Mrs. Smithson. My husband has gone to speak with Mrs. Smithson. I thought I would ask if you would like some tea."

"Yes, Mrs. Bell. That would be much appreciated."

He decided both he and the woman he visited might be a bit nervous in one another's company. Having something to do with their hands would be nice.

A few minutes later, Mrs. Smithson entered the parlor. Byron rose, quickly taking in her appearance.

She was pretty, with golden ringlets and pale blue eyes. He doubted she was but five feet in height. She came toward him, giving him a timid smile.

"Lord Bridgewater? I am Mrs. Smithson."

He bowed and didn't know whether or not to take her hand, so he didn't.

"It is nice to finally meet you, Mrs. Smithson," he said politely.

The door opened again, and Mrs. Bell entered, supervising a maid who rolled in a teacart.

"Oh, tea!" Mrs. Smithson declared. "How lovely for you to have thought of it, Mrs. Bell. Place the cart here, Anna. Yes, thank you."

The maid and housekeeper waited for instructions, and finally Mrs. Smithson seemed to understand the need to dismiss them. Something told Byron this poor woman never had visitors, which greatly saddened him.

"I will ring if we have need of anything else. Thank you."

The servants departed, and his hostess asked how he liked his tea.

"Just tea in a cup. Nothing added," he told her.

She poured out and handed him his saucer and cup. He waited, allowing her to add a healthy dose of sugar to her own tea and stir before he spoke.

"I suppose you are wondering why I am here," he began.

"Let me speak first, Lord Bridgewater," she said quickly. "I must thank you for your extreme generosity. Before you substantially increased the monies being sent to me, I had neither butler nor housekeeper. I managed the cleaning with Anna, the maid you just met. Thanks to you, I have hired adequate help, along with another servant, Ella, who serves as both a maid and nursery governess to Amity."

"I am sorry you were having to take on the cleaning, Mrs. Smithson," he apologized.

She looked at him—and burst into tears.

Byron set down his saucer, unsure what to do. Then he slipped an arm about her shoulders and simply let her cry it out. It took several minutes before her weeping subsided.

"Forgive me, my lord," she said, slipping a handkerchief from her sleeve and dabbing her eyes. "I have not cried like that in a long time. Not since I found out . . . well, a very long while."

"We should speak openly, Mrs. Smithson," he told her. "There are things which must be addressed."

"Yes, I suppose you are right." She picked up her saucer and took another sip of tea. "Cold already. Should I ring for a fresh pot?"

"No. It is not necessary," he assured her.

"Call me Verity," she said, surprising him. "I am Verity Truman, my lord. Not Mrs. Smithson. Your brother suggested I do so when he set me up in this establishment. I understand it is to save face, pretending that a Mr. Smithson existed at one time, but we should be honest with one another." She hesitated. "How much do you know?"

"I have the basic facts. That Bridgewater got you with child and then told you of his betrothal to Miss Bowles."

She shook her head. "I was such a fool. Bridgewater was handsome and quite charming. So very confident. I . . . did things with him. Things I should not have done. Amity is the result of my actions. I cannot say I regret what I did because my daughter is the light of my life, my lord."

"I know how convincing my brother could be. And you did not do these things alone, Miss Verity. Bridgewater was also a partner to . . . the events," he said delicately. "He was older. You were naïve. Do not solely blame yourself."

"It is hard not to, my lord. I went from a girl in love, stars in my eyes, to one who would give birth to a bastard," she said, no trace of bitterness in her tone, for which Byron admired her all the more. "Your brother explained how his father had arranged the betrothal to a neighbor's daughter, one who would not be making her come-out for years because of her tender age."

She took another sip of tea. "I know now that I was but a plaything to Bridgewater. Frankly, even if he had been available, I am not quite certain that he would have offered for me, even knowing the condition I found myself in."

That remark cut Byron to the quick. Because he believed it to be true. The brother he had worshipped had simply not been a very good man. He felt in his gut that she was right. Bridgewater would never have owned up to his responsibility. The fact that he could use his secret betrothal was a convenient excuse.

"Mr. Pilsbury told me that your family has abandoned you."

Tears welled in her eyes again. "Yes. If it were only Mama, she would never have done so. We would have retired to the country and lived a quiet life. Somehow, Mama would have found a way to adopt Amity into our family so that I could raise her."

She frowned. "Papa tells Mama what to think, however. In truth, she is terrified of him. I . . . I think he is . . . cruel to her. I have seen . . . bruises."

Anger welled inside Byron, but he did not interrupt her story.

"Papa berated me for hours once he knew, telling me how ashamed he was of me. How I had disgraced the Truman family name. That he simply could not acknowledge me or my babe, much less have us in his house, sitting at his table."

He could not imagine being so young and in her shoes.

"He gave me one week to make arrangements and leave his house. He forbade Mama from helping me. I told Lord Bridge-water of the circumstances. That is when he agreed to set me up here, in this house, with a cook and maid. I left my parents' house and came straight here."

She shook her head. "You cannot imagine the pain I felt when I read of my supposed death in the newspapers." She took a deep breath and expelled it. "Actually, Verity Truman is dead to Polite Society. I became Mrs. Smithson and will always be her."

"Is it true that Bridgewater never saw you again? Never came to see his child?" he asked, needing to verify that information.

"Yes. He had nothing more to do with me, other than sending the money. It was never enough. Oh, I know how ungrateful I must sound, and I do not mean to be, my lord. At least I had a roof over my head and food to eat. But thanks to you, I no longer have to scrub pots and floors and hang the wash out to dry."

He reached and took one of her hands, turning the palm face up, seeing the calluses still there. Rage filled him. If his brother were still here, Byron would have knocked him into tomorrow.

Releasing her hand, he said, "Miss Verity, you never need worry again about money. And if you find you need more, please send word to me through Mr. Pilsbury. As Amity gets older, I am certain she will need more than she has now. You mentioned one of your maids also serves as a kind of nursery governess. When the time comes, we shall hire a proper governess for Amity."

Verity burst into tears again, flinging her arms about him, burying her face in his chest. He could feel the wetness soaking through his waistcoat and shirt, but he merely stroked her hair.

She sat up, brushing the tears away. "Forgive me, my lord. Oh, I do seem to continually apologize to you." She paused. "Would you care to meet Amity?"

Anticipation filled him. "I most certainly would."

"I will be back with her in a moment."

Verity Truman left the parlor, and Byron sighed. He liked her quite a bit and hated the situation his brother had placed her in. She was between places. No gentleman in Polite Society would ever have her, due to the bastard babe she had borne. Others would feel her above them, so he doubted she would ever wed and have other children. To live in that kind of limbo, with no family or friends, must be terribly depressing.

Byron determined to continue to visit her—and come to some kind of solution.

She returned, holding the hand of a girl who was Verity's mirror image, only years younger. Amity had the same golden ringlets and blue eyes. Where her mother was timid, though, this girl had an eagerness about her and smiled at him.

"Do as we practiced, Amity," her mother urged.

The girl came to stand in front of Byron and made her curtsey to him. He remained seated, not wanting to loom over her, and offered his hand. She took it, and they shook.

"I am Amity Smithson," she informed him. "I am five years old. And who might you be? Mama said someone was here and wanted to meet me."

He wanted to be called Uncle Byron but thought that might be too confusing for the child, so he said, "I am Mr. Byron." He hoped sometime in the future she would call him Uncle Byron. This would be a start.

"Hello, Mr. Byron," she said. "Thank you for coming to see us. No one ever does. I see people when we go for a walk. Other children playing in the park, but Mama doesn't let me talk to them."

"I am very happy to come and visit you, Amity."

"Will you really come back?" she pleaded.

"I most certainly will," he promised.

The girl stayed a few more minutes, singing Byron a song and naming as many animals as she could, along with voicing the noises that they made. She had him laughing, something he had not done in a long time.

A servant slipped into the room, and he decided this was Ella, the maid.

"Miss Amity, it is time for you to eat."

The girl frowned. "Do I have to go, Mama?"

"Yes, my darling," Verity said, slipping an arm about her daughter. "Mr. Byron has to leave now."

"But I will be back to see you," he reminded the girl.

"Soon?" she asked.

"Soon," he responded.

The servant took the girl away, and Verity looked to him. "You do not have to come again, my lord. I do not expect it."

"She is my niece," he said simply. "I must come back."

Her mouth trembled. "Then from the bottom of my heart, I do thank you, my lord." She studied him a moment. "You will make for a much better marquess than your brother ever did."

"I am trying my best, Verity. And since I will be a frequent visitor, you must call me Byron."

When he left the house a short while later, he knew it had been the right thing to come and meet both Verity and Amity.

For now, he would keep these visits a secret from his mother, who had no idea the pair existed. He thought he might tell Aunt Flora and Uncle Hugh, though, thinking they would sympathize with Verity's situation.

Byron also hoped that Jacinda Bowles would be understanding and accompany him on these visits once they were wed.

CHAPTER TWELVE

MIRELLA THANKED THE maid and looked at her reflection in the mirror, pleased with what she saw.

Tonight was the opening ball of the Season, something she seemed to have looked forward to for all her life. It would be odd, not having any of her sisters or cousins there with her, but she knew how happy they were in their new lives and how Effie would enjoy her last carefree spring and summer at Shadowcrest with her animals.

A light tap sounded on the door, and Mama stuck her head in. Mirella waved Mama inside the bedchamber.

Tears misted her mother's eyes as she said, "Oh, Mirella, you look absolutely lovely. The soft lilac was the perfect choice of gown."

"Yes," she agreed. "This is the gown I would have worn to the first ball of my come-out last year. I thought it only appropriate to wear it tonight."

Mama smiled. "I have something else that I wish for you to wear this evening. Turn around and close your eyes."

Curious, Mirella did as her mother asked. She sensed Mama lifting something over her head and then an object brushed her neck. She decided it was a necklace.

"You may open your eyes."

Glancing down, she fingered the gold locket now hanging from her neck. Moving to the mirror, she looked at it.

"Oh, Mama! It is beautiful." She thought a moment. "Wait. I saw Georgie wearing one similar to this at her wedding. Allegra and Lyric, too. I thought to ask them about it, but we were so carried away in the festivities of the day, I forgot."

She turned to face her mother and asked, "Is this something you give to all your girls?"

Mama placed her hands on Mirella's shoulders. "Yes. I purchased these lockets for each of you shortly after your births. I had the jeweler engrave each one with the initial of your first name, and then once you had enough hair, I snipped a small lock of it to place inside."

Mirella brought the locket to her lips and kissed it tenderly. "This means a great deal to me, Mama. I will wear it with pride, knowing all the Strong women have done so." She thought a moment. "Did Pippa receive one? I cannot recall from her wedding day."

"Even though Pippa had no formal come-out, I did give hers to her before her wedding to Seth. So far, Georgina is the only one who has made a traditional come-out in our family, and she received hers on the opening night of the Season last spring. I gave Lyric and Allegra theirs before the house party began last summer. I hope this locket will bring you happiness and good fortune and that you find the man who is destined to be your soulmate this Season."

A knock sounded at the door, and Mama went to answer it. Mirella saw the captain standing there.

"I have been sent to hurry you along," he told them. "You know how impatient James can be."

"Fortunately, we are both ready," Mama told her husband, who brushed a kiss against his wife's cheek.

They left the bedchamber, with the captain offering each of them his arm, saying, "I cannot believe I will be escorting the two most beautiful ladies to the opening ball. Unfortunately, that means I have to attend that ball, wearing these clothes."

Mirella thought her stepfather quite handsome in his evening dress, but it was very different from the usual clothes he wore to Neptune Shipping each day.

When they reached the last set of stairs, he said to her, "This is your first shining moment of this evening, Mirella. I want you to descend the stairs alone so that your family focuses only on you." He kissed her cheek. "I could not be prouder of you, and I hope you will enjoy your time tonight and over the next few months."

"Thank you, Captain," she said. "I am happy you and Mama will be by my side at these events. It will help quell my nerves."

She stood back and allowed the couple to descend the stairs together. Once they had reached the landing and turned, now out of her sight, she slowly began her own descent. Moments later, she came into view of her waiting family in the foyer below, smiling at them, and seeing their smiles in return.

"Oh, Mirella!" exclaimed Sophie. "You look like a fairy princess."

Aunt Matty met her and embraced Mirella, kissing her cheek. "You look like a dream, my darling. I hope you have the time of your life tonight."

James gruffly said, "You are beautiful, Mirella. So much so that Drake and I may have to keep away the hungry wolves who chase after you."

Sophie swatted her husband playfully. "You and Drake will do no such thing, James. Mirella is a grown woman, and she can handle any social situation. That includes whether or not she wishes to spend time with a gentleman."

"Then I will make it widely known that both Drake and I will be present in the drawing room tomorrow afternoon if any suitor wishes to call upon my sister. They will have to talk to—and get through—the both of us before Mirella is available to them."

She laughed and went and tucked her arm through her brother's. "You are all sound and fury, James, and I know you mean well. Sophie is right, however. I can fend for myself. Besides, I believe Strong women are blessed with good judgment. Just look at the additions which have come into our family during the last year or so. I must deem a man incredibly worthy if he is to join the line of my brothers-in-law."

They went outside where the carriage awaited them and traveled to Lord and Lady Pance's. The couple was hosting the first ball of the Season, and Mirella saw how snarled traffic was getting to their destination.

"I have never asked about what to expect this evening," she said suddenly. "What actually happens at a ball besides dancing?"

Her sister-in-law smiled at her. "Besides dancing, at which you excel? We will first go through a receiving line, where we are greeted by our host and hostess. Then, we make our way into the ballroom, where your mother—who knows everyone in Polite Society—will introduce you to others."

"We will stake out a prime place in the ballroom," Mama added. "Because your brother is a duke, we will not circulate around the room. Instead, others will come to us. Once you have been properly introduced to someone, you may then accept a dance if the gentleman asks for one from you. You must always have that introduction first, though, Mirella. Most of those introductions will come from me, but you may, on occasion, be introduced by a third party to someone new."

"Do not forget the part about the number of dances," Aunt Matty reminded.

"Oh, yes," Mama said. "You only want to dance with a gentleman once in an evening. If, however, he asks for a second dance, he is demonstrating to you—and the other guests present—that he is most interested in you. If you return that interest, then you may accept a second dance from a suitor."

"And under no circumstances are you to ever dance thrice with a man in a single evening," Aunt Matty advised. "It is simply not done."

"Do not worry about me," she told everyone inside the carriage. "I do love to dance, and I want to meet as many people as possible tonight, both gentlemen and ladies. While my sisters and cousins have been my closest friends and always will be, I am looking forward to getting to know other ladies close to my age over the Season. Why, I recall Georgie talking about Miss Bancroft and how much she enjoyed their new friendship."

Mama smiled. "Yes, we all got to know Miss Bancroft quite well at the house party. She left it engaged to Viscount Tillings, and they wed close to the time your cousins did. Miss Bancroft was the most delightful woman. If she and Lord Tillings are present this evening, I will make certain that you make their acquaintance."

The carriage, which barely crawled along, finally came to a standstill. After a moment, a footman opened the door and said, "Your Grace, the coachman says this is as close as he can get you. You will have to walk the rest of the way."

"Walk?" Mirella asked. "It is that crowded?"

Mama nodded. "It is not unusual to do so. The opening ball of the Season is the most attended event. As time passes, not as many people will turn out for an affair, but they are all eager to catch up with old friends and see what others are wearing on this first night, as well as look over the group of girls making their come-outs. Almost aways, a ball is the only event of an evening, but on the nights no ball is being held? There will be other smaller, more intimate gatherings, such as a card party or musicale. Even though you love to dance, Mirella, I believe you will enjoy those events just as much. They give you more of a chance to converse with others and get to know them better."

She was glad to be learning all these things about the Season. She was now on the threshold of embarking upon her come-out, and excitement filled her.

James climbed from his ducal carriage, and the captain followed, with James handing each of the ladies down.

Her brother said, "I will escort Sophie and Mirella inside. Drake, you look after Dinah and Aunt Matty."

They walked a good five minutes before they arrived at their destination, cutting through stalled carriages along the road. They entered Lord and Lady Pance's townhouse and joined the receiving line.

As they stood waiting their turn to greet their hosts, Mama pointed out various people to Mirella. She listened carefully, trying to memorize as many names and faces as she could.

While searching for Lord Bridgewater.

She knew he would be in attendance tonight. She shouldn't be looking forward to seeing him, but she was. Part of her hoped he would ask her for a dance, and yet she thought it would be unwise if he did so. She would have to wait and see if Lord Bridgewater approached her and asked for a dance before she decided to award one to him or not.

As far as other gentlemen went, Mirella had already made up her mind that she would not reject any requests for a dance with her, wanting to give all gentlemen an equal chance to make her acquaintance.

They finally reached the front of the line, and Lord and Lady Pance greeted James and Sophie.

James said, "I have the honor of introducing you to my sister, Lady Mirella Strong. Tonight, she is making her come-out into Polite Society."

Lady Pance eyed her with interest. "Oh, don't you look lovely, Lady Mirella. We have already met several of the girls who are making their come-outs this Season, but you are—by far— superior to them in beauty and grace."

"Thank you, Lady Pance," she said humbly.

While she knew she was quite pretty, Mirella did not feel comfortable with others complimenting her looks. She wanted to be more than her looks to others. More than a sister of a duke. She wanted to be Mirella.

Mama, the captain, and Aunt Matty also greeted their hosts, then the six of them entered the ballroom. Her eyes swept across it, seeing it was already quite crowded. She spied a quartet of musicians and anticipation filled her. Her feet itched to dance.

"Over there," Mama said, steering their group to a place where they could see and be seen by others.

Immediately, people appeared before them, some as couples and others as individuals. She noticed every single individual happened to be male. A few had a hungry look in their eyes, as if they were on the hunt for prey. She would have to use all her intelligence to discern which men were simply wishing to claim her as some trophy and which ones truly wished to get to know her.

Her dance card began filling rapidly, and a small part of her wished she could save a number for Lord Bridgewater. She chided herself, knowing it was a strong possibility that he would not approach her this evening because of the way they had parted.

Then she caught sight of him, and her heart began to beat rapidly. If she had thought him handsome before, he was ten times so in his formal, black evening wear. He stood talking with a young man and woman. Mirella did not know if they were wed or possibly brother and sister. She decided the latter when she saw the young lady allow Lord Bridgewater to sign her dance programme. Matrons—even young ones—did not dance often, so she surmised the couple must be a brother and sister.

She studied the young woman the marquess would be dancing with at some point this evening. The girl was exquisite, with a dark cloud of hair and the face of an angel. Mirella wondered if this girl, too, might be making her own come-out this evening.

"Oh, there is Lord Bridgewater," Aunt Matty declared. "I hope he sees us. It would be good to visit with him."

Suddenly, she and the marquess locked eyes. An intense rush of unnamed emotions ran through her.

"Mirella?"

She broke the spell between them, turning to her mother. "Yes, Mama?" Then she saw Lord and Lady Benton had joined their circle.

Smiling, Mirella dipped a curtsey to the pair. "It is so good to see you again, my lord, my lady."

"It is delightful to see you, as well, my dear," Lord Benton said.

"And it is so odd being at a ball in town," Lady Benton added. "While we go to the assembly room in Grasmere and dance upon occasion, I do believe that I have missed being in a large, London ballroom."

Lady Benton gazed up at her husband. "You will need to dance with me at least once, Benton, before you vanish into the card room."

Something changed in the air, and Mirella knew Lord Bridgewater had joined them. She turned, drawing on all her strength to appear calm before saying, "Good evening, Lord Bridgewater. It is good to see you."

"I feel the same, Lady Mirella."

Aunt Matty stepped in, saying, "Let me introduce you, my lord, to those in my family whom you have yet to meet."

Her aunt swiftly went through the introductions, and Mirella felt lightheaded. She told herself above all else, she should not faint in front of the marquess and a ballroom full of guests.

"We are delighted Bridgewater has come to town for the Season," his aunt declared, beaming proudly at her nephew. With a twinkle in her eyes, Lady Benton added, "And we hope he will find his marchioness."

"I hope the same, Aunt Flora," the marquess said. "But it is good to see an old friend such as Lady Mirella." His gaze met hers. "Might you be able to accommodate me with a dance, my lady? Your cousin, Mr. Strong, said I should request to dance with you and that it would be him you danced with in spirit."

She only had two slots remaining on her dance card, the one after supper and the final one of the evening.

Curious as to which one he might choose, she handed her programme to him. He scribbled his name and returned it, smiling at her. That smile tugged on her heartstrings, and Mirella told herself not to fall victim to it.

"It was lovely meeting you all," the marquess told the group, bowing before departing.

As the others began chatting, Mama quietly said to her, "You did not mention how very handsome Lord Bridgewater is."

"Too handsome if you ask me," she said, glancing down at her programme.

He had taken the last slot on her card, which meant they would spend the final minutes of the evening together.

Mirella told herself not to worry about it. Not to think about him. She would enjoy this evening and then tolerate the dance with him. In fact, she would explain to him that she would prefer they did not dance in the future. Yes, that would be best and free her up to dance with other gentlemen.

The musicians began tuning their instruments, and her first partner of the evening, an earl, joined their circle.

"I am looking forward to our dance, Lady Mirella," he said to her.

"So am I, my lord," she replied, allowing him to lead her onto the dance floor.

CHAPTER THIRTEEN

BYRON WALKED AWAY from Lady Mirella and her family. It had not surprised him to find Aunt Flora and Uncle Hugh with the Strongs, especially because the couple and Lady Mathilda were so close. Mama, however, had not been with them. She had parted ways the moment they had entered the ballroom, saying she needed to catch up with her own friends.

As he had suspected, his mother had not seemed happy to see her sister and brother-in-law after a gap of several years. He had learned no visits had taken place after he left for his officer's training and headed to the continent and war. Mama's tight smile was so different from Aunt Flora's warm, gracious one. If he'd had a choice, Byron would have chosen his aunt and uncle as parents over his true ones.

He made his way around the ballroom, not talking with anyone for very long. He had seen a few classmates from his Eton and Cambridge days, and they had promised to catch up at White's. He had yet to avail himself of his membership at the club. He supposed it was a place for gentlemen to gather and gossip during the Season. It wouldn't hurt for him to drop by every now and then, just to renew old friendships.

It also might give him insight as to which gentlemen were courting Jacinda. Byron had made certain to head straight to her and her brother when he arrived this evening. He had skipped the receiving line, knowing his hosts did not know who he was and likely did not care. Uncle Hugh had been the one who suggested doing so, saying standing in receiving lines could be cruelly long. As a bachelor attending *ton* events, he said he often had skipped the receiving line, heading straight to the ballroom.

Byron did meet a few other young women and signed a couple of their programmes. It wouldn't look good for him to only dance with Jacinda and Lady Mirella, so he did not mind appearing on the dance floor with a few other girls making their come-outs.

He sighed inwardly, wishing that Lady Mirella were his lone dance partner this evening. Already, he didn't like Jacinda. He had hoped beyond hope that she might have changed from the spoiled child he remembered.

She hadn't.

While he would still offer for her, he wasn't ready to make that commitment at this point, deciding to abide by Uncle Hugh's advice. Byron told himself he would eventually speak with her brother and let Lord Hampton know of his intention of marrying her, but he wanted a bit of the Season to pass before he did so.

At least that was what he told himself.

And knew he was lying.

If he spoke with Hampton and they worked out the marriage contracts, the news would get out, sooner or later. For the moment—and for an amount of time he would not articulate—he wanted to be free of that entanglement.

Because he wanted to spend time with Lady Mirella.

Yes, it was wrong of him to do so. He did not want to lead her on, but he craved her company in a way he couldn't begin to fathom. Byron told himself he would be satisfied with a handful of dances over the next month with her. Perhaps even visiting her once or twice, just to see the number of suitors flocking to her. Then he would step away and voice a commitment to Jacinda. Or rather to Lord Hampton. He thought to deal with the brother first since Hampton served as his sister's guardian.

The musicians began tuning their instruments, so he knew the ball would begin any moment now. Yes, an older couple went to the center of the ballroom's floor, and he supposed they were the host and hostess for tonight's affair. He scanned the room and located Lady Mirella. She was easy to spot because of her auburn hair. Her lilac gown floated about her as she moved, and his throat grew thick with emotion.

Other couples were coming out now, forming groups for the country dance that would be played by the string quartet. He was glad he had not agreed to dance with anyone during this first set. This way, he could watch Lady Mirella. After hearing Caleb Strong call her the best dancer in the Strong family, Byron wanted to see her caught up in the music. He supposed it might be the same as when she played the pianoforte, all her attention devoted to the song.

The musicians struck up a lively tune, and the ballroom went into motion as dozens of dancers moved to the beat. His gaze followed Lady Mirella the entire time, thinking her the epitome of beauty and grace. By the dance's end, her cheeks were flushed and her smile wide as she looked to her partner. If Byron had been wearing his sword, he would have run it through the gentleman.

When had he become such an unreasonable, jealous man? He had never known envy before—and he did not like it one bit.

He recalled a phrase from Shakespeare's *Othello*, which had stuck with him from his school days. The scheming Iago had warned Othello to beware of jealousy, calling it a green-eyed monster, insinuating that Desdemona had acted in an adulterous manner. The accusation had ruined the romance between the couple.

Byron shook his head. He could not compare his relationship with Lady Mirella to the one which the Bard had created. Yes, he had been miserable ever since he fled Benbrook, knowing he loved Lady Mirella and could never act upon that love. But while

Desdemona loved Othello passionately, Byron entertained no thoughts that Lady Mirella held any romantic feelings for him, especially since she had called him a coward.

Still, she had agreed to partner with him tonight for the last dance of the evening. He had overheard his mother telling his aunt that it was a trend for the supper dance and the final one of a ball to be a waltz. Byron had felt obligated to ask Jacinda for the supper dance. It would allow them to spend more time in one another's company and help him lay the groundwork for his pursuit of her. So, he would dance that first waltz with Jacinda Bowles and the other with Lady Mirella. Despite knowing it was wrong, he knew he would draw comparisons between the two women after those dances.

He watched Lady Mirella's partner escort her back to her family and then went in search for his partner for the next set. After that, Byron retreated to the card room for an hour, returning in time for his supper dance with Jacinda. He found her standing with two other young ladies, one fairly pretty and the other quite plain. His intended was by far the beauty of the group. She would stand out anywhere, with her dark hair, blue eyes, and luscious figure.

Yet she did not appeal to him one whit.

Bowing, he said, "Miss Bowles, are you ready for our supper dance?"

She had been frowning, but now she turned to him, her smile insincere. "Ah, Lord Bridgewater. Yes, I am eager for our dance."

Stepping toward him, she placed her hand on his sleeve, ignoring the two ladies who had been standing with her. He could not believe she would not introduce her two friends. Once again, he reminded himself of the duty he would fulfill by making her his marchioness and led her onto the dance floor.

"It is to be a waltz," he told her.

"Oh, a waltz!" she cried girlishly. "I am quite excellent at the dance, according to my dance master."

"That is good to know, my lady," he said blandly, not liking that she boasted about her abilities. It made him wonder about her level of maturity. Again, he decided he could ignore that because they would never be close. Never be friends or true partners. She would be more of a brood mare, producing children for the, the two of them living very separate lives.

The dance commenced, and he moved her about the dance floor, immediately realizing the dance master had blatantly lied to her. Jacinda had no sense of rhythm and constantly bumped into him or trod upon his toes. Instead of a brief apology or demure smile, she looked at him with hostility, as if he were the one at fault.

Finally, the interminable dance ended. He breathed an inward sigh of relief.

"You are rather clumsy, my lord," she said, not mincing her words.

Byron could only stare at her, locking his jaw to keep it from hitting the floor. All this creature had going for her were her looks. Even then, the importance of those looks seemed to be diminishing by the minute.

"Shall we go into supper?" he asked neutrally, hiding the anger building within him.

"Oh, we must sit with Hampton and his many friends. My brother has asked all his friends to dance with me this evening. I am meeting so many different eligible bachelors. They have told me how beautiful I am and what a privilege it is to partner with me."

He was liking her less and less. No, truth be told, he did not like her at all.

The evening only went downhill from there.

They joined Lord Hampton at a large table which seated a dozen. His friends were rowdy, despite the presence of young ladies at it. He cringed inwardly, seeing others looking in their direction, hating that he was being lumped together with this loud, offensive group.

Worse, his conversation with Jacinda was incredibly boring.

When he asked any question of her, to get to know her better, she talked incessantly about how wonderful she was. Never once did she ask Byron a single thing about himself.

"Will you call upon me tomorrow, my lord?" she asked pertly. "You have not asked to do so. I am surprised at that."

He had not known that was how it was done. Pasting on a social smile, he replied, "I would be happy to have the privilege of calling upon you, Miss Bowles. After all, we have been neighbors in the country for many years, and I do hope we will be special friends."

She rolled her eyes. "No talk of the country, Bridgewater. I despise it. When I wed, I wish to spend the majority of my year in town. Either my husband will agree to that, or he can remain in the country."

His eyes widened. Living in town other than during the Season was the last thing he wanted to do. Byron wanted his children raised amidst the fresh, country air. He wanted to teach them to ride and allow them to play on the lawns. Take them for long walks and show them how to skim rocks along a pond.

Then again, if they were to live the kind of separate lives that most married couples within the *ton* chose, it might be better if Jacinda remained in town for most of the year, while he stayed at Bridgefield with their children. The trouble with that plan would be in getting her with child. He would have to compromise and live in town more than he would prefer, at least until he had the children he wanted.

No, that was wrong. By God, he was a marquess. She was a female. A husband should be the leader in a marriage. If he ordered her to the country, then she would need to please him and do as he requested.

Byron recalled how Lady Mirella had told him that she was a country girl at heart. He knew from watching her this evening that she would be at home in any grand ballroom, but she would prefer a life in the country.

"Blast," he murmured under his breath, frustration filling

him.

Supper seemed to be drawing to an end. He could no longer abide being around the chit.

Rising, Byron said, "If you will excuse me, Miss Bowles. I see an old friend from my Cambridge days and must speak to him. Thank you for doing me the great honor of dancing the supper dance with me."

She looked at him, and he saw she was bored by him. Still, she asked, "You will call upon me tomorrow, my lord, won't you?"

"I plan to do so, Miss Bowles. Good evening."

Never had Byron been happier to escape the company of a woman than at this moment. He hurried from the supper room, spying his aunt and uncle dining with Lady Mathilda and the Duke and Duchess of Seaton. Lady Mirella was not seated with them, and he wondered with whom she had spent the last hour.

He caught sight of her auburn hair, as a gentleman led her out a set of French doors.

Good God. She was going to the terrace—alone—with a man. The first night of the Season.

Without thought for the consequences, Byron followed the couple.

It surprised him to find a good dozen or more couples strolling around the terrace. Lanterns had been placed at intervals, and he saw some of the couples even held glasses of punch in their hands. Still, he did not think it wise for Lady Mirella to have gone outside with a man she had only met this evening.

He caught sight of them and followed slowly, at a discreet pace, wondering what he would say when he neared them.

They stopped when they reached the end, turning to face one another. He saw the smile she favored the gentleman with, and it was as if she had stabbed Byron's heart with a knife. Without thinking, he hurried toward them.

"There you are, my lady," he said, watching as the pair

turned toward him.

The gentleman appeared confused with Byron's sudden appearance, while Lady Mirella's eyes narrowed.

"What is it, my lord?" she asked, her tone sharp.

"Your aunt has need of you," he lied smoothly. "She sent me to find you. I happened to see you and . . . this gentleman . . . leaving the supper room."

"Is Aunt Matty all right?" she asked worriedly, her demeanor toward him changing in an instant.

"I am sure it is a small matter—but she did wish to speak with you immediately."

Byron stepped forward, claiming her hand and slipping it through his arm. "Come, my lady." With an apologetic smile, he nodded at her companion and led her away.

"I hope nothing is wrong," Lady Mirella said as they moved along the terrace. "That Aunt Matty is not feeling ill. If she is, we must leave at once."

"Your aunt is fine," Byron assured her, as they stepped through the doors and back into the supper room. "I merely thought you needed help . . . excusing yourself from the situation you had gotten yourself into."

"The situation?" She frowned. "Whatever are you speaking of, Lord Bridgewater?"

Sternly, he said, "Leaving to stroll in the gardens or on the terrace is a good indication that you are willing to kiss a gentleman, my lady."

She snorted. "And you nominated yourself to be my protector tonight, my lord?" she asked, her voice dripping with sarcasm. "I was enjoying my time with the viscount. And if he had asked to kiss me, I would most certainly have agreed to do so."

Lady Mirella removed her hand from his sleeve. "What I do not understand in the slightest is why you tried to prevent that from occurring. You have no right to meddle in my affairs, Lord Bridgewater. None whatsoever."

He caught her wrist as she turned to leave. "The first night, my lady? It simply does not look good to others. I would have thought you would have used better judgment," he chided.

"Says the man who kissed me and then ran home like a scared schoolboy," she hissed. "Let go of me. Now."

He did so, embarrassed by his foolish behavior. "My apologies, Lady Mirella. I was only thinking of your reputation."

"You may leave that in my hands, my lord. Not yours. In fact, I think it unwise if we dance together this evening. Or at any other event. Do not bother to come and claim me when the final dance is announced, Lord Bridgewater."

She whirled and left him, exiting the supper room. He supposed she would go and cool off in the retiring room.

Oh, he had handled that badly. About as poorly as he had ever done anything in his entire life.

But Byron was not going to be put off by her temper. He would apologize to her again. Profusely, if need be.

Because he had every intention of dancing the waltz with Lady Mirella at the end of this night.

CHAPTER FOURTEEN

MIRELLA FOUND HERSELF shaking with anger, and she slowed her pace, trying to get her emotions under control. She saw a footman and asked him directions to the retiring room, wanting to get away from the large group of people milling about.

Going down the stairs, she saw several ladies exiting the room the footman had steered her toward, and she smiled politely at them as they passed and she entered. Several women primped, holding hand mirrors. She went to one of the curtains which had been raised and stepped inside, lowering it, thankful for a few moments of privacy as she relieved herself.

Why had Lord Bridgewater interfered with her walk on the terrace?

He had ruined a perfectly nice time with a man whose name she could not even recall at the moment—because her anger at the marquess had wiped everything else from her memory.

Did he believe simply because he'd had the audacity to kiss her that he now possessed her?

The thought riled Mirella even further, and she forced herself to breathe slowly, in and out. One thing was certain. She could never have anything to do with him again. If, by some chance, Aunt Matty asked Lord and Lady Benton to tea and their nephew accompanied them, Mirella would announce that she had other plans because she refused to sit in the same room with Lord Bridgewater.

As far as dancing the final number of the evening with him? It was totally out of the question. She hoped no one had realized they were arguing. Thankfully, they both had kept their voices down, but he had taken hold of her wrist. The supper room had been emptying by that point, and she prayed no one had noticed that exchange between them. He said he had worried for her reputation, but his own actions had put hers into jeopardy. She would not exacerbate it by dancing with him.

Finally calm now, Mirella came from behind the curtain, seeing only one other lady present now.

It was the beauty she had spied Lord Bridgewater with earlier in the evening. The young lady smoothed her hair as she looked into a hand mirror held by a maid, slipping a pin from her hair to make an adjustment and then sliding it back into place.

Mirella went and washed her hands, accepting the small cloth given to her by another maid as a third removed the basin of water she had used.

She couldn't help it. Curiosity overwhelmed her, and so she moved toward this woman.

"I so admire the pearl earrings you are wearing, my lady," Mirella said, striking up a conversation between them. She knew it wasn't quite proper etiquette, since they had yet to be introduced, but she saw no harm in doing so since no other guests were present in the room.

The young woman smiled, and Mirella was struck by how flawless this woman's skin was and how even more beautiful she appeared at close range.

"Thank you," the woman said crisply. "They belonged to my mother. She is gone now."

"I am sorry you lost her, my lady," she said sympathetically, knowing how distraught she would be if she had been in this same position and lost her own mother.

The woman shrugged. "They look better on me than they ever did on her," she said matter-of-factly," shocking Mirella to her core.

"We do not know one another," the woman said. "Since there is no one here to introduce us, I will tell you that I am Miss Jacinda Bowles."

Maintaining her poise, she said, "And I am Lady Mirella Strong."

Miss Bowles' nose crinkled. "You were with a duke earlier. Yes, the Duke of Seaton, if I recall correctly."

"Seaton is my brother," she said proudly.

Again, Miss Bowles' nose crinkled, and Mirella read the condemnation on her face.

"He involves himself in trade," Miss Bowles said disapprovingly. "You will have a difficult time finding a husband because of it, even if he is a duke."

This woman's behavior was outrageous, angering Mirella even more than Lord Bridgewater's had.

"Yes, it is true that His Grace is actively involved in Strong Shipping, which was founded by my family several generations ago."

Miss Bowles pursed her lips. "He is *that* duke," she said dismissively.

"What do you mean by that, my lady?" Mirella challenged.

Clucking her tongue and shaking her head, the young woman said, "All of Polite Society knows of your brother and his most improper duchess. How she was shunned by the *ton* when she wed beneath her—and shunned further once she began soiling her hands by running her husband's business when she became a widow. Why, I have heard rumors that Her Grace still runs it!"

Mirella felt the need to defend her family, and yet she did not want to sink into the mire Miss Bowles rolled about in. "Yes, Her Grace is active in making decisions regarding Neptune Shipping, which my stepfather helps her to run."

"Well, since it appears that you are making your come-out,

Lady Mirella, I hope that you can acquire a husband quickly before they look too deeply into your family." Miss Bowles patted her hair. "As for myself, my reputation is spotless. Why, I have danced with a great deal of important men this evening, and they all have told me how marvelous I am."

Miss Bowles went on to toss out several names, many of whom Mirella herself had already partnered with tonight.

She did not like this woman one whit. Miss Bowles boasted, gossiped, and judged without thought. She was a type of poison which Mirella determined to avoid in the future at all costs.

Before she could excuse herself, however, Miss Bowles said, "I did partner with my neighbor for the supper dance. Lord Bridgewater. *He* has turned into quite a handsome fellow, if I do say so myself."

So, they were neighbors. Perhaps that was the only reason Lord Bridgewater asked Miss Bowles to dance. If he knew her true nature—and knew what a sour person she was—he might have tried to do Miss Bowles a favor by filling a spot on her dance card.

"I had not seen the marquess for many years before this evening," continued Miss Bowles, dispelling Mirella's theory. "Not since I was a child. I am pleased how he turned out, even having served in the army. Such a distasteful thing for a man to do."

She clamped her lips together, knowing she must watch herself around Miss Bowles. This opinionated female had no idea of how the British army kept their country safe.

Again, Miss Bowles rambled on. "My father and Lord Bridgewater were quite close, friends from the cradle. My brother holds the title now. Papa and the previous Lord Bridgewater were foolish enough to race one another when they were deep in their cups. Fortunately, that scandal occurred a couple of years ago. It will not affect my opportunities of making a suitable match this Season. I am stunningly beautiful. I will have my choice of husband."

Mirella knew this woman had exceptional looks without

being told so by Miss Bowles. It was all she offered, though. Mirella could only wonder how many men would vie for Miss Jacinda Bowles' hand. She had already seen into this woman's heart. Miss Bowles was a braggart, unsympathetic and egotistical. Not a person Mirella would ever associate herself with. She could not even bring herself to mouth a polite phrase and tell this woman it had been nice to meet her.

Instead, she said, "I hope you enjoy the rest of your evening, Miss Bowles."

Quitting the retiring room, her nerves unsettled by her encounter with Miss Bowles, Mirella could not help but wonder if Lord Bridgewater had danced with Miss Bowles out of obligation, seeing their fathers had been close. Miss Bowles had been so dismissive of her father and the phaeton accident, which Mirella knew had deeply affected Lord Bridgewater.

Should she warn him what a viper this woman was?

No, she decided she should have nothing more to do with him. Let the marquess dance with whomever he chose to do so. If he spent more than two minutes with Miss Bowles, he would learn for himself just how spiteful and selfish she was. It was not her responsibility to watch over him.

She returned upstairs to the ballroom and joined Sophie and Aunt Matty, who stood talking with Lady Benton and a few others.

"I see the men have abandoned the ladies," she said quietly to her aunt.

"Yes, I am certain the card room is packed now with gentlemen ready to escape all the dancing and gossip." Aunt Matty smiled mischievously. "I do believe, however, that those same men gossip even more than their wives and sisters and mothers do."

"May I speak to you a moment privately?" Mirella asked.

"Certainly, my dear," her aunt said, slipping her arm through Mirella's as they began to take a turn about the ballroom.

"I am curious, Aunt Matty. Do you know anything about a

Miss Jacinda Bowles?"

Her aunt cocked her head, thinking a moment. "Bowles. Jacinda Bowles," she repeated. "I cannot say that I do. Why do you ask?"

"Apparently, her family and Lord Bridgewater's are neighbors, and she is making her come-out this Season. I met her in the retiring room just now, and my impression of her was, shall we say, less than favorable."

"Oh, I do know the family, now that I can place them. Flora has met them a few times during visits to Bridgefield. From what I can recall her saying, the current Lord Bridgewater's father and Lord Hampton were constant companions from their youth. Flora mentioned that her sister despised Lady Hampton and thought the two Hampton children to be spoiled brats. Was that your impression of Miss Bowles?"

"Yes, Aunt. I admired her earrings and complimented her on them. She casually mentioned they were her mother's, and that her mother had passed, not expressing any sadness at all. The same was true when she spoke of her father. Frankly, I found Miss Bowles to be quite self-centered and opinionated."

Mirella spied Miss Bowles and said, "She is with her brother now, Aunt Matty," and told her aunt where to look.

"My, she is most beautiful," Aunt Matty murmured. "She will certainly turn the heads of many gentlemen. Despite what you have told me about her lack of character, Miss Bowles will, no doubt, have a large number of suitors based on her looks alone. Most *ton* marriages are business arrangements, Mirella. They are made for financial reasons or to increase a family's social status within Polite Society."

Her aunt paused, her gaze meeting Mirella's. "You are not expected to make that kind of marriage, my dear. Your mother has always wanted a love match for all you girls. I know it is what you want for yourself, as well. That is why James has told you not to rush into anything or feel pressured to accept the first offer which you receive. He and Sophie are set on you finding happiness and lasting love."

"I do want that for myself, Aunt Matty."

They continued making a circle about the ballroom, her aunt asking about various gentlemen Mirella had danced with and the kind of impressions they had made upon her. She mentioned how several had asked to call the following day.

"It is a bit too hard to converse during a lively reel or country dance. That is why I look forward to tomorrow, so that I might speak with these gentlemen individually."

"They will not stay long," Aunt Matty warned. "Gentlemen are taught that a quarter-hour is long enough for a visit, and they are to take their leave after that amount of time."

"Why so short a visit?" she asked, perplexed.

Her aunt chuckled. "Possibly because they have more than one young lady that they wish to call upon," she said knowingly. "But I do hope the gentlemen who choose to come and visit tomorrow will enjoy their brief time with you."

Just before they returned to their group, her aunt asked, "Is your dance with Lord Bridgewater coming up soon? I know he signed your programme earlier this evening."

"No," she said abruptly.

Aunt Matty's brows shot up. "That was a quick response. And not the one I anticipated, Mirella. I saw Lord Bridgewater sign your dance card."

She sighed. "He did—but we have had a falling out, Aunt. I asked that he not approach me for the dance."

"I see," Aunt Matty said. She patted Mirella's hand before slipping her own away. "If you wish to speak about this further tomorrow, I can come to the music room so that we have privacy."

Mirella wasn't certain just how much of what had occurred she might want to share with her aunt.

"I will think on it. If I need to ask your advice, I will let you know."

The musicians had returned to the dais, and a tall, gangly earl came to claim Mirella for their dance.

Despite appearing to be ever so awkward, the earl danced wonderfully, ending the dance with a smile and asking to call upon her tomorrow afternoon. She readily agreed, liking him quite a bit and interested to learn more about this gentleman.

She danced every number for the next two hours, finally taking a brief respite, with her partner bringing them both a cup of punch to sip.

Glancing at her dance card, she saw only one dance remained and would be played shortly. She spied Sophie and saw that James had returned to his wife's side, no doubt to dance the final number of the evening with her before they left for home. Mirella only hoped Lord Bridgewater would have the sense to leave her alone, as she had requested.

She went to join James and Sophie. By this time, the captain and her mother were also there.

"Have you enjoyed showing off the captain this evening, Mama?" she asked, not bothering to hide her smile.

Mama glowed as she said, "Every lady in this ballroom is envious of me."

"And every gentleman in the card room is out for his blood," James teased. "Drake had an excellent run of luck tonight, taking far more money than he lost."

They all laughed, and the captain said, "I am ready to dance now with my lovely Mrs. Andrews." He offered Mama his arm, and she took it, her gaze adoring.

James and Sophie also left for the dance floor, leaving Mirella alone. She thought to go and sit in the chairs provided for those ladies not dancing a particular number. Before she could move toward the section, however, she saw Lord Bridgewater making his way toward her, determination on his face.

Mirella did have her reputation to think of. She could not afford to cause a scene in front of an entire ballroom of guests. That would do far more to harm her than satisfy the anger she still carried inside toward this man.

The marquess reached her, smiling charmingly. "Are you ready for our waltz, my lady?" he asked innocently, as if he did not recall the previous exchange between them.

Mirella cursed under her breath, a word she had never uttered before. He must have read her lips because he began chuckling, which only irritated her further.

She had not known the last number closing the ball would be a waltz. That meant she would be held close in the marquess' arms the entire time the music played. She told herself to be stoic. To not come undone by his touch.

"I believe we had previously arranged not to dance together, my lord," she said haughtily.

"I think you did make that suggestion, Lady Mirella." He smiled again, causing her insides to turn to jelly. "One which I decided to ignore. I know you will do the right thing by honoring your commitment to me."

Though she had hoped to talk him out of it, Mirella realized it would not come to pass. She lifted her hand, placing it on his offered arm, and he led her onto the dance floor.

Smiling at him, she said sternly, "This will be the *only* time we ever dance together, Lord Bridgewater. Do not ask me in the future—because I will turn you down."

"Understood, my lady," he said, his arms coming about her as the music began.

CHAPTER FIFTEEN

BYRON HAD KNOWN that Lady Mirella would dance with him. She had exquisite manners and would not reject him in front of a packed ballroom. Moreover, he knew she would never create a scene in public. He had been counting on those two things. Now, he led her out onto the dance floor, already conscious of the floral scent he recalled from their time together in Grasmere.

He slipped his arm about her shoulders, his fingers lightly grazing her body, as he took her hand in his. The music began, and they began moving to the strains of the waltz. As he had observed throughout the evening, she was a graceful dancer. What was different now was that she wore a blank expression on her face instead of the joyful smile which had been present while she danced with others.

He was determined to see that smile again.

"You dance divinely, Lady Mirella," he complimented.

She remained silent, as if her face had been set in stone.

"I am only glad to finally partner with someone who understands music the way you do. Who feels the rhythm within it and can move accordingly. Why, I have had my toes trampled numerous times this evening. One of my partners could not distinguish her left from her right and constantly bumped into me and others. And one young lady had the breath of a dragon and almost knocked me down."

That did it. The corners of her lips turned up. She fought the smile, though.

"Surely, you are exaggerating, my lord."

"You will never know, will you?" he teased. "After all, I am a gentleman—and a gentleman never calls out a lady by name for her misdeeds on the dance floor."

He felt her relax, so subtle, and yet he was attuned to her like no other. Byron had kept to the basic steps of the waltz, but now he turned with her, her skirts whirling about them. As expected, the move broke through her icy exterior.

"There," he said. "A true smile from you now. I was beginning to think that you were not happy dancing the waltz with me."

"You are a skilled dancer, Lord Bridgewater," she told him. "Despite my personal opinion of you, I cannot help but enjoy partnering with someone who dances so well."

"Have you enjoyed this opening night of the Season?" he asked, curious about her perspective of the night.

"I have never disguised my love of dancing, so yes, my lord. I would say it has been a most successful evening because I have danced into the wee hours of the morning."

"You danced often," he said. "I know—because I have been watching you."

A blush stained her cheeks. "Have you?

"I have indeed."

They fell silent, and he twirled her about the dance floor, feeling as though they moved as one. The rest of the evening paled in comparison to these minutes Lady Mirella Strong was in his arms.

Suddenly, she said, "I met your neighbor tonight. She is quite beautiful."

She had met Jacinda?

"We spoke for a time in the retiring room. Miss Bowles said she had not seen you since childhood."

"While I told you that our fathers were close, my brother and I were never friendly with Cedric Bowles. He was a couple of years younger than I was and not someone either of us enjoyed being around. Miss Bowles was quite a bit younger. Because of that, I rarely saw her."

"She seemed pleased that you had asked her to dance this evening," Lady Mirella continued. "Miss Bowles is . . ." Her voice trailed off.

Byron knew what Lady Mirella wanted to say—and couldn't—because as a lady, she would never disparage someone else.

"From the little I recall about her, she was always a handful," he said truthfully. "Mama was not fond of Lady Hampton, and Miss Bowles was greatly influenced by her mother."

The dance would end soon, and he did not want to be speaking of Jacinda during his last moments with Lady Mirella.

Out of the blue, she asked, "Are you going to call upon me tomorrow, my lord?"

It was the last thing Byron intended to do. He would be going to Lord Hampton's tomorrow afternoon to pay a call upon Jacinda instead. He needed to see who his competitors might be and make certain both she and her brother understood that he was a most interested suitor.

Instead, what came out of his mouth surprised him.

"Yes, Lady Mirella. I intend to call upon you tomorrow, if only to count the number of hearts you have stolen this evening."

She giggled, a sweet sound which he wished he could hear every day from her. That every day he awoke with this woman in his arms and had the privilege of being her husband.

But it could never be. His sense of duty was too great. He must abide by the decision he had made regarding taking a marchioness, the one his father had chosen.

And yet Byron found, as the last strains of the waltz sounded, that he could not tell her that he had changed his mind and would not come to see her.

Glancing over her shoulder, he caught sight of where the matrons sat observing the dancers. His gaze connected with that of his mother's, and she looked pleased. Aunt Flora and Lady Mathilda sat with Mama, both of them beaming at Lady Mirella and him. Byron knew he had compounded mistake upon mistake this evening.

He had danced with Lady Mirella when he should not have done so.

He continued to compare her to Jacinda.

Worst of all, he had committed to calling upon her, giving her false hope about them.

Byron wished he could tuck tail and rush back to Bridgefield. Of course, he had done that very thing last autumn when he had first met Lady Mirella. She had called him a coward then.

She would call him far worse once she realized he had misled her so badly.

The waltz ended, and he held her close a final moment, breathing in that fresh, floral scent which he would never forget. Then he placed her hand on his sleeve and escorted her from the ballroom floor.

"There is Mama and the captain," she said, and he led her in their direction.

From the angle he observed the couple, he thought Mrs. Andrews might be with child.

Lady Mirella turned to him, smiling, a radiant smile which was like sunshine washing over him. For a moment, Byron experienced a pure rush of happiness.

"It does my heart good to see how happy Mama is with the captain. She spent so many years in a loveless marriage, with Papa barely acknowledging her. The captain has been so good for her, and she has been good for him, as well."

"Do you think they might have children?" he asked.

"Oh, Mama is with child now. She has shared with us that it will be the only one they will have, because of her age, but I am so looking forward to having a new little brother or sister.

Already, the captain has been a wonderful stepfather and embraced my sisters and me, claiming us as his own. In the eight months they have been wed, he has been more a father to me than my own ever was."

They reached the couple and were joined by the Duke and Duchess of Seaton.

Her Grace asked, "How was your evening, Lord Bridgewater? I heard this is the first Season you have attended."

"It was most interesting, Your Grace," he replied. "If you will excuse me."

Byron bowed to the group, and though he hated the commitment he had made, Byron said, "I will see you tomorrow afternoon, Lady Mirella."

He worked his way through the crowd, meeting up with Uncle Hugh along the way.

"How was your card game this evening?" he asked.

"I won more than I lost, which is always a pleasant surprise," his uncle shared. "I did lose twice, however, to a Mr. Andrews. He was with the Duke of Seaton, who introduced him around. Apparently, they are somehow related by marriage. The man had a wicked run of luck."

"Andrews was formerly Captain Andrews," Byron informed his uncle. "A sea captain, not an army one. Andrews wed Seaton's stepmother last summer."

"Ah, the convoluted relationships in the *ton*." Uncle Hugh tossed an arm about Byron's shoulder. "I hope you enjoyed your own evening, dancing with a string of pretty young girls."

He did not answer because they had reached his mother and Aunt Flora. Thank goodness, Lady Mathilda was nowhere in sight.

"Shall we go to our carriage?" he asked.

Byron took Mama's arm, escorting her, while Uncle Hugh claimed Aunt Flora.

It took more than half an hour to work their way through the crush of guests and toward their carriage a few streets away. He handed up his mother and then Aunt Flora, following Uncle Hugh into the carriage. The light of dawn breaking let him know just how different the hours in town would be from the ones he had observed in the country.

He braced himself, waiting for Aunt Flora to bring up Lady Mirella, which he thought would be inevitable. Instead, it was his mother who mentioned her first.

"I noticed you danced with several young ladies this evening, Bridgewater," Mama said. "The last girl, in particular, was quite beautiful, even if she did have reddish hair. Flora tells me that she is Lady Mirella Strong, and that you made her acquaintance at Benbrook when you were last there in September."

"Yes, Mama, I did meet Lady Mirella, along with her aunt and youngest sister. All three ladies were delightful."

Mama nodded. "I must say, Bridgewater, that you and Lady Mirella looked as if you belonged together. Of all the couples on the dance floor for that waltz, the two of you danced superbly, better than any other couple. It was as if you had been dancing with one another your entire lives."

"I suppose I am glad that I took those dance lessons in Bridgehampton," he said casually.

Byron saw the hope on his aunt and uncle's faces, and he knew the decision he had made regarding a wife would greatly disappointment them. Mama, as well, since she had no love for the Bowles' family.

He had to stop dallying with Lady Mirella, however. Yes, he had fallen in love with her months ago and still loved her, but she was too great a temptation for him to be around further. He would stick to his plans.

And that meant declaring for Jacinda Bowles as soon as possible, despite Uncle Hugh's advice against doing so.

Deciding to start with informing his own family, Byron said, "I have an announcement to make. One, I acknowledge, which most likely will not please any of you."

Uncle Hugh looked puzzled and said, "There is no need to

hide your feelings from us about Lady Mirella, Bridgewater. Yes, you only reacquainted yourself with her this evening, but when your heart knows, it knows. That is how it was with Flora and me."

His uncle slipped a hand around his wife's and added, "If you believe it might be too soon to declare your intentions to her and her family, at least you can call upon her and simply tell her you wish to get to know her better. The way you look at her, it is obvious what your feelings are toward her."

Uncle Hugh's words were like a knife twisted in Byron's gut, especially because his uncle already knew what Byron had planned. Obviously, he was still trying to influence Byron, hoping he would change his mind.

"Let me clarify matters," he said brusquely.

But the words simply wouldn't come. He saw anticipation on his aunt and uncle's face and could sense it from his mother, who was seated next to him.

Forcing himself to say the words, Byron said, "I do not intend to make Lady Mirella my marchioness. My choice for my bride will be Miss Jacinda Bowles."

His aunt audibly gasped, while his uncle looked bemused by the announcement. Byron dared a glance at his mother and found her mouth hardening.

"You are doing this out of a sense of duty, aren't you?" she accused, her tone bitter. "Just because your father wished to unite our families through marriage, seeing your brother and Jacinda wed, it does not mean that you have to follow through with those plans, Bridgewater."

When he remained silent, Mama's tone softened, her eyes now pleading with him. "Please. Do not do this to yourself. You know how I felt about Lady Hampton. Her daughter is ten times worse than she was. You have not been around the chit for many years, but I watched her grow up. Jacinda is cruel, Bridgewater. She will make you most unhappy."

"Marriage is a business arrangement, Mama," he said stiffly. "I intend to speak with Lord Hampton tomorrow about drawing up new contracts so that his sister and I might wed."

"You simply cannot do this, Byron," Aunt Flora insisted. "We see how you look at Lady Mirella. How she looks at you. Why, I think one—or the both of you—are already in love."

"Love has nothing to do with marriage," he said dismissively. "I am the Marquess of Bridgewater. I decide my own fate. My mind is made up, and none of you will change it. No further discussion will be required."

Byron fell silent, gazing out the window at the darkened streets being lit by dawn's first light. He must bury the feelings he had for Lady Mirella Strong.

And the best way to do that was to announce his betrothal to Jacinda Bowles.

Chapter Sixteen

Breakfast was a silent affair. Byron went through the morning post after he finished, setting aside a few items he would give more attention to in his study as he sipped his tea.

Beyond a brief *Good morning*, no one else had said a word. Forks clicked on plates as everyone ate in silence. He decided he wasn't in the business of fixing things in this instance. He felt no need to apologize for his choice of a bride. As he had told them, he was the marquess. Whom he wed was his affair alone. They did not have to like—or even support—his choice.

It troubled him that it would alienate him further from his mother. They had never had a close relationship, and he had hoped to repair it after he came home from war. That hadn't been the case. As far as Aunt Flora and Uncle Hugh went, he believed the couple upset with him now, but they would forgive him in the end.

He did worry how Jacinda would treat his relatives. They would not be together often, but he would expect her to show respect to her elders, even if she would never have a close relationship with his family.

Or him.

For a moment, Byron questioned why he was doing what he was doing. It would be so much easier to ignore Jacinda and Lord

Hampton and follow his heart, pursuing Lady Mirella. Yet ingrained in him was such a deep sense of obligation and duty, knowing a marriage between a Balfour son and a Bowles daughter was what his father had wanted. Even expected.

He rose, excusing himself, and retreated to his study. The stack of invitations on his desk grew by the day. He sorted through them now, deciding he would ask Mama to reply to the newest of them in the affirmative, for the four of them. He did not know which events Jacinda would attend, and so he did not want to lose any ground to another gentleman by skipping any of them.

Usually, a secretary would take on such a duty as responding to invitations, but his brother had not had one. When Byron had questioned Paulson about it, his butler had informed him that the previous Lord Bridgewater had not bothered responding to any invitations. He merely showed up at the affairs he wished to attend. Byron thought that unconscionable, but it did sound like Dawson. His brother would not have cared if he alienated any of London's hostesses. After all, he was secretly betrothed and in no need to remain on the good side of anyone.

He thought again of his plan to announce his betrothal to Jacinda as soon as possible and decided that would not be feasible. From the little he had been around her last night, he understood she was reveling in making her come-out and attending the many social events. If he pressed her too early, she might reject him outright—and he wasn't having any of that.

Instead, he decided to go with the plan he had first hit upon. He would take Lord Hampton aside this afternoon and make the necessary arrangements with the viscount. Once again, Jacinda would be left in the dark about the plans made on her behalf, but he supposed many parents amongst the *ton* did the same each Season. A dutiful daughter would simply obey and follow through with the arranged marriage.

Then he thought of how Lady Mirella wished to make a love match, as others in her family had done. A deep yearning filled him, need for her so great that it was almost a physical ache he carried inside him. He would carry through with his commitment today, but he would refrain from calling upon her in the future. If their paths crossed at a social event, he would be polite but distant.

And he knew now never to ask her to dance again.

Byron had dreamed of Lady Mirella when he had finally fallen asleep. He had stripped off his clothes and fallen into bed, not bothering to wash, because he could still detect the faint scent of her perfume on him. In his dream, he had kissed her. Made love to her. He had awakened with an aching cock and an emptiness which would never be filled. Still, he would do his duty and link the Balfour and Bowles families, get his heir off Jacinda, and then see that they went their separate ways.

He thought how happy his aunt and uncle were after so many decades of wedded bliss, knowing he would never experience the same satisfaction in the marriage he made. It did not matter. He would have his marchioness. Get his children. Most importantly, he would never return to town for the Season again. He would be happy to send Jacinda to London and let her be with her friends. Even her lovers, once Byron had his heir. It was common amongst the *ton*. No one would think twice of it, as long as his wife could conduct any affair discreetly.

By not attending the Season, he would not have to see Lady Mirella ever again. He would not see her with the husband she chose and have to curb his jealousy of the man. He would not have to see her mature, growing more lovely with each passing year. He would not have to meet her children or see her relatives or even think about what they might have had together.

He pulled out his pocket watch and saw it was time to make his two calls. Naturally, he would call upon Jacinda first. She was his priority. He rang for Paulson and ordered his carriage to be readied. Trepidation filled him as he rode through the London streets, thinking about approaching Lord Hampton regarding his sister.

Cursing, he told himself that he was a bloody marquess. He should have no fears. He was doing his duty in choosing a bride, one familiar to him. By Season's end, they would wed, and he would get her with child as quickly as possible.

But his thoughts meandered, and he went back to those moments with Lady Mirella atop Helm Crag. Closing his eyes, he could feel her in his arms once more. Taste the sweetness of her. Those kisses had been the most memorable of his life.

Opening his eyes again, he thought of a simple solution. He would not kiss Jacinda. Oh, a perfunctory one every now and then, but he did not want to share something as intimate as the kisses he and Lady Mirella had shared. In a way, the kisses were more special and private than the act of making love might be. Byron would save that small part of him and her. It was theirs alone.

He reached Lord Hampton's townhouse and saw other carriages lining the streets. The butler admitted him, directing him to the drawing room. Looking about, he doubted any of the gentlemen present had an iota of the true Jacinda Bowles. Yes, they looked upon her beauty and were taken in by it, yet they had no idea of who she truly was. Byron had hoped for the best and been disappointed last night after their shared supper. Her conversation was limited, and her shallow nature had been apparent. He wondered how many of these men would continue to vie for her hand once they got to know the true Jacinda.

Probably most, he told himself. After all, weren't a majority of these men the same as he was? Looking for a woman to wed and not really caring much about her. He couldn't blame any of them if they continued to admire her strictly for her looks.

Without speaking to Jacinda, he drew Lord Hampton aside, taking him to the far corner of the drawing room.

"Thank you for calling today, Lord Bridgewater," the viscount said. "As you see, my sister is proving to be quite popular."

"I wish to wed Miss Bowles," he said flatly.

"What?" Lord Hampton looked shaken by the sudden announcement.

"I know you are aware of the marriage contracts drawn up for your sister and my brother. That they were legally betrothed and would have wed after this Season played out."

"Yes," the viscount said, questions in his eyes. "What of them? The marriage settlements are obviously null and void because of your brother's . . . passing."

"There is no need to tread warily, Hampton. The both of us know that Bridgewater and Hampton were drunk when they raced one another that day in Hyde Park. My brother's death put an end to the plans our fathers had of uniting our families." He paused. "I am willing to take my brother's place and wed your sister."

"You . . . would do that?" Lord Hampton asked, his shock evident.

"I would," he said firmly, his commitment to family now voiced.

"Jacinda is . . . well . . . my sister is quite headstrong, my lord."

"I can deal with that."

The viscount studied him. "I believe you can."

"I do not think it wise to tell her of this now. She did not know of the previous betrothal. I think we can refrain from mentioning this one for a month or two. Let her enjoy her come-out Season. Dance and flirt. Then when engagements start being announced, you can take her aside and share with her that her future is secure."

Hampton's laugh sounded like a pig snorting. "I will not be telling Jacinda anything, my lord. *You* are to be her husband. I think it wise this information comes from you."

Byron had not particularly liked Hampton, but he thought the man weak.

"I will do so," he promised. "In the meantime, I will have Mr. Pilsbury, my solicitor, get in touch with your solicitor if you will provide me with his name."

"It would be the same man who negotiated the previous marriage settlements, my lord," the viscount told him. "He has handled our family's affairs for many years now."

"Then I will have Pilsbury write to him, and the two of them can handle the negotiations. Would you be fine with a similar arrangement as the one our fathers came to regarding the betrothal?"

Byron eagerly anticipated the viscount's answer, thinking if Hampton wavered, he would agree to forgo Jacinda's dowry to further tempt the man.

"Absolutely, my lord."

Not that he needed her dowry, but he was glad the contracts could stand as previously drawn up.

"I will notify Pilsbury of our intentions then, Hampton." He glanced up, seeing Jacinda smile prettily at the circle of men about her. "For now, I will go and spend a bit of time with my future marchioness."

"I will not say a word of our arrangement to Jacinda, Bridgewater," Lord Hampton said. "She is quite headstrong. I believe the news of her betrothal will be better coming from you."

Byron nodded. "Then I will let you know when I am going to approach her. For now, I will play the besotted suitor."

He left Hampton and moved across the room. Two of the men were saying their goodbyes to Jacinda. Byron looked at the other two sternly, and they took the hint, also taking their leave.

That left the two of them alone, and he said, "Good afternoon, Miss Bowles. I have come to call upon you."

She batted her eyelashes at him. "I received your lovely floral arrangement, Lord Bridgewater. By far, it is the largest of all which have arrived today."

"Good. I wanted it to stand out. I am most interested in you, my lady. I intend to be your most faithful suitor."

He knew not to stay more than a quarter-hour, thanks to Aunt Flora, and was surprised how long those fifteen minutes stretched out. Jacinda talked only of herself or of her other suitors. He had never met a more self-centered person. She was concerned solely with herself. No other topic seemed to interest her. He found it hard to listen to her as she went on and on and was happy when a pair of gentlemen arrived and could take his place.

Waiting for her to wind down, he finally got in a word and said, "I see you have two new suitors who have come to call upon you. You must give them your full attention, my lady," he told her. "I would, however, request that you save a dance for me this evening. The supper dance," he insisted, knowing how bored he would be in her company.

She smiled flirtatiously. "I will do so, my lord."

"Perhaps we can sup alone. I would prefer to have you all to myself."

She tittered at the suggestion. "Of course, my lord. I am certain that, as a marquess, you are used to getting your way. I am happy to accommodate you."

He took her hand. Lifting it to his lips, he brushed a kiss upon her knuckles. "Thank you, Miss Bowles. I look forward to this evening."

Byron took his leave, returning to his coach. His driver asked where he was off to next, and he instructed him to head to Mr. Pilsbury's office.

He climbed into the vehicle, a wave of nausea passing through him. He told himself he was doing the right thing, and yet it felt so very wrong. Sitting back against the cushions, he wondered how long he would be able to stomach courting Jacinda.

Byron did not let his thoughts roam toward what marriage with her would be like.

When he arrived at the solicitor's, the clerk greeted him immediately, saying, "Good afternoon, Lord Bridgewater. I was not aware you had an appointment today."

"I don't," he said crisply. "I only need five minutes of Mr. Pilsbury's time. Is he available?"

"One moment, my lord."

Soon, the clerk ushered Byron into Pilsbury's office, where the solicitor greeted him warmly.

"How might I assist you today, Lord Bridgewater?" the older man asked.

"It is a simple matter," he replied. "Do you recall how we spoke of the marriage settlements which had been signed by my father and Lord Hampton several years ago?"

"Yes, of course. We spoke of them when you returned to claim your title."

"You said you still had a copy of the documents. If so, use them as a reference. Set up a time as soon as possible with Lord Hampton's solicitor and update these contracts, inserting my name where my brother's had been. All other items are to remain the same, just as my father wished."

Pilsbury nodded. "I see. So, no changes are to be made."

"None. Once you and this solicitor have rewritten them, contact me at once. I will wish to review them before we meet with the current Lord Hampton in order to sign them."

"I will handle this matter immediately, my lord," the solicitor guaranteed. "May I extend my congratulations to you on your betrothal?"

"Do not put the cart before the horse, Pilsbury," he warned. "Only when both parties have signed will I accept your good wishes on my upcoming marriage. Good day."

Byron quit the offices, returning to his carriage. Though it was later than he wished, he instructed his coachman to take him to the Duke of Seaton's townhouse. He would keep his word and call upon Lady Mirella.

Because he had to let her know they had no future together.

Obviously, they would run into one another during the various events of the Season, but he needed her to understand that while he would be polite, he intended to keep his distance from her. She needed to know that so she could look forward—and not behind her.

When he arrived at the square where the ducal townhouse stood, it surprised him it was not more crowded with carriages and hansom cabs. He had seen so many vehicles at Hampton's and assumed the same would be true here. Then again, he was much later than he had originally intended to be. Perhaps the bulk of Lady Mirella's callers had already come and gone.

Byron left the carriage, his heart heavy, and approached the Seaton townhouse. He had no idea how he would get Lady Mirella alone.

Much less have the courage to tell her he wished to have no more to do with her.

CHAPTER SEVENTEEN

MIRELLA LOOKED INTO the mirror, pleased with the gown the maid had chosen for her. Mama also nodded her approval.

"You certainly know how to wear a gown, my dear. Come, let us go downstairs before your suitors come calling. You need to see the many bouquets which have been arriving all morning."

They started down the corridor, Aunt Matty joining them.

"Oh, isn't it exciting to have a young person in the house and gentlemen calling," her aunt declared. "I have just come from the drawing room, and it is filled with the most beautiful flowers."

Georgie had told Mirella that suitors would send elaborate floral arrangements to her once the Season began. The larger the arrangement, the more the gentleman's interest in her supposedly was. She couldn't help but wonder what Lord Bridgewater's flowers would look like.

Her feelings were mixed regarding the marquess. On one hand, she was certainly aware of the physical attraction which lay between them. He was also intelligent and entertaining to be around. She had thought to keep him at arm's length, even when the waltz began last night, but somehow she kept wanting to give him another chance. That was why she had asked if he planned to visit her today, and she had been pleased when he answered in the affirmative.

They entered the drawing room, and she exclaimed, "Oh! It is like entering an indoor garden."

On every surface, she saw gorgeous arrangements of flowers. Their sweet fragrances filled the air. The room was an array of color. It overwhelmed Mirella to think all these beautiful bouquets were for her.

"It is quite lovely," Mama said. "We should go about the room and see which gentlemen have been thoughtful enough to send you flowers."

Before each arrangement sat a card, and Mirella picked up the first one, reading the name of the suitor who had sent that particular bouquet.

"There are so many," she observed as they stepped to the second one.

"And quite large," Aunt Matty noted.

"I recognize most of the names on these cards," she said as they strolled about the room, examining each bouquet as she noted its sender. "There are a few, however, which I am unfamiliar with."

"That means you have admirers you have yet to meet," Mama informed her.

Two maids entered the drawing room, one carrying an arrangement that dwarfed her. The other maid held one which was small and artfully arranged, with a unique combination of flowers in it. The servants set down the flowers and placed the cards in front of them.

Mirella worked her way around to these final two offerings, opening the card to the larger of the two, recalling the earl she had danced with as she saw his name. Then she picked up the final card and opened it, realizing the mistake she had made.

"I am sorry, Mama. These are for you. From . . . Lord Bridgewater."

She handed the card to her mother, and Aunt Matty peered over Mama's shoulder as both women read it.

"He is a clever one," her aunt said, smiling broadly. "Sending flowers not to you, but to your mother."

The gesture puzzled her. She did not understand the reasoning behind him doing so. His bouquet was also outshone by all the others. Still, she liked the mixture of flowers in the arrangement.

"I will be certain to thank Lord Bridgewater when he stops by today," Mama said.

James and the captain entered the drawing room, Sophie with them.

"Are you ready for all your callers?" Sophie asked, her eyes bright. "Looking about the room, I see that you will have many of them visiting with you today."

"And we will be here to see if they are worthy of you or not," James inserted, crossing his arms over his broad, muscular chest.

Mirella looked from him to the captain, who now mimicked his friend's stance, and couldn't help but laugh. "The two of you are quite intimidating. It will be interesting to see how many of them you scare away and how many pass your imaginary test."

Powell opened the door, announcing the first callers of the afternoon, and Mirella became swept up in her duties. She recognized most of the gentlemen who came through the door and tried to spend a few moments alone with each of them before they departed. All the while, she was conscious of new arrivals, disappointed each time when Lord Bridgewater's name was not declared.

The afternoon grew late, and the number of callers finally thinned. She knew that teatime would be at hand soon—and still no appearance by the Marquess of Bridgewater. Her disappointment turned to anger. She should have known not to count on him. Her resolve firmed, deciding she had been right all along to want to have nothing to do with him.

Then she heard the butler announce his name, and Mirella focused on the last two gentlemen before her, giving them her full attention and ignoring this last arrival. Even as she smiled and nodded, appearing interested in what the pair had to say, she was aware of the marquess and his location in the room.

The two gentlemen she spoke with took their leave, and Lord Bridgewater came toward her. He bowed and took her hand in his, raising it to his lips and brushing a light kiss upon her fingers. A sizzle of awareness rippled through her.

"You decided to call rather late, my lord," she said sternly. "It is almost time for calls to end."

"My apologies, Lady Mirella. I found I had unexpected business to attend to with my solicitor. I came straight from his office. Did you entertain many suitors this afternoon?"

She waved a hand around. "Judge for yourself, my lord. The bouquets are an indication that I most certainly did. Thank you, by the way, for sending one to Mama. I am certain she will tell you how appreciative she is of it."

His gaze pinned hers, causing a rush of warmth to race through her.

"I thought it important to acknowledge the mother who brought such a remarkable lady into Polite Society," he told her. Then his face grew serious. "We must speak about something important, my lady."

"What?" she asked, her heart beating rapidly.

Surely, he was not about to offer for her. And if he did—what would she say?

Mirella did not love him. At least, she did not think she did. All she knew was this pull between them. An attraction was not enough for a marriage, though. She needed the love which might spring from that attraction before she would even consider wedding a gentleman.

She felt herself blush, feeling foolish because she doubted the marquess was about to propose marriage to her, yet that had been her first thought.

James appeared at her elbow, along with Sophie. Greetings were exchanged, and Sophie smiled rightly at Lord Bridgewater.

"We were about to take tea, my lord," Sophie said. "Would you care to join us?"

"Thank you for the invitation, Your Grace," Lord Bridgewater replied. "I would be happy to do so."

They crossed the room and took seats, and the marquess said to her, "We must speak after tea ends. It is urgent." He paused. "And private."

"Certainly, my lord," she responded, wondering what might be so pressing, something that could not be said in front of others.

Again, she prayed that he would not offer marriage. Her head told her she must immediately turn him down if he did so. Her heart, on the other hand, remembered those incredible kisses—and might tempt her to say yes.

They were a lively group at tea, talking about last night's ball and the upcoming events during the next week. Lord Bridgewater indicated he would be attending all of them. She vacillated on whether she was happy to hear that or not. Mirella still was having trouble deciding whether or not she wanted to be around the mercurial marquess. So many decent gentlemen had called upon her today. None seemed to hide his interest in her. Yet Lord Bridgewater swung back and forth, totally confusing her.

She decided she would hear him out before making any decision regarding him.

"It has been delightful spending this hour with you," the marquess told the group. "I appreciate your kind invitation, Your Grace. I will see you all this evening."

As he rose, Sophie said, "Mirella, why don't you walk our guest out?"

"Of course," she responded, coming to her feet and accompanying Lord Bridgewater from the drawing room.

She knew what her sister-in-law did, trying to give the pair a few precious moments alone.

They moved down the corridor and before they reached the stairs, he halted.

"I must speak with you now," he insisted. "Not in the foyer where a footman will be on duty. What I have to say to you is private, my lady."

Her heart thumped against her ribs as she composed herself. "Yes, my lord?"

He took her hands in his and smiled at her, but she saw the sadness in that smile.

"I think every day of that moment at the top of Helm Crag," he said earnestly. "About those kisses we shared. That entire day with you is the highlight of my life."

A chill ran through her. "I, too, have thought about that day fondly," she told him.

Angst filled his face. "That memory is one I will forever cherish, Lady Mirella. You must understand that. But I cannot give you false hope. I will no longer be calling upon you. I will never ask you to dance with me again. I cannot do so—because I am soon to be betrothed to another."

It was the last thing she had expected him to say to her. Hurt immediately filled her. Mirella felt herself start to tremble, and his hands tightened about hers. She could not stand the sight of him, much less tolerate his touch. Quickly, she jerked her hands from his and took a few steps back, needing to put distance between them.

"Then why on earth did you lead me on, my lord?" she asked angrily. "Why are you speaking so fondly of kisses between us?"

Sadness filled those gray eyes. "Because that memory is the happiest moment of my life, and I will never be that happy again. Goodbye, Lady Mirella. I will see myself out."

He turned away, moving down the stairs.

When he reached the landing below, she called out to him. "Lord Bridgewater."

He paused on the landing, not looking up.

"Who is to be your marchioness?"

Slowly, his head came up until their gazes met. "Miss Jacinda Bowles."

They looked at one another a long moment before he looked away and hurried out of sight.

Mirella had known the answer. Somehow, she had known it

all along. Perhaps he had even known he would offer for Miss Bowles before he even came to Grasmere last year.

Yet he had kissed her. Made her come alive. Caused her to feel things she had never experienced before.

It made more sense to her now, his rapid departure from Benbrook. The marquess had been tempted by her and had had to leave in order for their feelings not to grow stronger for one another. Why he had asked her to dance last night, though, still bothered her. In his mind, it possibly had been his way of saying goodbye to her.

She would always have that waltz. Those kisses.

They would be all she ever had of him.

Somehow, she managed to keep the tears at bay until she reached her bedchamber. Entering it, she locked the door before falling on the bed, pressing her face into the pillow to muffle her sobs. As she wept, Mirella's broken heart finally spoke its truth.

She loved Lord Bridgewater.

And he could never be hers.

CHAPTER EIGHTEEN

BYRON ALLOWED KELLER to dress him for this afternoon's garden party. He was already tired of the social swirl of the Season. In the past two weeks, he had attended seven balls, two routs, and a musicale. One evening had been devoted to the theatre. Another, the opera. Last night, he had gone to a card party, hoping the much smaller affair would bring him some relief. Instead, he had not been able to concentrate on the cards in his hand, which angered Jacinda. She had been his partner for the evening, thanks to Byron speaking privately with the hostess before gameplay began. His betrothed-in-the-making had pouted. Then sulked. Then demanded that she be paired with a new partner. The fuss thoroughly embarrassed him.

It seemed his intended bride had the maturity of a five-year-old, something which grated on his nerves. She also was incredibly judgmental, making fun of others' looks or their ensembles. He had danced with her at each ball, four of those times claiming the supper dance, and she had bored him beyond measure.

He had invited Jacinda and Lord Hampton to attend the opera, taking along Mama, Aunt Flora, and Uncle Hugh. He thought it might be a good way to have her interact with his family. Jacinda had been short with his aunt and uncle, and she had offended his mother. What had been said, he couldn't say, only that Mama had acted indifferently to Jacinda the entire evening.

In the carriage on the way home, Mama had pleaded with him to reconsider marriage to Jacinda, but he said the marriage settlements were already being written. Upset after a week of not hearing from Pilsbury, Byron had gone directly to the solicitor's office, only to learn that Lord Hampton's solicitor had left town to bury his father. Pilsbury assured Byron that he had completed all the necessary documents on his part, and he would see that the other solicitor did the same upon his return from York.

In the meantime, Byron tried to woo Jacinda, both at the events and when visiting her on a daily basis. She blew hot and cold, sometimes flirting outrageously with him, and other times ignoring him altogether. It gave him insight into what their future together would be like. He had yet to find a sympathetic bone in her body and wondered if she would be willing to turn all care of their children over to him. Somehow, he could not picture her being maternal. He certainly did not want their children to have her disposition, must less be influenced by her in any manner, as she had by her own mother.

Slowly, her suitors had begun fading away. She still had plenty, but he believed as those gentlemen spent more time in Jacinda's company, even her attractiveness faded when coupled with her disposition. It didn't matter. He had made the arrangements with her brother. As soon as Pilsbury had things drawn up and Byron had looked over the details, he would inform Jacinda of their upcoming nuptials. He was more than willing to allow her to enjoy the rest of the Season before they wed, but he had decided to rein her in a bit by letting her know of the betrothal once all parties had signed.

Once the Season ended, he would insist upon their marriage taking place immediately. Instead of waiting for the three weeks for the banns to be read in Bridgehampton, at the church their families both attended, he thought it might be wiser to purchase a special license after the ink had dried on the marriage contracts. That way, no waiting period would be necessary. He hoped she would be increasing by year's end and give birth to their first child by this time next year.

The worst part of the past fortnight had been whenever he spied Lady Mirella at an event. As promised, he had avoided her as much as possible, going nowhere near her when gentlemen were signing her programme. She continued to be quite popular with the eligible bachelors of the *ton*, and Byron couldn't help but watch her as she danced with them.

They had spoken twice when their paths crossed, once at the musicale and a second time in the foyer of the theatre. She had been with her brother and sister-in-law and an earl who Byron had attended university with. They had not been friends and only recognized one another in passing. He wished he knew more about the earl and whether he was suitable or not for Lady Mirella. It only showed how foolish he was, thinking he might hold sway over her if he discovered something about the man and tried to get her to stop seeing him.

For the hundredth time, Byron told himself that Lady Mirella Strong was not his concern. After this Season, he need never see her again. He would allow Jacinda to come to town for each new Season, but he and their children would be perfectly happy remaining at Bridgefield. When those children grew older, perhaps he would take them for a month or two up to the Lake District. Grasmere was always lovely in the summer, and Aunt Flora and Uncle Hugh would be delighted to host them.

Especially if his marchioness remained in town.

Keller finished tying Byron's cravat and then helped him slip into his coat.

"Thank you," he said dismissively, and the valet was smart enough to leave the room quickly, having become attuned to his employer's mercurial moods.

Since he still had half an hour before they were scheduled to leave for this afternoon's garden party, he decided to go to his study. On his way to it, he came across Paulson.

"My lord, you just received a package from Mr. Pilsbury. I placed it on the desk in your study."

"Finally," he said, thanking the butler and heading to see if it might be the documents he had anticipated.

Closing the door, he found the package, wrapped in brown paper and secured with twine. He cut through the twine and unwrapped it, finding a letter atop a sheaf of papers.

Lord Bridgefield —

Enclosed you will find a set of the marriage contracts between you and Miss Jacinda Bowles. Lord Hampton's solicitor returned from York yesterday, and we have agreed to everything in principle within these documents.

As requested, I am sending you these settlements since you wished to read through them before Lord Hampton received his own copy. Please feel free to make any notes you choose to on what I have sent. My clerk will prepare fresh copies for both you and Lord Hampton to sign.

If you have any questions or further need of me, please let me know.

Your humble servant,
P. Pilsbury

Byron set aside Pilsbury's note and began reading. Everything was very straightforward. Hampton would provide Jacinda's dowry. In return, Byron would provide dowries for any female issue from the marriage. A monthly amount of pin money had been established, as well as provisions for his marchioness if he passed before she did. That included her taking up residence in the dower house upon her widowhood. He had not suggested that his own mother do the same although he had learned that had been in the agreements signed when his parents wed. Byron felt Bridgefield was large enough and saw no need for Mama to leave the main house. She might choose to do so on her own, though, when Jacinda became his wife.

He saw nothing to change in the documents and withdrew fresh paper to dash off a quick note to Pilsbury, instructing him to move forward in the process. The sooner he and Hampton had signed the marriage settlements, the better. He would request that Hampton and his solicitor meet them in Pilsbury's office the day after tomorrow to complete the process and sign the settlements.

A knock sounded on his door, and Paulson appeared. "Your carriage is waiting, Lord Bridgewater, as are your mother and the Bentons."

While he would prefer writing the note and sending it on to Pilsbury, his mother was a stickler when it came to being on time to events. He supposed he could write the solicitor once they returned from the garden party and have it delivered first thing tomorrow morning.

"Very well," he said, rising from behind his desk and heading to the foyer.

"There you are, Bridgewater," Mama said. "What kept you?"

He did not want to suffer in disapproving silence in the carriage on the way to the garden party by mentioning the marriage contracts, so he merely said, "Just a bit of business, Mama. Are we ready to go?"

They went the few blocks to where the event was being held. Byron thought it ridiculous to have the carriage readied when they traveled such a short distance, but he dare not approach Mama and tell her that they should walk to an event.

The coachman dropped them off, promising to return in two hours' time. As they moved along the pavement, they caught up with Lord Hampton and Jacinda.

"Miss Bowles," he said. "I am delighted to see you. Don't you look lovely this afternoon?"

"I always look lovely, my lord," she said pertly.

"She should. I paid enough for her wardrobe for the Season," Hampton grumbled, falling into step beside Byron as Jacinda hurried her pace and moved away from them. "She'll be all yours soon, including the cost of her wardrobe."

"You will find a bride of your own and still be paying those costs in the future," he reminded the viscount. "As for my betrothal to your sister, I just received a copy of the marriage settlements before we left the house. I read through them and found no fault. They are practically identical to the previous ones written up, simply substituting my name for Lord Linden's, my brother's title at the time of their creation."

"Then I have no need to read them myself," Hampton said, causing Byron to stifle a laugh since he never believed the viscount would have done so in the first place.

"I will send them back to Mr. Pilsbury then, telling him to have copies drawn up for the both of us and Miss Bowles, as well. Hopefully, that might be accomplished tomorrow. We can then meet the following day and place our signatures on them."

"Just let me know," Hampton said, appearing bored by their conversation.

They were admitted into the house and led by a footman to the gardens. Byron caught sight of Jacinda passing through the French doors onto the terrace. By the time he reached them, however, she was nowhere in sight. The terrace was crowded, as was the area on the other side of it. The gardens lay beyond that.

Since he had lost his chance to speak with his intended for now, Byron asked his mother and aunt if they would like some punch. Both wished for some, so he and Uncle Hugh located the punch bowl and requested two cups be poured. As they turned, he spied a man he did not know but had instantly loathed when he learned his identity, that of Verity's father.

Lord Hall.

The only bright light in Byron's life in recent weeks had been his visits to Verity and Amity. The little girl was bright and personable and had quite stolen his heart. Verity was quiet and unassuming, and they had grown closer during his visits. He found her to be a decent person and a good mother. It was a shame her father had disowned her over a tragic error in judgment. Even at that, Byron could not view Amity as a mistake.

He did not know when or how—but he planned to confront Lord Hall before Season's end.

"Something wrong, Bridgewater?" Uncle Hugh asked.

"No. I just saw someone I do not like in the least. It is nothing, Uncle."

They returned to his mother and aunt. By now, Lady Mathilda had joined the pair.

"Good afternoon, my lady," he said, not wishing to address her familiarly as Aunt Matty, something he easily could have done so had he married her niece.

Passing the cup of punch to Mama, he said, "I am off to make the rounds."

"Bridgewater has no love of small talk," Byron heard Mama say as he left them.

Moving through the large group, he decided to go through the gardens so he wouldn't have to make that small talk his mother had mentioned.

Unfortunately, the gardens were populated with strolling couples, arm-in-arm. He recalled his own walk that day through the Benbrook gardens with Lady Mirella.

Would everything he saw and did for the rest of his life remind him of her?

Byron truly wanted the best for her. How could he not, when he still loved her? He only hoped that she would find a man worthy of her, one who would love and cherish her all his days. He had seen her dancing with everyone from the shyest of men to known rogues—and everyone in-between. At least she was giving a good number of bachelors a chance of capturing her heart.

He began moving briskly through the gardens, past couples sitting on benches and those stopping to look at certain blooms. When he reached the end of the path and saw a large gazebo there, he started to return the way he came—because he saw a couple kissing and wished to give them some privacy.

But he hesitated a moment, studying the pair. The gentlemen had his back to Byron and was tall and broad enough that he blocked most of the women he kissed so enthusiastically. Only her gloved hands were visible, wrapped around his neck, along with a bit of the hem of her gown showing, a pale yellow in color.

The same shade Jacinda was wearing.

Byron strode toward the pair, yanking them apart. He recognized Viscount Percival, whom he had seen dancing with Jacinda and Mirella both.

"What are you doing, Bridgewater?" demanded Jacinda.

Lord Percival merely flushed a bright red and said, "We have been caught, Miss Bowles. I will not see you ruined. I will wed you at once."

"You will not," Byron spat out. "Miss Bowles is *my* intended."

"What?" the couple both cried in unison.

"Leave. Now," he commanded, scowling at the viscount.

Much to his surprise, Jacinda went and slipped her arm through Percival's arm. "You cannot tell me what to do, my lord. And you are certainly *not* my betrothed."

"Not yet," he told her. "But your brother has already agreed to the match. In fact, I received the marriage contracts today from my solicitor. Copies will be made tomorrow, and then Lord Hampton and I will sign them the following day."

Her jaw fell open.

"Did you know about this?" Lord Percival demanded.

"No! Not a thing, my lord. This is the first I am learning of it."

"Miss Bowles was betrothed before," Byron said. "To my brother."

"What?" Jacinda exclaimed, stepping away from the viscount. "I have no idea what you are babbling about, Lord Bridgewater. Perhaps the sun is too hot today, and it has affected your speech."

"You know our fathers were the closest of friends," he began, and she nodded.

"What of it?"

"Their dream was to see our two families united through marriage," he explained. "When you were only ten years of age, your father and mine had marriage settlements drawn up. My brother was to wed you when you came of age at the end of this Season."

Fury filled her eyes. "I was never told such a thing!" she said, her face turning bright red. "You are lying. Father would have told me of such a plan."

"You were ten, Miss Bowles," Byron said flatly. "A mere child. I was with my brother when our father told him the news. Linden was given no choice in the matter. He grudgingly agreed to the marriage simply because the marriage contracts had already been written and signed by the two men. A betrothal contract is almost as good as actually being wed is what I understand."

Jacinda frowned, shaking her head. "But your brother is dead. Surely, that means the contract means nothing now, wouldn't it?" she asked Lord Percival.

"I would think so, my lady."

"Yes, they did become null and void—until I offered for you in my brother's place."

He watched them both wince.

And realized they were in love.

His thoughts swirled madly, and he took several deep breaths, trying to calm himself and focus.

"Of course, even though Hampton and I agreed to them, they have yet to be signed," he stated, wanting to gauge their reaction. "So, no betrothal exists at this point. Nothing is official until your brother and I sign the documents."

Lord Percival pleaded with him. "Do not do so, Bridgewater. I beg you. I wish to wed Miss Bowles." He glanced at Jacinda. "And she wishes to be my viscountess."

Byron had two choices.

He could demand that she honor the agreement he and Lord Hampton had previously come to.

Or he could gift her with her freedom—and receive his own in return.

In the end, he decided there was no choice at all.

"I will destroy the contracts," he said quietly. "But you will have to be the one to speak to your brother, Miss Bowles."

The viscount spoke up. "She will not have to do so alone, Bridgewater. I will be with her. I will offer for her."

"I am certain Hampton will agree to put aside your previous agreement, my lord, if you ask him to do so," Jacinda said, her voice shaking.

"Very well," Byron agreed. "When shall the three of us speak with him? I believe we should all be present."

The couple glanced at one another, and Jacinda said, "Tomorrow at noon. I will skip tonight's ball. Tell Hampton that I have a headache. It will give me time to prepare what to say to him."

"Very well. I will arrive at noon tomorrow, along with Lord Percival. We will sit and have a civil discussion." He paused, smiling at her, relief filling him. "Your brother wants what is best for you. If you have found happiness with Lord Percival, I cannot see how he would object to it."

"You do not mind?" she asked worriedly.

"I was merely trying to do what my father—and yours—had wanted done, my lady. I believed my duty was to my family, but I will not stand in your way to finding happiness."

Not when it meant that he had a chance to be with Mirella.

"I will leave you so that have some privacy. However, I suggest you forgo any more kissing for the moment. It would not be wise to be caught doing so by someone else."

"Thank you, my lord," the viscount said fervently. "Thank you from the bottom of my heart."

"And mine," Jacinda echoed.

Byron returned to the garden party, his heart light. He was now free to pursue the woman he loved.

He only hoped that she was willing to give him another chance.

CHAPTER NINETEEN

MIRELLA STOOD TALKING with Lord Morrow. Rather, she stood and smiled, occasionally nodding her head without speaking. The earl was actually carrying on a one-sided conversation with himself. He was wrapped up in describing things about his estate. His family. A hunt he had participated in last autumn. He switched topics rapidly and randomly, so quickly that she could not get in a word to graciously excuse herself and move on. He did ask her questions—which he then proceeded to answer for her. Lord Morris merely rambled on. And on. And on.

Never had she been so bored or so miserable.

The Season, which she had looked forward to her entire life, had turned out to be most dismal. Yes, overall, she was enjoying the various events and activities. The music played at each ball was wonderful, and she danced as many of the dances as she could in her new, beautiful ball gowns. She had also attended events beyond balls. As Mama had assured her, Mirella really had fun at these other social affairs, as well.

But there was a yawning emptiness inside her that grew each day. That emptiness was where Lord Bridgewater should be in her heart.

It had cut Mirella to the quick when he had informed her that he would be marrying Miss Bowles. She would not wish that woman upon anyone, especially the man she loved.

She had pushed these feelings of love for him deep inside her, telling no one of them. Her heart yearned for a man she could never have, which was utterly foolish. Her situation was similar to Aunt Matty's, in that Mirella loved a man and would never be able to wed him. The biggest different was that Aunt Matty's lieutenant had left for a new continent and a good reason, while Lord Bridgewater would remain in England to vex her. Mirella had no idea how she would be able to go on, Season by Season, seeing the marquess and his marchioness at events night after night in the years to come.

The only thing which comforted her was that she believed, he, too, would be as unhappy as she was, which was a very selfish thought to have. She had no idea why the marquess was wedding his neighbor, but she had a good idea that he knew exactly what he was in for by doing so. Without a doubt, it would be a typical *ton* marriage, one in which the husband and wife led vastly different—and separate—lives from one another.

Effie had joked about being the Aunt Matty of the Strong family, traveling from household to household to see and spoil all the nieces and nephews. Mirella could now see herself in that role because she could not envision herself wed to anyone but Lord Bridgewater.

Still, she had to give the gentlemen of this Season a chance. That was why she stood here, listening to the tedious monotone of Lord Morrow. She also allowed any number of suitors to visit with her every afternoon. She listened to them. Sympathized with them. Smiled at them. Even flirted a little with them.

All the while, her heart cried out for a man who had done her terribly wrong, and yet he was the only one Mirella feared she might ever love.

She doubted she would find love again, much less so quickly. That meant another Season and most likely, more hopes dashed. It was as if her life stretched out as endlessly as this conversation, and Mirella wondered if she should simply remain in the country come next spring. They actually had some nice neighbors near Shadowcrest. Perhaps she might find she had something in common with one of them and make a quiet marriage in Kent.

Her heart told her that would not be the case. She sighed, wondering how she could escape Lord Morrow's monologue.

Suddenly, her body tingled, a familiar awareness settling over her that gave her a moment of hope. She glanced up and saw Lord Bridgewater had joined them.

"I hate to interrupt your conversation, but Lady Mathilda has asked to speak with her niece immediately," the marquess informed the couple.

Mirella knew this was a rescue mission on Lord Bridgewater's part and decided to play her role in the escapade.

"Oh, I hope it is not the headache. Aunt Matty felt one coming on in the carriage on our way here. If that is the case, we must leave the garden party." She turned to Lord Morrow. "If you will excuse me, my lord?"

"Of course, Lady Mirella," he said, immediately turning away to look for a new audience.

Seconds later, he joined two ladies who were speaking to one another, and Mirella could only hope they would not be stuck with Lord Morrow as long as she had been.

She turned to Lord Bridgewater, who had a twinkle in his eyes. He offered her his arm, and she placed her fingers upon his sleeve, feeling the electricity between them as she did so.

"This way, my lady," he said, steering her up the steps of the terrace and through the French doors so they were once more inside the house.

She looked about, seeing a few scattered tables had been set up, with mostly elderly guests seated at them. He guided her to a table in the corner, far away from the other occupied ones, and seated her.

Taking the seat next to her, Lord Bridgewater said, "I guess you surmised by now that your aunt is not in not great need of you." His lips twitched in amusement.

"The last time you interrupted me and took me away, I was most angry with you." Mirella paused. "This time, however, I must express my extreme gratitude to you, my lord. I thought I might never escape Lord Morris."

"I was passing and saw you trapped by him," he shared. "He is known for dominating every conversation he is a part of."

She laughed, relaxing for the first time in weeks. "I could not get in a word edgewise," she confided. "Lord Morrow was full of himself, spouting opinions and giving me his life history. I am thankful you came to my rescue, my lord."

They sat for a moment, drinking in one another, and then Mirella thought nothing had changed. He was still unavailable to her. He had only helped her because he must have seen how miserable she had been in Lord Morrow's company.

Pasting on a smile, she asked, "When will your betrothal be announced, my lord?"

"No announcement will be forthcoming. At least not to Miss Bowles."

Mirella felt herself grow faint. The blood rushed to her ears, and she gripped her hands, which lay in her lap.

"Miss Bowles and you . . . decided against a marriage?" she asked.

"I believe that you tried to warn me before, Lady Mirella."

"Warn you? How?"

"You tried to let me know just how unsuitable Miss Bowles was for me. I chose to ignore your advice because of a sense of duty."

He was making no sense at all. "Duty? To whom?"

The marquess reached under the table and took one of her hands. Even though it was gloved, she could feel his tremendous heat through the material. Mirella's eyes darted about the room, but only two tables were occupied now, and they were far from them.

He squeezed her fingers gently. "I listened on occasions too numerous to count to my father speaking of family. Father constantly lectured Dawson and me on family obligations, instilled in us how duty to family was the most important thing, above all else. I grew up with a sense of knowing I must give my all to my family because of the constant lectures he hammered into us. These thoughts were so drilled into me, that I never questioned them once."

He fell silent a moment, but he held her gaze with those mesmerizing gray eyes.

"When I left for the army, I received more of the same, only now my family consisted of my fellow officers and the men serving under me. My duty was to them, along with king and country.

"Then I became the Marquess of Bridgewater—and all those memories of what family meant came flooding back, along with the numerous obligations which accompany the title. I did my best to learn about my new role in society and how to care for my land and its tenants."

Understanding filled her, and Mirella said, "You had told me your father and Lord Hampton were very close to one another. And Miss Bowles is Lord Hampton's daughter."

He nodded. "You are beginning to understand. Although I knew Jacinda was entirely wrong for me, my father had wished for our families to be united through marriage. He betrothed my brother to her when she was but ten years of age. Dawson hated that the choice of a wife had been stolen from him. In a way, I suspect it is why he turned so wild in the years before his death."

"He was rebelling because the choice had been removed from him," she said. "But what of Miss Bowles? What did she think of this betrothal?"

"Miss Bowles had no idea the marriage settlements even existed. She was to be told when she came of age, during her come-out Season. When I returned from war and claimed my title, I met with my solicitor and asked Mr. Pilsbury about those very contracts. He told me they would be voided now, due to my brother's death."

She squeezed his hand. "But you felt a deep sense of obligation, didn't you? You decided you must do what your father had wished. What your brother could not do. *You* would be the one to sacrifice your happiness and wed Miss Bowles."

The marquess nodded solemnly. "Even though I knew it was a mistake, I still pursued that course of action," he admitted. "I had the contracts drawn up."

She tensed, knowing that a signed betrothal contract was almost as good as a marriage ceremony having already taken place. She tried to pull her hand from his, but he tightened his grip.

"Wait," he said softly. "I must say the rest of this to you."

He had already bared his soul to her, so she thought she might as well listen to what he had to say.

"Go ahead," she encouraged.

"Those very contracts arrived at my residence just before I left to attend this garden party," he shared. "I read over them, sinking deeper into the mire, knowing I was committed to a course of action my father would approve. My plan was to meet with Lord Hampton and sign these settlements in two days. Thankfully, that will not happen now."

His words confused her—and yet gave Mirella hope.

"Something happened. Here. At this garden party this afternoon."

He smiled wryly. "You are most astute, Lady Mirella. Yes, something did occur which changed the course I was set upon. It is allowing me to walk a new path. The one I preferred all along."

Her mouth grew dry, and her heart slammed against her ribs painfully. "What happened?" she asked softly, almost afraid of his answer.

"I came across Miss Bowles kissing another gentleman in the gardens. I have been calling upon her each afternoon, trying to win her over or at least have her like me a bit. I wasn't certain that would ever happen, but I had already made the arrangements with her brother. I knew Lord Hampton would honor the signed marriage contracts, and Miss Bowles would have no choice but to follow through."

With his free hand, he raked his fingers through his hair, and Mirella itched to do the same to him.

"I informed her that the contracts had been drawn up and would be signed soon. While I do not like her in the slightest, I could see how, when I told her of the arrangements which had been made for her, that her heart was breaking—and that of the gentleman she was with. Suddenly, everything became clear to me. Either I could insist that the completed contracts be signed and be stuck in a loveless marriage with an angry wife for the next several decades.

"Or I could give Miss Bowles the freedom to marry this fellow."

His gaze pinned hers. "And I could follow what my heart has been whispering to me all along."

Tears filled Mirella's eyes. She blinked several times and then said, "What are you saying to me, Lord Bridgewater?"

"That ever since we met, I have wanted to get to know you. I have wished to spend time with you. I know you seek a love match, Lady Mirella. What I am asking of you is your forgiveness. And not only that, I would like the chance to court you. Can you find it in your heart to give me yet another opportunity?"

Her heart was singing as she viewed him through watery eyes. Mirella already loved this man with her whole heart, but she did not think it appropriate to declare her feelings for him at this time.

At least, she had a chance with him now. A chance she had thought already passed her by.

"There is nothing to forgive, my lord," she said. "You pursued what your father had wished for. What parents dream of for their children—and what their children desire—are often two very different things, however." She smiled at him. "Yes, Lord Bridgewater. I would be happy to give you the opportunity to woo me this Season. I would understand, however, if you needed to take some time to heal emotionally from the trauma you have experienced. You saw a life with Miss Bowles. That dream has now dissipated."

The resolve in his eyes took her aback. "No, my lady, I need no time to go and lick my wounds. I am committed to seeing if the two of us suit. And if love can grow between us, especially after what I have shared with you."

Mirella already loved him. It would be up to this man to see if he might open his heart and love her in return. Only then, once he had voiced those feelings for her, would she be free to declare what was in her own heart.

She pulled her hands from his and rose. He followed suit.

"Perhaps you would care to come to tea tomorrow afternoon, Lord Bridgewater."

"I will happily accept that invitation to tea, my, lady, but my question is this—will you allow me to engage you for the supper dance at tonight's ball?"

Her heart sang as she said, "I would be happy to do so, Lord Bridgewater. Most happy, indeed."

CHAPTER TWENTY

MIRELLA GOT READY for tonight's ball, her excitement greater than it had been on the opening night of the Season. She was going to dance with Lord Bridgewater.

It would be a new start for them.

She dismissed the maid and took a final look in the mirror before she left her bedchamber. Going three doors down, she tapped lightly on her aunt's door.

Aunt Matty opened her door and said, "Won't you come in, Mirella? You look as those you need to talk."

Crossing the threshold, she waited as Aunt Matty closed the door. Without a word, she flung herself into her aunt's arms, giddy with joy.

Mirella released her aunt, and the older woman chuckled, saying, "I know you are fond of me, but this is more than that, isn't it?"

"I am to dance with Lord Bridgewater tonight, Aunt. The supper dance. He requested it of me this afternoon."

"What has changed, my dear? You are radiating happiness."

"For the last couple of weeks, he has had nothing to do with me. The day he came to tea, he told me he would soon be betrothed to Miss Bowles. He said that he would no longer be asking me to dance with him and could not even be around me."

Mirella sighed and began pacing the room. "He was doing it all out of a sense of duty, Aunt Matty. Because of his father."

Her aunt cocked her head. "How so?"

She explained how Lord Bridgewater and Lord Hampton's closeness had led to them drawing up marriage contracts for two of their children to wed, but Lord Bridgewater had died soon after, not seeing the plan come to fruition.

"Once the new Lord Bridgewater, the current one's brother, died while racing his phaeton against Lord Hampton, *this* Lord Bridgewater experienced extreme guilt. I gather he had never been close to his father, who had favored his heir apparent. Out of some misguided sense of duty to his father, Lord Bridgewater wished to unite their families, just as his father had wished would be done years ago. He did not even *like* Miss Bowles," Mirella declared.

Aunt Matty nodded sagely. "Liking someone has very little to do with wedding them. Surely, you understand that our family is much different from other families in Polite Society." She paused. "No betrothal was announced between Lord Bridgewater and Miss Bowles, however. And now Lord Bridgewater wishes to dance with you again?"

"Would you believe Miss Bowles fell in love with someone else? How, I cannot imagine, because Lord Bridgewater is a most incredible man. She did, though, and when the marquess told her of their upcoming betrothal? It broke her heart. Lord Bridgewater decided to free her from the agreement, which she had never agreed to in the first place. He said the marriage contracts had yet to be signed, so they were not official—and now they never will be."

She captured Aunt Matty's hands in hers. "He wants to woo me. Even when he told me he could no longer see me again— because of his sense of obligation to Miss Bowles—Lord Bridgewater mentioned the day we had spent together at Grasmere. He called it the happiest of his life, and the kisses we shared were memorable."

A knowing light came into her aunt's eyes. "So, you have kissed him."

"Yes," she declared, not bothering to hide her smile. "He is the most divine kisser, Aunt Matty. I had thought it good that I had been kissed before the Season began, so that when I did kiss another man, I would know what I was doing."

"And have you done so?"

Mirella shook her head. "I simply couldn't. I wanted to. I thought that I might compare his kiss to others, but I realized no one else would ever be Lord Bridgewater." She shrugged, smiling sheepishly. "I thought I was destined to be on the shelf the rest of my life because I could not see myself committing to another gentleman."

"Now, though, you have a new chance. Make a new start with your marquess, Mirella," her aunt advised. "Obviously, he is a good one. First, he was willing to sacrifice his own happiness for family, which you hold dearly. Second, he was gentleman enough to not dally with you while he was wooing another woman. Third, he was wise enough to let go so that both he and Miss Bowles might pursue their own happiness with others."

"Oh, Aunt Matty, I do love him. I have for the longest time. I do not want to tell him this, however. He knows I seek a love match, and I do not want to pressure him into declaring for me unless he truly does come to love me."

Her aunt kissed Mirella's cheek. "I think you very wise, Niece. Get to know him better. Let him come to know you better, as well. Exchange a few more of those marvelous kisses. I have a feeling that Lord Bridgewater will declare for you in the very near future."

They went downstairs and found James and Sophie waiting. Mama and the captain soon joined them, and they went to the carriage.

On their way to the ball, Mirella said, "I have asked Lord Bridgewater to come to tea tomorrow afternoon. I hope you do not mind."

Her brother's brows arched, and she quickly looked to Mama.

"You know you may always ask anyone you wish to stay for tea, my dearest," Mama told her. "Does that mean Lord Bridgewater might be calling on you tomorrow afternoon?"

"Oh, yes, Mama," Mirella said fervently. "In fact, I think he will become a regular caller."

"That is wonderful," Sophie declared. "I quite like Lord Bridgewater."

"Why the sudden change?" the captain asked, his brows knitting together.

"I know you are being protective of me, Captain. I am appreciative of it. Lord Bridgewater and I needed a bit of time apart to explore other . . . friendships. We have mutually decided to spend more time with one another, however."

The captain nodded, satisfied with her answer. "That sounds as if it might be serious between the two of you, Mirella."

"I expect it will be," she said.

"Then you will have my support. Your mother's, as well," he assured her.

"And ours," James declared, warming Mirella's insides. She had hoped her family would welcome Lord Bridgewater's pursuit of her.

They arrived at the ball and went through the receiving line. She looked about, not spying the marquess, nerves flitting through her. For a brief moment, a seed of doubt crept in, but she dismissed it. He would be here. He would dance the supper dance with her.

Their group entered the ballroom, and she saw Lord Bishop lingering near the entrance. He had begun paying her special attention during the last few social engagements, and he made his way toward her now.

"Good evening," he greeted the group, his focus solely on her. "Good evening, Lady Mirella."

He took her hand and kissed it. I would like to request a dance with you this evening."

She handed her programme to him and before she could say anything, he had written his name where the supper dance was. Mirella bit her lip, unsure how to handle the matter.

Then a voice said, "You will need to choose another dance, Lord Bishop."

It was Lord Bridgewater.

"I say, Bridgewater, I got here first. And I will dance with—"

"You signed for the supper dance," the marquess said. "That is a waltz. Lady Mirella will be dancing all her waltzes with me," he stated firmly.

For a moment, the two men stared at one another, and Mirella realized they had reached some secret, silent understanding.

"I see," Lord Bishop said, scratching through his name and glancing to her. "My lady, would you be interested in dancing the opening set with me?"

She smiled at him. "I would delighted to do so, my lord."

Lord Bishop wrote his name at the top of her programme and instead of returning it to her, handed it to the marquess.

She watched as he scrawled his name next to where Lord Bishop's had been and also added it to the last dance of the evening. He returned it to her, grinning like a schoolboy.

"I hear you are coming to tea tomorrow afternoon," James said, looking Lord Bridgewater up and down.

To his credit, the marquess did not flinch under the duke's scrutiny. "Yes, Your Grace. Lady Mirella was kind enough to ask me to do so. I will be calling upon her tomorrow afternoon and will stay if it is agreeable to you and Her Grace."

Sophie spoke up. "We would be delighted to share in your company tomorrow, Lord Bridgewater. Is there anything specific you might like for our cook to make for you?"

"I am fond of blueberries," the marquess revealed. "In scones. Tarts. Even by themselves."

Sophie smiled sweetly at him. "Then I will make certain Cook prepares something with blueberries in it, my lord."

"Thank you, Your Grace," he said graciously and turned back

to Mirella. "I will see you later this evening, my lady. I hope you enjoy dancing this evening with your many partners."

"Thank you, my lord," she said, watching him leave the ballroom entirely.

That could mean only one thing.

It was early—and he would be asking no other lady to dance. He was retreating to the card room.

"My," Mama said. "Lord Bridgewater is making quite a statement."

"How so?" the captain asked.

Mama explained, "First, Lord Bridgewater was quite assertive, telling Lord Bishop that Mirella is only dancing waltzes with him. Lord Bishop, in turn, will spread that news to the other eligible bachelors who have been vying for Mirella's hand. Now, he has quit the ballroom entirely, meaning he will be in the card room and not dancing with anyone else."

The captain nodded in understanding. "So, not only has he declared his affection for our Mirella, Bridgewater is making a deliberate point by not dancing the rest of the evening. I like that," he proclaimed. "I like him."

His gaze connected with Mirella's. "What do you feel about this turn of events, Mirella?"

Her cheeks heated as she said, "I am in favor of them, Captain. Very much so."

"Then we are, as well," her stepfather said.

Her dance card filled, not as quickly as it had in the past, though. She understood that Lord Bishop had quickly put out the word that Lord Bridgewater had all but declared for Mirella. The men who signed her programme tonight were a few of the ones who had called upon her previously, but the majority of them were the rogues, gentlemen with a bit of a fast reputation and ones not ready to settle into marriage just yet. Mirella understood that the more serious of her suitors would now fall away, seeking other female companionship at these balls. It would be safe for her to dance with the rakes because not only were they not interested in marriage—they understood that Lord Bridgewater was.

An immense sense of relief flooded her. She would still be able to enjoy dancing at these balls, and yet she—and others— would know of Lord Bridgewater's extreme interest in her.

It would only be a matter of time before he offered for her. Mirella could only hope that when he did, it would be out of love.

She decided to lose herself in the music, enjoying each dance thoroughly. During the last lively reel, which was played just before the supper dance, she caught sight of Lord Bridgewater on the sidelines with James and the captain. The marquess watched her dancing, a slow smile lighting his handsome face. Mirella danced. Not only for herself. But him.

The reel ended, and she found herself out of breath as she thanked her partner, who returned her to Lord Bridgewater. That, in itself, spoke volumes, and Mirella glanced about the ballroom, seeing hundreds of eyes on the two of them.

"Have you enjoyed yourself this evening, Lady Mirella?" Lord Bridgewater asked.

"Very much so, my lord."

"I enjoyed watching you dance," he said, his eyes darkening as he gazed at her.

She knew that meant something. What, she wasn't exactly sure of, but the marquess looked as if he wished to gobble her up.

Taking her hand and placing it on his sleeve, he led her to the very center of the ballroom, saying, "I do not have to ask if you know that every eye in this room is upon us at the moment."

Smiling at him, she said, "Yes, I feel them. I do not believe I have ever been such an object of interest by so many."

"You, my lady, are a diamond of the first water," he praised. "And long after your beauty fades, your lovely auburn hair turning white and your face lined from the smiles you have given over the years, I will be there. Still looking at you in wonder."

They weren't exactly words offering marriage, but they were so much more than that. Lord Bridgewater was telling Mirella that he would be there with her, decades from now.

He placed an arm about her and took her hand in his, and she believed his eyes shined down at her in love.

CHAPTER TWENTY-ONE

BYRON AWOKE, EACH day seeming to be a good one now, thanks to having let go of the idea of wedding Jacinda Bowles. He realized now how misguided his actions had been.

And how he had almost missed out on the love of a lifetime.

Of course, he hadn't told Mirella that he loved her yet. He had tried to let her know in other ways. In the way he looked at her. How he treated her. The courtesy and respect which he showed her and her family. He told himself that he did not want to rush her or force her into a marriage with him.

He had even waited to kiss her again. The tension building between them as each day passed was palpable.

Today, he would kiss her. Declare his undying love. Ask her to be his wife.

Not a day had gone by that he had not seen her during the last two weeks. Of course, they saw one another at *ton* affairs. Byron knew their names were coupled by others. He had also visited the Seaton household every single day. He had taken tea with all those who lived in the house, as well as a more intimate tea with only her mother and stepfather present. Lady Mirella had played the pianoforte for him on several occasions, and each time he was in awe of her talent.

Tomorrow, he had been invited to the christening of *Sophie*, the new ship which had taken two years to be built. It was named after Her Grace and would be the crown jewel of all the sailing vessels at Neptune Shipping Lines, the shipping company owned by the Duchess of Seaton. He knew the invitation had been extended to him because the duke and duchess already looked upon him as family. All the household treated him thus, and Byron was ready to make it official.

He arrived at the Seaton townhouse an hour before tea was to begin, hoping to gain a few moments with Mirella, away from her callers, so he might declare his affection for her. Mrs. Andrews had asked him to come take tea with them today, and he had readily agreed to do so. Lady Mirella's mother was one of the kindest women Byron had ever known. He already thought of the babe she carried as family to him.

Dursley, the footman, admitted Byron. "Good afternoon, Lord Bridgewater."

"No use in seeing me to the drawing room," he said, smiling. "I believe I know my way by now."

"Lady Mirella is not there, my lord," Dursley informed him. "She is practicing in the music room. She said you were to be brought there when you arrived. If you would follow me."

Byron did as requested, and the footman tapped lightly on the door and opened it, announcing him.

"Lord Bridgewater is here, my lady."

He caught sight of her sitting at the pianoforte, wearing a gown of soft green. She smiled.

"Please, come in, my lord. Thank you, Dursley."

The footman stepped aside so Byron could enter the room, and then the servant closed the door behind him.

They were alone.

His heart sped up as he moved toward her. She rose, and he took her hands, raising them both to his lips, kissing each one.

And not releasing them.

"Why are you here and not in the drawing room so that you can visit with your callers?" he asked.

She grinned. "You may have noticed that the number of gentlemen calling upon me has dwindled. I stopped the slow trickle and made it known that I would not be entertaining any suitors today. Or any other day."

Now, his heart slammed against his ribs. He stepped toward her, releasing her hands and pulling her into his arms.

"Why on earth would such a beautiful creature do that?" he said, his voice low and rough.

"Because I only want to see you, my lord."

Her honest declaration moved him. Byron saw her love for him shining in her Strong eyes. He bent, softly brushing his lips against hers.

Lifting his head, he said, "Then it makes what I wish to say easy."

He paused, knowing there would be no going back after he spoke the words she longed to hear. It didn't matter, though. He didn't want to have that life.

Byron wanted a new life with this woman, one the two of them would build together over the years to come.

"I love you," he said. "I have loved you since Grasmere. Fool that I was, I still doggedly pursued the idea of making Jacinda Bowles my wife. I knew we would both be unhappy in the marriage, but I was trying to bring to life the vision my father had of what our family should look like."

He gently kissed her. "But my heart always belonged to you, Mirella. It did from the start. I hope you can see a life with me because it is the only life I wish to lead. I love you more with each passing day. Please tell me you love me, my darling. That you will promise to be my marchioness. My friend and lover. Mother of our children."

Her eyes misted with tears. "I lost my heart to you at Grasmere, my lord. You have been its owner all these months. Not me. I do love you. So very much. I want a life with you. I want to share everything with you. Especially children."

"Then I will be the happiest man each day from now on," he

told her. "And not only will I love you until the end of time, I will tell you I do every day of our lives. I only ask one thing of you."

"What?" she asked breathlessly.

"Call me Byron. Aunt Flora and Uncle Hugh do when we are alone."

Her radiant smile stole his breath. "I believe I can do so, Byron."

His name on her lips sounded like heaven.

Tightening his arms about her, he said, "The only time you should call me Bridgewater when we are alone is if you are angry or upset with me. That will be my clue that I have done something wrong, and I promise I will right things between us."

Her hands came up to cradle his face. "I will remember that, Bridgewater."

He frowned. "You are already upset with me?"

"Of course, I am. Because you have yet to kiss me thoroughly, Bridgewater. So much that I cannot breathe. So long and hard that I cannot even think. So—"

He cut her off, his mouth seizing hers. A time for gentle, tender kisses would come.

Now was not that time.

Byron kissed her with all the love he felt for her. She eagerly returned his kisses, and they spun out of control. That subtle, floral scent which clung to her invaded his senses, driving him wild. He couldn't wait for the time when she wore that scent— and nothing else—and was in his bed.

Her fingers pushed into his hair, tightening almost painfully, but he continued to kiss her. His tongued delved deep, investigating everywhere inside her mouth, leaving them both breathless. He broke the kiss, gazing into her cornflower blue eyes, thinking she was the very air he breathed. That she gave life to him and purpose for all he did.

He seized her mouth again with his, the kisses hard, wild, and demanding. Wanting more of her, he scooped her up, startling her, a rich laugh bubbling up as he went to a chair and sat, bringing her into his lap. Byron slipped one arm about her waist and used his free hand to capture her nape, bringing her closer until their lips touched. A sizzling desire flooded him as they continued to kiss.

His hand dropped to her breast, and Byron kneaded it, hearing her moans. He broke the kiss, his lips trailing down the column of her throat, nipping it as he went. Dipping his hand into her bodice, he lifted her breast. Freed now, he licked the nipple, hearing her gasp.

Raising his head, he saw the dazed look on her face. "Do you like that?" he asked.

"Yes," she said, panting. "Very much. You should do it again," she encouraged.

"I will."

He took his time, feasting on her breast, sucking hard, laving the nipple, all as she squirmed and sighed. Byron lifted his head, blowing cool air on her nipple, seeing it stand at attention for him. He lowered his head, devouring her again, need for her growing with each minute.

Knowing he must stop, he grazed his teeth a final time against the nipple and eased her breast back into her gown.

"It feels larger," she said in wonder. "My . . . breast." Pinkening slightly, she added, "I never thought I would say that word in front of a man."

He kissed her. "I am not just any man, Mirella. I am your betrothed. The man who will explore every inch of your body. I will touch you in places you have never dreamed of being touched. And you will like it."

"I will like it," she echoed solemnly. "Oh, Byron. I know I will like it. I like *you*. I had always wanted to love the man who became my husband, but I understand now that liking him is also important."

He kissed her again, both of them laughing as they did so.

Breaking the kiss, he told her, "I like you very much, Mirella. And I love you more than I thought possible."

She sighed, toying with the hair at his nape. "I believe love is the most marvelous thing in the world."

He smoothed her hair. "I never believed that. I never believed in love. Until I met you."

Kissing her tenderly, he thought of how wonderful their life together would be.

"I must stop kissing you now," he told her.

"Why?" she asked, deliberately thrusting out her bottom lip in a pout.

"Because your lips are already swollen as it is—and we are due to take tea with your family soon. I don't want them to know what we have been up to."

She laughed, that musical sound that he would hear for the rest of his life. "Oh, Byron, they have come to tea *frequently* with swollen lips. They will understand. Especially after we share with them our news."

He frowned. "Should we do so, Mirella? I thought I should meet with your mother and the captain. Or possibly His Grace before we said anything."

"That is not necessary," she told him. "We will tell them at tea."

"If that is what you wish," he said, kissing her again because he simply had to do so—or perish.

After a few more heated kisses, he stopped. Rising with her in his arms, he set her on her feet.

"It might be wise to go and wash your face. And secure a few stray locks that have come loose," he advised.

She smiled at him. "I will do so. You can go to the drawing room. The others will be there soon."

Mirella took a step away, but Byron caught her wrist, yanking her back to him. He kissed her again.

"Just something to tide me over," he said, causing her to giggle.

This time, she captured his face with her hands and leaned up on tiptoe, kissing him.

"There. We are even."

She left the music room, and he watched her go. Pride swelled within him. He found it hard to believe the most adorable, beautiful creature in the world had agreed to become his marchioness.

He thought it might be appropriate to have her family over for dinner to meet with his. Byron didn't know if his mother had ever been introduced to Mirella. If not, it was time the two women met. Aunt Flora and Uncle Hugh would be so pleased at the news. He only hoped Mirella's family would also be happy.

Running his hands through his hair to make certain it was tamed, he glanced down to see if he looked presentable. Byron went to the drawing room, a place he had visited many times, and found only Mrs. Andrews present.

"Ah, Lord Bridgewater, come and join me," she said. "The others will be along shortly."

He did so. "How are you feeling, Mrs. Andrews?"

Her hands went to her belly. "So, you know. I suppose others do, as well. I knew I would start to show once the Season got underway. I had told Mirella that I would go to all the events with her, but I may taper off. As it is, she has James and Sophie to escort her."

"And me," he volunteered. "I am happy to come to the townhouse and go with her to any event."

She eyed him with interest. "In what capacity, my lord?"

"As her betrothed," he replied.

Mrs. Andrews smiled, and Byron could see Mirella in that smile.

"I am so pleased to hear this, my lord."

"I have only just asked her to become my wife. I had thought I should speak with you and the captain, but Mirella did not think it necessary."

"No, my girl has always been one to know her own mind. The decision was always hers to make." She paused. "I believe the two of you will suit admirably."

"I do love her, Mrs. Andrews. I am only sorry I wasted a few weeks when I could have spent them at her side."

"You learned from your mistake, my lord," she assured him. Glancing up, her face softened. "Hello, my love."

Byron turned, seeing the captain approach. He brushed a tender kiss upon his wife's brow and took the seat next to her.

"Thank goodness I was able to stay at work this afternoon and not have to chaperone smitten suitors in the drawing room," he grumbled good-naturedly. "With *Sophie* being christened tomorrow, there was more than enough work to do in the Neptune Shipping offices."

"They are betrothed, Drake. Mirella and Lord Bridgewater."

The captain beamed at Byron. "Congratulations, my lord. You have just made the best decision of your life."

"What decision?" the duke asked, entering the room with his duchess and Lady Mathilda.

"Oh, please tell me the good news is a betrothal," said Lady Mathilda.

He couldn't help but grin. "It is, Aunt Matty."

Suddenly, everyone was hugging him and shaking his hand. Even though Mirella would be marrying into the Balfour family, Byron felt so welcomed by these Strongs.

"You couldn't wait?" he heard, turning to see his fiancée. Guilt raced through him. "It just . . . came out. Your mother could wrench secrets out of any French spy within minutes."

She joined him, slipping her arm about his waist. "I am not angry. Just tickled that you blurted out our news."

"How could I not?" he asked. "I am in love—and I want the entire world to know."

CHAPTER TWENTY-TWO

MIRELLA AND HER mother left the house and crossed the square, eager to see their family members who had come into town for today's ship christening. Word had come just after dinner last night that Georgie, August, and little Alexandra had arrived in town, accompanied by Effie. Since they were committed to attending a rout, Mama had sent word they would like to visit this morning before they went to the London docks. It would be the first time that they had been able to see Alexandra, and she and Mama were looking forward to meeting the newest Strong.

"Of course, I understand that she is not actually a Strong," Mama said.

"She is half-Strong," Mirella proclaimed. "That is good enough. Besides, the other half of her comes from August, and there isn't a kinder man on the planet than Georgie's marquess."

"It is convenient that August's townhouse is directly across from ours," Mama said. "Oh, I cannot wait to see my grandchild."

The butler admitted them as Georgie came sailing down the stairs, looking happier than Mirella had ever seen her.

Georgie flew into Mama's arms, embracing her tightly, and then turned to Mirella. The sisters hugged.

"You look absolutely wonderful, my dearest," Mama told

Georgie. "Motherhood obviously suits you."

"We cannot wait to meet Alexandra," she said. "Is she in the nursery?"

Georgie smiled. "She is. With her father. I have told August I am not certain why we even engage a nursery governess because he is with the babe so much."

Mama smiled approvingly. "I knew he would be a good husband and father."

Her sister led them upstairs, telling them that Effie was in the barn, helping a mare deliver her colt.

"I told her this colt better be born and Effie bathed and dressed in time for us to make it to the ceremony," Georgie said. "She promised she would."

"She better," Mama said. "I have missed my baby so much."

Mirella laughed. "Do not let Effie hear you calling her a baby, Mama. She would resent it."

"I cannot help it," Mama said. "It is hard for me to believe that this time next year, she will be making her come-out."

They arrived at the nursery and saw August cradling his daughter in his arms, telling her some story.

Georgie smiled indulgently at them. "You do realize that Alexandra does not understand a word of what you are telling her."

He grinned. "Not yet. But she will. Sooner than you think. Why, Alexandra is going to be more intelligent than both her parents combined."

Rising from the chair, he came toward them, handing the baby to her grandmother. Mama beamed down at the little one. "Welcome to our family, sweet Alexandra," she said softly, the babe looking up with round eyes. "And soon, you will have someone to play with. Your aunt or uncle."

Mama chuckled. "It will seem odd, a niece being older than her aunt or uncle."

Mama handed the babe to Mirella, and she held the precious bundle close. Alexandra cooed at her, and Mirella fell instantly in love with her niece.

They remained in the nursery a few more minutes until the nursery governess chased them out, saying it was time for the wet nurse to feed Lady Alexandra.

"Let us go to my sitting room," Georgie said. "It is more cozy than the drawing room."

August accompanied the three women down the stairs and said, "Since we are in town, I have a few things to attend to in my study. I will see you this afternoon at the christening of *Sophie*."

He excused himself, and they went to the sitting room, where Georgie said, "Tell me everything about this Season, Mirella." She smiled. "And do not leave a single thing out."

"Today, you will meet Lord Bridgewater. He is my betrothed," Mirella informed her sister.

Georgie squealed in delight, throwing her arms about Mirella and hugging her tightly. "Oh, I was not expecting that news. You have only written once and did not name any gentleman when you did. I do not blame you, though. I know just how difficult it is to steal a moment to pen a letter when you are so busy."

"The engagement only happened yesterday," Mama commented. "We learned of it at teatime."

"Well, tell me about your intended. Who is he? What is he like? Where is his country seat located?" Georgie asked. "Oh, I do hope it is close to Edgefield."

"I find it hard to know where to begin," she protested. "I first met Lord Bridgewater when Effie and I went with Aunt Matty to Benbrook in the Lake District. During the house party last year."

"Oh, I do recall his name being mentioned. He is . . . the nephew of Lord and Lady Benton?"

"He is Lady Benton's nephew," she confirmed. "Though they never attend the Season, the Bentons have done so this year because they knew Lord Bridgewater would be perusing the Marriage Mart for a bride."

"Since he holds the title, does he still have his mother?" George inquired.

"He does. I have not been formally introduced to her, however. I am certain that will occur at tonight's musicale. I do not know when we are going to announce our betrothal to Polite Society."

"Why not do so at your ball?" Georgie said. "Surely, James and Sophie are holding one in your honor. They did for me during my come-out last Season."

"Sophie and Mama have made plans for one," she said. "But I had been a bit reluctant."

"Why?" Georgie pressed.

"Lord Bridgewater and I have had a bit of a rocky road leading up to our engagement," Mirella explained.

"Then I must hear all those details before I meet him," her sister proclaimed.

"Do not hold anything you hear against the marquess," Mama cautioned. "Lord Bridgewater is a good man, and it is apparent that he loves your sister very much."

"Now, I am truly intrigued," Georgie said. "Start at the beginning.

Mirella explained how she had been drawn to Byron during their meeting at Grasmere and how they had kissed during that time. She did not look at Mama, a bit embarrassed talking about such personal matters with her mother present.

"The Season began, and I was eager to know more about him," she shared. "Then he told me that he was to be betrothed to one of his neighbors and that we could no longer share an acquaintance."

"Was this betrothal arranged by his parents?" Georgie asked. "Before his father passed and he claimed his title?"

She chuckled. "It is far more complicated than that."

Mirella detailed the situation, punctuated by her sister's frequent reactions and comments. Finally, she brought her tale to a conclusion with yesterday's offer of marriage.

"So, you see, Georgie, Lord Bridgewater believed he was doing the right thing by offering for Miss Bowles."

"It is fortunate that he decided to give both this Miss Bowles and himself the freedom to pursue their separate happiness with others."

"You will not hold any of this against him? Judge him harshly when you meet him?" she asked.

"Do you love him?" Georgie asked pointedly.

"With all my heart."

"And he loves her," Mama chimed in. "Lord Bridgewater was quite vocal about his feelings toward Mirella at tea yesterday."

"Then I am satisfied," her sister said. "I simply want you to be loved and adored, my little sister. It sounds as if you are."

Georgie embraced her again, and Mirella felt relief, having crossed that hurdle.

They spent the next hour talking about nothing but Alexandra and what the babe had been doing. Georgie shared what a good father August was and how the birthing experience had brought them even closer together as a couple.

"I am so happy to hear that, Georgie," Mama said. "I know Pippa is happy from the few letters which have made their way back to England. It is only fitting that you, too, have found happiness with your husband. Will Alexandra be attending today's christening?"

Georgie laughed. "I doubt it. August does not want to stay in town long at all, Mama. The moment we drew near, he talked about how foul the London air is and how he worried about his daughter breathing it in. No, we are destined to leave for Edgefield tomorrow morning. Effie will be going with us. We will remain in the country until next Season."

"Do not forget the house party I am holding for the family at the end of this Season," Mama reminded. "Pippa, Seth, and little Adam will be home by then. I wanted us to all come to Shadowcrest and spend time together for at least a week."

"It will be exciting to introduce Alexandra to Adam and George. Will George be coming to the christening today?"

Mirella laughed. "James carts George about everywhere. This

is too important a day for James and Sophie for George not to be present. Even if he does nap through the entire event."

Mama rose. "Mirella and I will take our leave now. You need to get some rest before this afternoon's ceremony. I know how difficult it is birthing a child, and you did so just a month ago."

"I quite forgot to ask how your health is, Mama," Georgie said contritely. "Do you even feel up to holding this house party? I know the burden of its planning will rest with you since Sophie has no interest in these types of affairs. You will be giving birth in September, shortly after the house party ends."

"To have all my ducklings and their spouses and children under one roof means the world to me, Georgina," Mama replied. "Do not worry about me. I have done this many times."

"What, Mama? Hold house parties—or give birth?" teased Mirella.

"Both," Mama said smartly, and they all burst into laughter.

She and Mama returned to the Seaton townhouse, and Mirella went to the music room to practice. After she put in a good two hours, she went up to her bedchamber. She was still debating between two different gowns and finally chose one of pale yellow. The maid dressed Mirella's hair, and she went downstairs, finding Byron waiting in the foyer.

"I did not know you were here," she apologized.

"I only just arrived."

He took her hands in his and brushed a soft kiss against her cheek, causing those lovely tingles to ripple through her.

"Did you and Mrs. Andrews get to visit with your sisters this morning?"

"Only Georgie because Effie was assisting a mare who was giving birth. Effie should be at the christening this afternoon, however. And the best part was we got to meet Alexandra. Oh, Byron, she is a miniature Georgie, with blond fuzz and a sweet smile. August is so protective and loving toward her."

"I look forward to meeting her, as well as Lord and Lady Edgethorne. Will they be at tonight's event?"

"No. It is surprising how motherhood has changed Georgie. She has no interest in going to a social affair this evening. In fact, they are returning to the country tomorrow morning."

Mirella told Byron how August did not want his daughter breathing in the dirty London air, which had him roaring in laughter.

"At least I will be able to meet them this afternoon," he said. "We must also think about our wedding, Mirella. We have not discussed those details yet. Since it is your come-out, I assumed you will wish to finish out the Season."

"I have not even thought of it," she admitted. "I have been basking in the thought of you loving me." She hesitated. "I really do not think I can wait that long, Byron."

He slipped his arms about her and kissed her enthusiastically, despite the presence of the footman on duty by the door.

Breaking the kiss, he said, "You would make me the happiest of men if we were to wed sooner. Of course, I know you want your family to be present at the ceremony."

She frowned. "Mama is going to hold a house party at the end of August once the Season is done. She wants the whole family to gather since Pippa will be home from her honeymoon by then, and Lyric and Allegra will have given birth to their babies, as well. I suppose that would be the ideal time to wed because they all would be at Shadowcrest."

"Do not wait, Mirella," her mother said firmly.

Turning, she saw Mama had joined them. "How much did you overhear, Mama?"

"Only that the two of you are eager to start your lives together, and yet you are torn because you want your family at the wedding."

Mama took Mirella's hands in hers. "Lord Bridgewater is to be your family now, my dearest. You will always be a Strong and have the love of your brother, sisters, and cousins, but your loyalties must always lie with him. He is your priority. If it were me and I were so in love with this handsome marquess?" Mama teased. "Why, I would get a special license and wed as soon as possible. Our family can always celebrate your marriage in August when we all come together at Shadowcrest."

Tears welled in her eyes. "You do not mind, Mama?"

"I want what is best for you and Lord Bridgewater, Mirella. The two of you need to discuss the matter, but I believe I have already offered a perfect solution. Wed now and allow the family to celebrate the two of you later."

Mama released Mirella's hands, and she turned to Byron. "What do you want?" she asked.

He took her hands and squeezed them. "I want you. You are—and always will be—the most important thing in my life. I will say that I wish for Aunt Flora and Uncle Hugh to be present at the ceremony, whether we hold it here in town or at Shadowcrest."

Mirella bit her lip, unsure what to do. "All Strongs wed in the Shadowcrest chapel," she told him. "It would be impossible for Allegra and Lyric to come to the wedding, no matter where we hold it. They are both too far along to travel any distance by coach."

Her gaze met his. "I would still like to marry at Shadowcrest, but I wish to do so as soon as possible. Would you mind traveling to Kent for the wedding? It is not far, and we can always return here for the rest of the Season."

"We can do whatever you wish, my love," Byron said, his gaze adoring.

Mama clucked her tongue. "I think a Shadowcrest wedding would be lovely, but now that the two of you have found one another, do you really wish to continue with the Season? The Season will always be there, but I believe a honeymoon would be in order instead."

Her heart told her that her mother was right, and Mirella said, "I have gotten from the Season exactly what I wanted. A husband who will love and cherish me always. Mama is right, Byron. We should go to Shadowcrest and wed in the chapel and then go on our honeymoon. I would be happy to spend it at Bridgefield, getting to know the estate and your people."

He brought her hands to his lips, tenderly kissing her fingers. "That sounds perfect." Her fiancé looked to Mama. "How soon might a wedding take place in Kent?"

"How about a week from today, my lord?" Mama responded with a smile. "That will give you time to purchase the special license and for the rest of us to return to Shadowcrest and make the necessary preparations."

Mirella looked at the man she loved in wonder. This time next week, she would be the Marchioness of Bridgewater.

CHAPTER TWENTY-THREE

BYRON ESCORTED MIRELLA and her mother outside to his waiting carriage. Aunt Matty had left half an hour earlier with George and his nanny. James had sent the ducal carriage with a request that his aunt bring his son and nursery governess to Neptune Shipping early.

As he handed them up, Lady Effie rushed across the square.

"Might I ride with you, my lord?" she asked.

"Of course, my lady. It is nice to see you again."

She flung her arms about him. "Oh, I am so happy that you and Mirella are going to wed!"

Grinning, he hoped he would be the recipient of many of Lady Effie's enthusiastic hugs over the years.

"Not as happy as I am," he told her. "Your sister has changed my life for the better."

He assisted Lady Effie into the carriage and then joined the others, sitting next to his betrothed. Byron took her hand, not worried about hiding his affection for her now since these Strongs were an affectionate lot.

"Were you dancing when Lord Bridgewater asked you to marry him?" Lady Effie asked her sister. "Or strolling on a terrace at midnight?"

"When did you become such a romantic?" asked Mirella. "I

do not recall you asking the others about details regarding their engagements."

Lady Effie grinned. "I just wanted to see what you would say in front of Mama. I know you had to have kissed Lord Bridgewater, Mirella. More than once. Georgie has told me that kissing is important. So has Lyric."

His intended's face went red, and everyone laughed.

"Kissing is quite important, Effie," Mrs. Andrews told her youngest daughter. "If you have any questions about it, you can ask me."

The young lady looked taken aback. "Oh, no, Mama. I would never ask you. That is something that sisters share between themselves. Besides, other than kissing? I do not think you have much to tell me at all. After being around animals so much, I understand how they mate and give birth. You should have seen the mare foaling her little one yesterday."

"No details are required, Effie," Mrs. Andrews said crisply. "I am certain neither Mirella nor Lord Bridgewater wish to hear about it."

"Well, giving birth is a true miracle," Lady Effie said.

Mirella laughed. "I believe Mama is well-versed in that particular art, Effie. What do you think of Alexandra?"

"Oh, she is a darling babe. I barely have been able to hold her, though, because August monopolizes her all the time. Even Georgie has to beg him to allow her a turn," Lady Effie revealed.

Byron already knew that Seaton was besotted with his son. Hearing Lord Edgethorne was the same with his daughter helped Byron to realize that he would not have to hide his affection for his own children. That was the beauty of marrying into the Strong family. They were fiercely loyal toward one another and unashamed to openly show affection. He liked that they didn't shuttle their children off, rarely to be seen. It let him know that he and Mirella would be actively involved in the lives of their offspring, not to mention numerous nieces and nephews.

They had left in plenty of time, and still London traffic

crawled, making their journey considerably longer than planned. By the time they reached the docks and left the carriage behind, he learned the ceremony would start in less than a quarter-hour. He spied the Duke and Duchess of Seaton and the Marquess of Alinwood, their nine-month-old son. They moved in that direction, and the women began passing the babe around.

Lord and Lady Edgethorne joined them, and Mirella introduced Byron to her sister and brother-in-law. The marquess gave him a hearty welcome, pumping Byron's hand enthusiastically. He did his best not to gawk at the man. It was obvious the marquess had been to war and come home worse for the wear. Lord Edgethorne wore a black eyepatch to cover his missing eye and had facial scarring, yet he seemed as jovial as any man Byron had ever met.

Then he watched as Edgethorne turned to introduce his wife to Byron. Before she even looked at him, her gaze turned upon her husband. In that moment, the love this couple had for one another was palpable. Lady Georgina was one of the most attractive women Byron had ever met. She could easily have wed her choice within the *ton*, yet she had fallen in love with this disfigured marquess. It told him how real love truly was.

He took her hand. "It is an honor to meet you, my lady."

"Love my sister," the marchioness advised. "That is all that I—and anyone in this family—will ever ask of you. And please, call me Georgie."

Beaming, Byron said, "I am proud to be joining this family, and I will do my best to love Mirella and keep her happy."

"I have always known my sister would make an excellent mother." She studied him. "I believe you will make for a wonderful father, Lord Bridgewater. You will find us a large, loving family. I hope you will enjoy getting to know your future relatives. There are many of us."

"I am Byron, Georgie. And I look forward to meeting all the Strongs and their spouses."

A familiar figure joined them. "Have you heard about all

these superstitions?"

He thrust out a hand. "Mr. Strong. It is good to see you again."

Caleb Strong shook Byron's hand. "I wouldn't have missed this for the world." He looked over his shoulder. "What a ship!"

The new ship stood, tall and proud, next to the docks.

"I heard the christening could not take place on a Thursday or Friday," Caleb said. "James was telling me he learned from Sophie that Thursday is named after Thor, the god of storms. Sailors are a superstitious lot and would never sail on a ship launched on a Thursday."

The Duke of Seaton joined them, his squirming son in his arms. "And Fridays are also out due to Christ's crucifixion taking place on that day. Sophie told me even the British navy refuses to launch a new vessel on a Friday."

The duchess arrived, slipping a hand through her husband's arm. "I hope all of you will be able to stay after the christening occurs and board the new ship. James is going to helm *Sophie* and sail her along the Thames."

Byron had not been on a ship since he had returned from the continent and war. This occasion would be a much happier one than his previous voyage.

He was introduced to Mr. Fex, who had drawn up the plans for *Sophie*, and the architect's father-in-law, Mr. Purdy, who owned and operated the shipyard where the vessel had been built.

"It is time," Her Grace said.

They all moved closer to where the new ship was docked, standing next to its middle. He slipped an arm about Mirella's waist as they watched Caleb hand the duke a bottle of champagne for the ceremony. Byron noted it was more than the Strongs present. Looking at the large crowd, he saw a mix of people, supposing some worked in the shipping offices and warehouse of the company, while others were sailors or curious passersby.

The duke signaled for quiet, and all conversation ceased.

"Today, we come to name this ship, *Sophie*, after my wonderful wife."

As the crowd chuckled, Byron was again amazed at the openness of affection, both verbally and physically. He understood how unique these Strongs were, and he would do his part to let Mirella and all her family know just how much he treasured her.

His Grace continued with a very brief speech before handing the opened bottle of champagne to his wife. She held tightly to the bottle, splashing its contents against the side of the ship, saying, "I name thee *Sophie*!"

Cheers erupted, while the duke took his duchess in his arms and kissed her. She said something to him, which caused the pair to smile and kiss again.

Byron caught the couple's enthusiasm and kissed Mirella.

"I love you," he told her—and kissed her again for good measure.

He broke the kiss and saw the captain and Mrs. Andrews kissing, along with Lord and Lady Edgethorne.

"Come aboard, all you Strongs and loved ones!" cried the Duke of Seaton.

He helped Mirella up the gangplank, and Her Grace gave her family the grand tour of the ship, pointing out all the things that made this ship stand out from others in the Neptune Shipping fleet. As they moved throughout the ship, Mirella explained to him how Strong Shipping was Neptune's greatest rival and that all of London had been shocked when His Grace did not force a merger between the two shipping empires upon his marriage to the former Mrs. Grant.

"You see, Sophie still wanted to run the business that was hers. James understood that. He understood *her*," Mirella explained. "He had the marriage settlements drawn up so that Sophie would retain ownership and control of Neptune Shipping. While Strong Shipping will go to George one day, their other children will run their mother's company, both males and females."

Byron couldn't help but marvel. "Your family is most unique, my love."

She beamed at him. "You are now a part of us, Byron. Oh, I know soon I will no longer be a Strong in name, but I will always be one in spirit."

He kissed the tip of her nose. "I would not have it any other way," he assured her.

They completed their tour and returned to the top deck, where His Grace steered the ship with ease. Mirella told Byron how her brother had been a ship's captain before he became the duke.

"Seth also captained a ship before he took his title from his uncle. He is now Lord Hopewell," she explained. "His country estate is next to Shadowcrest. Pippa was friends with Seth's uncle long before she met Seth himself because he was always away at sea."

"I assume Lord Edgethorne was in the military before he claimed his marquessate?"

"Yes, August was a captain before his injuries. He sold his commission and came home to heal from his wounds. His brother, whom he was very close to, had been ill most of his life. Fortunately, August was able to see him once more before Lord Edgethorne passed. August then claimed the title. Georgie fell madly in love with him last Season."

He brushed his lips against her brow, his arm going about her waist, pulling her close to him. "I am only glad we met at Benbrook. You have proven so popular this Season, I am not certain you would have given me a second glance if we had not earlier been acquainted."

Mirella gazed intently at him. "I think you are wrong, Byron. I feel in my bones as if I have always known you." Then she smiled. "Of course, it was brilliant on your part to kiss me at Grasmere because I dwelled on those kisses for months!"

He returned her smile. "I did, too, love. I never forgot them—or you."

They stood on the deck, his arm fast about her, watching the people and sights along the Thames. When the Duke of Seaton pulled *Sophie* back into her slip at the docks, they had been gone a good two hours. He could taste the river on his lips and smelled it in Mirella's hair as he brushed his mouth against it.

"I will want you to meet my mother at tonight's musicale," he told her. "We will need to share with her—and my aunt and uncle—that we are now betrothed."

"And also share our wedding plans," she reminded him. "By this time next Tuesday, we will be husband and wife."

"I do like the sound of that," he told her, eager not only for the wedding ceremony, but the wedding night.

Already, Byron knew he could not be parted from Mirella. Though Bridgefield had rooms for its marchioness, ones which his mother still occupied, he did not want his wife using them. Oh, she could store her gowns there. Even bathe and dress in them. But nights were to be spent in his bed. Their bed.

A shiver of anticipation ran through him.

Mirella, naked and their bed, her long, auburn hair spilling about her.

Next Tuesday couldn't come soon enough.

CHAPTER TWENTY-FOUR

BYRON FELT ON top of the world as he entered the breakfast room. Mama and his aunt and uncle were already present. He greeted them and took his seat, a footman immediately pouring a cup of tea for him.

He had purchased the special license at Doctors' Commons yesterday before going to the christening ceremony of *Sophie*. He had also introduced his mother to Mirella last night, and Mama had been at her most gracious, complimenting his fiancée and asking questions about her family and the upcoming wedding.

Aunt Flora and Uncle Hugh had pulled him aside to express their delight in his choice of a wife. After the couple attended the wedding at Shadowcrest, they planned to return to Benbrook, Aunt Flora saying their work in town was now done.

His mother would finish out the remainder of the Season. She had told Byron that once she arrived at Bridgefield, it would be to live in the dower house. When he protested, telling her there was plenty of room, she had replied that it was time for Bridgefield to embrace its new mistress. Mama instructed him to have Mrs. Jarrod pack up all her things and have them moved to the dower house so that the marchioness' rooms would be freed up for Lady Mirella. Byron did not tell Mama of his plan to have Mirella only use those rooms a short while each day. Some things mothers did not need to be privy to.

Byron had already gone to Mr. Pilsbury's office, instructing him to meet with the Duke of Seaton's solicitor as quickly as possible. Byron told Pilsbury to give the man whatever he requested in the marriage settlements, even it proved to be more than he had been offering Lord Hampton. The solicitor had agreed to do so, and a meeting for Byron and His Grace to go over those contracts had been set for tomorrow afternoon.

That meant only one thing was left to do, something which might prove to be a bit difficult.

He had to tell Verity and Amity goodbye.

Byron had yet to tell Mirella of their existence and his support of them. With her kind and generous nature, he did not see that to be a problem. Next Season, he even hoped he could bring Mirella to meet the pair. Time was limited now, however, and Mirella and her family would be leaving town tomorrow afternoon once the marriage contracts were signed. They would be returning to Shadowcrest in order to make the wedding preparations. That left no time for him to take her to meet his niece and her mother.

Still, he had visited them a couple of times a week during the Season, and Byron believed he owed it to Verity to let her know of his upcoming marriage and early return to the country. He feared Amity would take his absence hard. The girl had never had a father figure in her life and had attached herself to him. Perhaps the day might even come when he and Mirella could host Verity and Amity at Bridgefield for an extended visit. Once he told his wife about the pair, Byron had a feeling she would insist upon that very thing.

"How are plans progressing for the wedding?" Aunt Flora asked him.

"Our solicitors have already met, and His Grace and I will go to Pilsbury's office tomorrow at one o'clock to sign the marriage settlements. Once that is completed, the duke and his family members who are in town will return to Kent, where they will see things are readied for next Tuesday's ceremony."

"When are we to leave for Shadowcrest?" Mama asked.

"I have told Her Grace and Mrs. Andrews that we would travel down Monday morning," he replied. "That will give us the rest of the day to settle in, and the wedding will take place in the chapel on the grounds the next morning."

"When will you take your bride to Bridgefield?" Uncle Hugh asked.

"After the wedding breakfast concludes," Byron said. "We will only be a few hours away from Mirella's childhood home, and I believe we will be frequent visitors to Shadowcrest. Her mother has her own manor house nearby when she and the captain are not residing in town."

Mama's nose crinkled a bit. "I am a bit . . . surprised that Mrs. Andrews is having a child at her age."

Yes, there was the judgmental woman he knew so well. Byron glared at her until Mama's eyes fell to her plate.

"Mrs. Andrews is still young enough to bear a child," he chided gently. "That is her and her husband's business. I hope you will pray that they have a healthy child, Mama."

She glanced up. "Of course, Bridgewater," she assured him. "After all, she is a former duchess. She can do anything."

He wiped his mouth with his napkin in order to hide his smile.

They finished with breakfast, and he called for his carriage so that he might go and visit Verity and Amity a final time.

Paulson volunteered, "Preparations for your departure are going smoothly, my lord."

He had informed his butler, who in turn had notified the staff, that Byron, along with his aunt and uncle, would not be returning to town for the remainder of the Season. Only his mother would see it out before she returned to the country.

"That is good to know, Paulson," he said.

The carriage now ready, Byron went outside and told his coachman to take him to St. John's Wood. He settled back against the cushions, thinking where he would be this time next week.

Home. With his wife.

He and Mirella had exchanged a few quick, heated kisses, but Byron was ready to consummate their marriage as quickly as possible. He had never desired a woman as much as he did Mirella and looked forward to coupling with her frequently. She had taken to kissing quickly, and he could not wait to explore more carnal activities with her.

The vehicle began to slow, and he sat up expectantly. When it came to a halt, he opened it himself and bounded down the stairs the footman had placed for him, hearing Amity's squeal of delight.

Byron glanced to his left and saw his niece and her mother moving toward him, returning home from a walk. Amity broke away from Verity and ran to him. He focused all his attention upon the girl as he knelt. She flung herself into his arms, and he hugged her tightly. Having been around the five-year-old, he now knew how much he wanted children of his own.

She gave him kisses all over his face, causing him to laugh, and he rose, lifting her onto his shoulders, a new round of squeals sounding.

Verity greeted him. "She enjoys your visits so much, Byron."

He brushed a quick kiss onto her cheek. "Shall we walk?" he asked.

Her brow furrowed, but she nodded, falling into step with him.

As they moved along the pavement, he said, "I have come to say goodbye for now."

"I knew this day would come," Verity said sadly. She came to a halt and gazed up at him. "I almost wish you had not come to say your final farewell, my lord."

Immediately, he noticed she no longer addressed him as Byron.

"It is not what you think, Verity," he told her. "I have recent-ly become betrothed."

Before he could continue, she shook her head. "Your fiancée does not approve of us," she said, bitterness in her tone. "I wish you had never come calling upon us, my lord. My daughter's heart will now be broken."

Verity reached up and took a protesting Amity from his shoulders, setting her daughter onto the ground, holding her hand tightly.

Glaring at him, she asked, "Will your new wife also insist that you stop your payments to us? I need to know in order to make plans."

Byron understood how protective Verity was of Amity. He couldn't blame her for being so prickly. She had experienced far more hardship than a woman of her age and breeding ever did, and he wanted to assure her that he was not abandoning them.

"First of all, I have yet to tell Mirella about the two of you because we just became engaged. And no, my obligation to you will not cease simply because I am taking a wife. I want Mirella to meet the two of you."

Verity looked at him in disbelief. "Are you certain about that, my lord?"

"Actually, I am," he insisted. "My betrothed is the kindest person I have ever met. She is not one to stand in judgment of you, Verity. Of course, I plan to tell her about the two of you. I even hope to have you come and visit us at Bridgefield."

Fat tears began to roll down her cheeks. "You would do that?" she asked, wonder in her voice.

"I most certainly would. Give it some time. I want to wed and have a honeymoon with my new wife, but I promise you that we will ask you to Bridgefield to visit us once we are settled."

"I am sorry to have judged you so harshly, Byron," Verity apologized. "But I think it would be wise for you to tell your betrothed about us as soon as possible."

He knew things were right between them once more since she had returned to addressing him by his Christian name.

"That is good advice, Verity. Mirella should meet you now

and not later. Let me go and talk with her now. If it is convenient, we will return to visit with you today. If she is otherwise engaged, I will try to bring her to see you and Amity tomorrow morning, since she is leaving town with her family tomorrow afternoon for Kent. We are to be wed there Tuesday next."

"Again, I did not mean to react so poorly," Verity said. "You are not—and never will be—your brother."

"Let me walk you back," he suggested.

Byron did so, holding Amity's hand as he did so. When they arrived, he gave the little girl a noisy kiss on the cheek.

"Are you already leaving?" Amity asked.

"Yes, but I will be bringing someone back to visit you soon. A very nice lady with beautiful red hair. She is going to be my wife."

"What's a wife?" the small child asked.

He thought a moment. "When a man finds that he loves a lady very much, he wants to spend all his time with her. It is called marriage. They are wed by a clergyman, and then they live together in the same house. If they are lucky, they even have children together."

Amity digested that information a moment and then said, "My papa doesn't live with us. He died."

Deliberately avoiding looking at Verity, Byron said, "Yes, he did. But you still have your mother—and you will have Mirella and me to love you."

The little girl frowned. "Mirella?"

"That is the name of the lady I love and will wed," he explained. "You may call her Aunt Mirella, and you can call me Uncle Byron."

"Aunt Mirella. Uncle Byron," the girl echoed and then smiled. "I like that."

"I am glad you do. Your aunt Mirella and I will come to see you either today or tomorrow, and then we will be going to the country until next spring. Perhaps you might like to come and visit us there." Thinking of her age, he added, "We could even put you atop a horse and see if you might enjoy riding."

Amity's eyes lit up. "I could ride a horse?" she asked in wonder.

"Yes."

She hugged his leg tightly, and Byron smoothed her hair affectionately.

"I will bring Mirella either later today or tomorrow morning, Verity. Definitely before we leave for Kent."

Tears glistened in her eyes as she said, "Thank you, Byron. You are a very good man."

He went to his carriage and instructed the coachman to drive to the Seaton townhouse. If Mirella were free now, he would ask that she accompany him to St. John's Wood. Usually, in the mornings, she practiced her pianoforte. He thought she would not mind giving up a bit of her practice time to meet Verity and Amity.

His carriage turned into the square where the Duke of Seaton's townhouse stood. He exited the vehicle and his footman said, "My lord, may I speak to you a moment?"

"Not now, Bryson," he said. "We can do so once we return home."

"But my lord—"

"I said later." He frowned at the footman, who nodded and returned to the back of the carriage.

Byron approached the door and knocked briskly. Dursley opened the door, his eyes going wide when he spied Byron standing there.

"I am here to see my fiancée," he declared. "Is Lady Mirella available?"

The footman did not smile, nor did he step aside to allow Byron entrance into the foyer.

Powell appeared and said, "I will handle this, Dursley."

The footman visibly relaxed and scurried away as the butler stepped into the open doorway.

"Lady Mirella cannot receive you, Lord Bridgewater." His tone was firm. "I must ask you to leave."

"Come, now, Powell. You know we are to be wed in less than a week's time. I insist upon seeing my intended. I know I am interrupting her practice time, but it is very important that I speak with her now."

The butler's face hardened. "I am afraid there will be no wedding, my lord. Lady Mirella has given instructions that you are never to enter this household again."

Before he could react, the door closed in his face. Byron stood there, stunned.

CHAPTER TWENTY-FIVE

IRELLA AND AUNT Matty breakfasted together. James and Sophie had already left for their shipping offices, trying to get as much work in as possible before the family departed for Kent tomorrow afternoon. James would be signing the marriage settlements on her behalf, and he had already shared with Mirella the terms currently being drafted by the two solicitors. He called them very favorable and told her how much he approved of her marriage to Lord Bridgewater.

Mama was breakfasting in her room, something she had begun to do during the past week. Mirella suspected that once Mama and the captain returned to town following the wedding, they would only attend social events of the Season sporadically, if at all. Her mother was now five months along, and without the need to escort her unmarried daughter to social events, she would most likely forgo them and rest. Mama had taken up sewing again, making things for the coming babe.

As for Byron and her, they had decided they were done with the Season. His aunt and uncle would be returning to the Lake District after the wedding, and she and her new husband were traveling to Bridgefield, where they would remain until next spring. Mirella was eager to see her new home and settle into it before the house party they would attend at the end of summer.

She could not wait for Pippa and Seth to meet Byron. If she were lucky, Mirella might even be carrying a child of her own by the time her sister returned to England.

She excused herself and instead of going to the music room, she made her way to the kitchens.

Cook greeted her. "Ah, Lady Mirella, I have those blueberry scones you requested." The old woman asked a scullery maid to fetch them.

"Thank you for baking them, Cook. They are for Lord Bridgewater. He is mad for blueberries and enjoyed your tarts so much the other day. I thought to surprise him with these scones."

The scullery maid brought a basket to Mirella, and she accepted it. Drawing back the checked cloth, she saw a good dozen scones nestled inside the cloth.

"I plan to take these to Lord Bridgewater now," she told Cook. "Thank you again."

"That man has put a smile on your face, my lady. I hope your kind gesture puts one on his, as well," Cook said.

Mirella collected her bonnet and reticule and asked Mrs. Powell if one of the housemaids might be allowed to accompany her on a few errands, and the housekeeper agreed to allow Elsie to act as a chaperone. Since James and Sophie had taken the grand ducal carriage and Aunt Matty had told Mirella at breakfast that she was using the second one to go visit a friend, Mirella asked a groom to saddle a horse for the cart.

Elsie grew round-eyed as the groom left. "But . . . I don't know how to drive a cart, my lady."

She laughed. "Well, it is a good thing that I do. I have grown up doing so in the country."

"Where are we going this morning?" the maid asked.

Indicating the basket she held, she said, "I had Cook bake something special for Lord Bridgewater, so we will drop these at his townhouse first. Then we are going to the shop where I purchase my art supplies."

Mirella had not brought her paints to town because she knew

she would have little time to herself and had preferred to practice the pianoforte during it. She had always planned, however, to replenish her paints before she returned to the country because the store she patronized in London always had a large array of colors in stock. She would take up her painting again in earnest once she arrived at Bridgefield. She had branched out from her usual landscapes and had been testing out a few portraits over the last year. Perhaps she might even try to paint Byron's portrait once they settled in at Bridgefield.

The last paintings she had created before the Season began, though, had been of Grasmere. She had an artist's eye for detail and had painted several landscapes of the places Byron had taken her to on their outing, even replicating Mr. Wordsworth's Dove Cottage as best she could. Her favorite work from all those she had done of Grasmere had been one of the view atop Helm Crag. Mirella decided because that place held special meaning, she would give Byron the canvas as her wedding present to him. She hoped they would return to Grasmere someday and climb to that same spot with their own children in tow.

The groom appeared, driving the cart. He got out and helped her into it, and Elsie scrambled up to sit beside her. Mirella placed the basket of scones at her feet and took up the reins. It felt good to be behind them. She had not driven since she had left Shadowcrest, nor had she gone riding in Hyde Park while in town. She hoped Byron enjoyed riding as much as she did since it was the best way to get about the country.

Traffic was fairly light in Mayfair, and they turned on the street where his townhouse was located. As the horse approached, she saw him dash from the house and into his carriage. Curious as to where he was off to in such a hurry, especially since she knew he had already purchased their special license, Mirella decided to follow and surprise him, thinking he might be going to White's to peruse the morning papers and visit with friends over tea.

"Aren't we going to stop and deliver the scones?" Elsie asked when Mirella did not slow the cart and turned onto the next street instead.

"No. That is Lord Bridgewater in the carriage in front of us."

"You are following him?" the maid asked, sounding unsure.

"Yes."

"But is that a *good* idea, my lady?" Elsie pressed.

"I think it is a grand one," she said airily. "The day is a pretty one. It will be nice to be out for a longer drive than we anticipated."

The maid looked uncertain but fell silent.

They went through Marylebone and skirted Regent's Park. Mirella wondered where on earth Byron was headed. Then she thought perhaps he might be going to a jeweler's for her wedding ring. Oh, it wouldn't do at all if she followed him there!

His carriage turned down a residential street, and curiosity got the better of her. The vehicle was far ahead of her cart, but it now came to a stop. She would be able to catch up with it within the next minute or so and see whom he might be calling upon.

Her betrothed exited the carriage and even from this distance, she heard the squeal of a small child. Mirella saw a woman on the pavement near the carriage. A young girl broke away from her, and she raced toward Byron.

Mirella pulled up on the reins, befuddled as the girl threw herself at him, kissing his face several times. Blood rushed to her ears in a loud whoosh as she froze, watching the scene unfold. Byron casually swung the child onto his shoulders and brushed a kiss on the woman's cheek.

"No," she whimpered, tears springing to her eyes.

He had a child. And another woman.

"Go, my lady," Elsie urged. "Quickly!"

Blindly, she lifted the reins again, flicking her wrists slightly to encourage the horse to move forward. The couple had begun walking along the pavement, facing away from her, but Mirella would have to turn left just before she reached them as they walked on the right side of the street. Otherwise, she would have to pass them and move up the street, and she couldn't risk being seen.

As she guided the horse down the street, she passed his carriage. The footman on the rear met her gaze, and Mirella bit her lip, tears beginning to fall. She kept driving, averting her head and looking to the left as she turned left onto the street, praying Byron would not look in her direction.

She drove a few blocks and found her way out of the neighborhood. All the while, Elsie sat beside her, not uttering a word.

When Mirella reached the large thoroughfare they had traveled upon earlier, she relaxed, knowing she was not lost and could find her way home.

But her heart had been shattered by the betrayal she had witnessed.

They reached Mayfair, and she returned the cart, the same groom coming out to take charge of it. She thanked him, polite as always, and took up the basket.

Handing it to Elsie, she said, "Take these. Eat them. Dump them. I do not care what you do with them. I will never eat a blueberry again, not as long as I live."

The maid accepted the basket, and Mirella took off, tears blinding her. She retreated to the gardens for five minutes, trying to calm herself.

Byron had betrayed her in the worst possible way. Although she knew many gentlemen of the *ton* kept mistresses—and even had children by them—she was not the kind of woman who would happily share her husband with anyone.

It was over. Her dreams of love and a life with him died within her. Thank goodness they had yet to announce their betrothal. Georgie had explained to Mirella that any time a broken engagement occurred in Polite Society, the lady was always blamed. And shunned. Whether she had broken the commitment or the man had, the *ton* looked down their noses at the lady, while taking the gentleman's side.

At least this way, no one would be the wiser. Oh, some

would certainly suspect, but since no formal announcement had been made nor the item placed in the newspapers, others would merely gossip at the apparent falling out between Lady Mirella Strong and the Marquess of Bridgewater. She would have to attend tonight's affair with her head held high, and under no circumstances would she speak to Lord Bridgewater.

She decided she would pen a letter to him, letting him know she no longer wished to wed him. She would give no reason for crying off. It would be up to him to figure out how his sins had driven her away. The only person who might clue him in would be his footman. He had been the same one who had ridden with the carriage when they had taken it to the christening ceremony. Mirella was certain he had recognized her. Yet she doubted the servant would speak up.

Going inside, she found Powell, taking the first necessary action.

"Powell, I know you take your orders from His Grace, and I assure you that I will speak with him the moment he returns to the house." She swallowed painfully. "However, something has arisen, and I believe it in my best interest to take preventative action."

The butler's brow furrowed. "Yes, my lady?"

Mirella realized she was talking in circles, not explaining herself clearly at all.

"I am asking that you do not grant Lord Bridgewater entry into His Grace's residence," she said. "I do not know if he will make an appearance, but if that occurs, under no circumstances are you to admit him."

"I see," Powell said, sympathy flashing in his eyes.

"There will be no wedding," she declared. "We will not be going to Shadowcrest until the Season ends. Cancel all arrangements and packing if you would."

Mirella would not turn tail and run to hide in the country. That would only make the gossip ten times worse. Instead, she would remain in town and dance with every eligible bachelor she could. She would talk and laugh and flirt as if nothing was wrong in her world. She only hoped Lord Bridgewater would take the high road and not spread any gossip about her.

"Yes, my lady." The butler eyed her for a long moment. "I am sorry things did not work out."

Her throat tightened. "Thank you, Powell."

Retreating to her mother's sitting room, which was just off the foyer, Mirella found paper and ink. She had no idea what she would write but knew she must do so. Lord Bridgewater must receive her note before this afternoon. She did not want him to call upon her or try and take tea with the family. She wanted to communicate to him that she did not wish for him to approach her this evening, as well.

She spread the paper in front of her, waiting to dip her quill into the inkwell until she knew what to write—and worried she would hover over the page for a very long time.

"Just begin, you ninny," she told herself.

She scrawled *My dear Lord Bridgewater* and stopped.

"No," she said aloud. "You are not mine, and you are certainly not dear to me. In fact, you are quite the opposite."

Mirella set aside the paper and took out a fresh piece, writing *Lord Bridgewater.*

Nothing came to her.

How was she to write to the man who had trampled upon her heart? Part of her wished to rush to James—the captain, too—and tell them of her fiancé's betrayal. The pair would pummel and pound the marquess until nothing was left of him, meaning no polite note need be written to him. Of course, she would never do such a thing, nor would she allow the two men to do so. Mirella knew she would never be able to tell her family the entire story. She would have to say something, however trivial it might sound. Though she knew Mama and Sophie would press her for details, she could not provide any because her brother and stepfather *would* likely beat Lord Bridgewater black and blue if she told them about the scene she had stumbled upon.

No, she would only go so far as to share that she had discovered something distasteful about the marquess and had reconsidered the marriage, finding it in her best interest to break all ties with him. They would respect her wishes.

It also meant she would have no one to share her story with. Mirella would have to keep things bottled inside her from now until forever. Her sisters and cousins, loving her as much as they did, would betray her confidence and tell what she had shared.

Then Mirella realized she did have someone she could speak with.

Aunt Matty . . .

Though her aunt's beloved had not betrayed her, he had left her for his army career. She knew Aunt Matty would keep her secrets.

Relieved that she would be able to unburden herself, Mirella took up her quill again, only to be distracted by a carriage stopping in front of the window which looked out upon the square. Her heart slammed violently against her ribs as she saw Byron get out of it and move toward the front door.

Quickly, she leaped to her feet and raced across the room, cracking the door open so she could hear the exchange. By now, Powell would have had time to assemble the footmen and direct them not to admit the marquess to the ducal townhouse.

She heard the knock and the door opening, listening to the exchange first between Dursley and Lord Bridgewater and then Powell and the marquess. Grateful that the servants had stood their ground against the intruder, Mirella closed the door again and returned to the writing table. This time, she wrote quickly and with conviction.

Lord Bridgewater —

I have had a change of heart regarding our betrothal and am informing you that I no longer wish to wed you. I intended to marry a man who was filled with honor and decency—and have discovered you possess neither.

Save your protests because I am a stubborn creature. Nothing you might say will convince me to change my mind.

Please do not call upon me or even speak to me at future social affairs. My family is quite loyal, as you have seen, and so approaching them will also do you no good.

I hope that you are gentleman enough not to speak ill of me or any of the Strongs. In return, I will keep silent about you and your disappointing behavior.

Lady Mirella Strong

She read through it once, happy with the strong wording. Once the ink dried, she folded and addressed it, glancing up to make certain his carriage had vacated the square.

Mirella left the sitting room and went straight to Powell.

"I have a note for Lord Bridgewater," she explained, passing it to the butler. "I would like it delivered at once. Hopefully, it will persuade him not to appear on His Grace's doorstep again."

"The marquess did come by to see you, my lady."

"Yes, I saw his carriage outside the window. Thank you for standing up to him, Powell. I know it was difficult to do, but you acted admirably. I will certainly let His Grace know."

"Thank you, my lady."

She went to the music room, doubting she could play, but knowing no one else would be inside it. Mirella sat in a chair, too numb to even think. All she knew was she had loved—and her foolishness at falling in love with the wrong man had destroyed her.

CHAPTER TWENTY-SIX

BYRON SOMEHOW WALKED back to his carriage, his head held high. He would not cause a scene in front of His Grace's townhouse. He had gone cold inside, moving as if he were underwater. He climbed the steps to the carriage and fell against the cushions, dropping his head into his hands as the door closed. His coachman pulled away, and he glanced out the window, watching the townhouse pass by.

He remained stupefied by Powell's words.

No wedding.

No entrance.

What had changed in the space of less than half a day? Only last night, he had been with Mirella, his shining light. Everything had been fine between them. Yet something vile and horrible had occurred. Something had been said to her, something that blackened his name so severely that she no longer wanted to see him, much less become his wife.

Could it be Jacinda Bowles behind this sudden change? Or her brother?

He doubted it. Rumor had it that Viscount Percival was on the verge of offering for Miss Bowles. Byron could not see Jacinda wanting to ruin that. And Lord Hampton would be glad to have his obstinate sister taken off his hands.

Then who?

His carriage arrived at his townhouse, and he hurried from it, retreating to his study and locking the door behind him. He could not bear to see anyone at the moment. He needed time alone to understand what had just happened. How to solve it. There had to be a way.

Because without Mirella, Byron would lose his own way.

Forever.

A knock sounded at the door. Byron ignored it. A few moments later, the knock came again.

"My lord, you have received a letter from Lady Mirella. The messenger said it was urgent."

Quickly, he sprang to his feet and raced across the room, flinging open the door. He snatched the note from the silver tray it rested upon.

"Tell the messenger to wait," he ordered. "I may wish to send my reply."

Paulson looked apologetic. "The messenger said none was expected. He is gone, my lord. Of course, if you have need, I can send a footman with your reply to Lady Mirella."

Disappointment filled him. Without a word, Byron turned and closed the door. He returned to his desk and sat, placing the letter atop it. Staring at it. Willing it to carry inside an apology. To say what he had heard from Powell had been a mistake.

His gut told him otherwise.

So, he sat and closed his eyes. If he didn't see it, it did not exist. Because he knew when he opened it, the words would gut him.

Cursing, he opened his eyes. By God, he had confronted French bastards left and right, running his sword through them as he led charges on the battlefield. He should not be so bloody terrified of a note from a woman.

With trembling fingers, he reached for it. Opened it. Read it. *And wept . . .*

Hurt sliced through him. Then anger. How dare Mirella think

he did not possess honor and decency? Then doubt crept in.

What if he didn't have honor or decency? What if his life had been a lie?

Byron had always tried to do the right thing his entire life, whether anyone knew of it or not. He recalled listening to a sermon at church when he was no more than seven or eight years old. The clergyman who delivered it said that Christ told his disciples not to perform righteous deeds so that others saw you do them. That you were not to bring attention to your good deeds in order to win the praise of your fellow man. He stressed you must keep your good deeds a secret—and God Almighty would be witness to your actions and repay you a thousandfold.

He had taken that message to heart, never drawing attention to what he did, knowing others benefitted from the good he brought into the world. That, in itself, was reward enough to him.

For the life of him, Byron could not understand why Mirella had turned on him so. What had poisoned her against him? Someone had sabotaged him so convincingly that the woman who loved him wanted nothing more to do with him.

Another knock came at the door. He was in no mood to see anyone, be it relative or servant.

"Go away!" he shouted, knowing that would suffice.

It didn't.

The knock sounded again.

He would have the head of whoever stood on the other side of that door. Every bit of wrath boiling inside him would be taken out on whoever disturbed him.

Marching toward the door, he flung it open and saw one of his footmen standing there. He had always liked Bryson, who was an affable fellow and polite as they came. The servant always went the extra mile to see to his duty and Byron's comfort. Suddenly, the rage emptied, and he felt limp, almost as if he might pass out.

"My lord, I must speak with you," Bryson said, urgency in his voice.

He recalled how the footman had asked to do so earlier today, but he was so weary.

"No, Bryson. I cannot. I am spent. Perhaps tomorrow."

He began to close the door, but the footman boldly placed his foot so that the task could not be completed.

"My lord," Bryson said. "You may dismiss me if you wish— but you *will* hear me out."

Byron was so taken aback, he stumbled backward. Quickly, his footman rushed forward, taking him by the arm, leading him to a chair. He feared he might burst into tears again.

Bryson returned and closed the door before coming to stand before his employer.

"I will give you this—you are persistent," he said, trying to gain control of his emotions and the situation.

"Lady Mirella saw you. With Mrs. Smithson and the girl."

Confusion filled him, swirling, keeping him from forming a coherent thought. All he managed to get out was a very weak, "What?"

Kneeling next to him, Bryson forced Byron to look at him. "When we went to see Mrs. Smithson today. Lady Mirella was there. I can't explain why or how, but she was driving a cart. She saw you with the child. And the mother." The footman paused. "I am afraid she leaped to the wrong conclusion, my lord. That *you* were the girl's father—and that Mrs. Smithson was your mistress."

His jaw dropped. Bryson had been in the household when Dawson had been the marquess. He might be among the handful of servants who knew of the relationship between Byron's brother and Verity. He had never spoken of Verity and Amity to his family, much less his servants. He merely gave the address in St. John's Wood to his coachman and was taken there. Yet this servant had referred to Verity by the name she had assumed.

"Were you entrusted with setting Mrs. Smithson up in her household?"

Bryson nodded. "I helped to move her to where she now resides, my lord. Keller and I were the ones to do so. His lordship confided quite a bit in Keller. The two of us helped find the house where Mrs. Smithson now resides. It was Keller and I who picked her up at her father's house and took her and her things there."

"I see."

Byron's thoughts continued to swirl, but he began to make sense of them. He replayed the scene in his mind today. Amity racing toward him, enthusiastically kissing him. His fond greeting to Verity. Placing his niece on his shoulders and strolling with Verity. If Bryson was right and Mirella had seen that, no wonder she was so angry and had broken their betrothal. It disappointed him that she had not spoken to him in person. Then again, if he were despicable enough to tell her how much he loved her while secretly keeping the knowledge of a mistress and child from her, it did not surprise him.

Mirella was no shrinking violet. She believed him to be disingenuous. If he lied about a mistress and bastard, she would think he lied about everything.

Including loving her.

Raking his hands through his hair, he told Bryson, "I am sorry I did not listen to you sooner. You tried to tell me. Warn me. I refused to listen."

"I understand, my lord. But you did listen now. That is what is important. Should I have the carriage readied so you might go to Lady Mirella?"

"No, I will walk. It will be quicker." He rose, offering the footman his hand. "Thank you, Bryson. I hope knowing what you just shared will save me."

The footman grinned cheekily. "Good luck to you, my lord."

Byron looked grimly at the servant. "Thank you. I will need it."

MIRELLA APPEARED AT tea, composed and in control of her emotions. She would not weep. She would merely state facts.

Everyone was already present when she arrived. Mama smiled at her fondly, causing the first crack in her exterior. The captain indicated for her to take a seat next to him. Sophie was in the midst of pouring out and handed her a saucer as Mirella took her place.

She took a sip of the hot tea, firming her resolve.

Setting it down, she said, "I must speak to you about a grave matter. It involves Lord Bridgewater."

"I thought the marquess would be joining us for tea," Aunt Matty said. "Unless James has scared him off."

James laughed. "He is too much in love with our Mirella to ever let that occur."

That burst her dam. The floodgates open, Mirella's tears began streaming down her cheeks.

"What is it, my dearest?" Mama asked, the concern in her voice driving yet another knife into Mirella's heart.

"He has a child!" she cried. "And a mistress."

Silence filled the drawing room. No one moved. No one said a word. She stood, all eyes on her, hurt and rage filling her.

The captain shot to his feet. "I will see him strung up," he said, his tone deadly.

"No, you will not," she scolded. "Sit."

He eyed her a moment, and Mirella saw new respect for her in his eyes. He took his seat.

With everyone staring at her now, eyes filled with shock and disbelief, she said, "I learned of this little family today. I saw them together with my own eyes. I wrote to him, calling off our engagement. I also asked Powell to make certain that the marquess is not to be admitted into the house."

James balled his fists. "I am with Drake. We will find this worthless piece and give him the lesson he deserves."

"No one will be beating anyone," she said crisply. "I have asked him not to speak to any of us. We will ignore him. This is all I wish to say about the matter." Mirella paused, swallowing. "I beg you not to approach me or ask to discuss it further."

Mama reached and took Mirella's hand. "I know you are hurting."

She withdrew her hand. "I am. But your sympathy will only leave my wounds open. If I am to heal, I must do it my way, Mama. Please understand that I am not shutting you out to be cruel."

"It is your way of surviving," Aunt Matty said.

"Yes." She stood, resolute. "I will attend tonight's event. I will not be a coward."

"Is that wise?" Sophie asked. "I am not trying to question you, but you are quite fragile now, Mirella. We all can see that. No one would think the worse of you if you skipped an event or two."

"I cannot let him think he has won. And he will if he keeps me from the Season. I will need all of your support like never before, but I am determined to attend tonight's affair."

"If that is what you want, that is what we will do," the captain said.

Suddenly, the doors flew open—and a disheveled Lord Bridgewater came racing through them. He slammed the doors behind him, throwing the lock. Immediately, pounding occurred and shouts sounded from the other side of the door.

Turning, he said, "I do not know how long the doors will hold because your servants are determined to keep me out, Your Graces. But I must speak to Lady Mirella."

Both James and the captain came to their feet as Lord Bridgewater hurried across the room. Mirella's worst nightmare was now being played out.

"I will tear you limb from limb," the captain threatened, balling his fists.

She leaped to her feet and raced to stand between her relatives and the marquess.

"No one is to touch him," she declared.

Then Mirella turned and slammed her fist into her former fiancé's nose. Blood shot from it, spilling onto his snow-white cravat. Her fist ached something awful, but she looked stoically at him.

"If you still have something to share with me, my lord, feel free to do so. I have nothing to hide from my family. I promise I will keep my hounds at bay. Say your piece—and leave."

He pulled a handkerchief from his pocket and held it under his nose. "You pack quite a punch, my lady. I hope after you hear what I have to say that I am never on the receiving end of it again."

"Enough!" James roared. "You are not welcome here, Bridgewater. Leave."

The marquess tossed his handkerchief to the ground. "I will not, Your Grace. Not until Mirella learns the truth."

He turned to her. "You think you saw me with my mistress and child. Who you really saw was my niece. My brother's bastard child—and the woman he ruined."

Mirella fainted.

CHAPTER TWENTY-SEVEN

"S HE'S COMING TO."

Mirella heard the voice from a distance and stirred. She was enveloped in warmth and reluctant to open her eyes. Then she felt a cold, wet cloth placed upon her brow.

And inhaled the scent of Byron.

Her eyes flew open, and she saw her family gathered around her, concern on their faces. She turned. Her gaze met Byron's. She realized she was in his arms and began wriggling, trying to escape.

"No, love," he said softly. "Be still. You fainted."

Indignantly, she told him, "I have never fainted."

His lips twitched in amusement. "Never say never."

Everything came rushing back to her. Seeing him with the woman and child. Penning the scathing note to him. Byron bursting through the doors of the drawing room.

"Is what you said true?" she asked quietly.

He nodded solemnly. "I would like to tell you about them if you are ready to hear it." He glanced up. "Might we have some privacy?' he asked of the others.

"Of course," Mama said, the captain slipping his arm about her.

"No," Mirella protested. "They need to know the truth as

much as I do." She smiled at him. "Besides, you know I will only go and tell them everything anyway. This way, I will not leave anything out."

"Very well," he agreed, looking about the room. "Have a seat if you will," he encouraged the others.

As they sat, she said, "You can put me down now."

He stroked her cheek with the back of his fingers. "That is not something I am willing to do, love."

A rush of warmth ran through Mirella. He loved her. He truly loved her—and not another woman. He had not been unfaithful to her.

"I am sorry I leaped to the wrong conclusion and did not give you a chance to explain yourself to me," she said.

"And I am sorry I had not thought to tell you of Verity and Amity," he responded. "I was going to. When I visited them this morning, I told them all about you and promised to bring you to visit later today or even tomorrow."

"Oh, dear," she fretted.

"Do not worry. Let me tell you about them first."

He told his story to them all, but Byron only looked at her as he spoke.

"I have already told you how much I thought of my older brother growing up. He was my inspiration in all I did and taught me everything I learned as a boy. I wanted to be just like him when I grew up, but Dawson wasn't the man I thought he was."

Byron paused, swallowing, and Mirella knew how difficult this was for him. She placed her hand to where his heart beat steadily and encouraged, "Go on."

She knew he was repeating some of his story for the benefit of her family when he said, "When I received word of Dawson's death, it almost destroyed me. I returned to England and found out the circumstances of his death and that of Lord Hampton's. I also learned that he had spent a majority of his time in town, drinking and gambling, neglecting Bridgefield and our tenants. Already disillusioned by his behavior and the manner of his death,

I was further shocked to learn that Dawson had fathered a child."

She knew Dawson's death had been a severe blow to Byron, as well as learning he was not the saint Byron had once thought. But to learn that his brother had fathered a child out of wedlock must have cut Byron to the quick.

"When he found out the young lady in question was increasing, he blithely told her he could never wed her because he was already betrothed. This betrothal had occurred when Dawson had just completed university. Jacinda was only ten and one at the time and was not told of it."

Mirella heard the bitterness creeping into his tone.

"He used that young lady shamelessly, and then he discarded her. Oh, Dawson was gentleman enough to provide her with a place to live, but my brother provided very few funds for her. Her family disowned her. Her father even placed a death notice in the paper, saying his daughter had died of a fever."

The women present gasped. Mirella turned to look at her relatives and saw the hard look in the eyes of both James and the captain.

Byron continued, saying, "I thought the yearly amount settled upon her was small, so I had my solicitor double it. Still, I was not ready to meet this woman or her child, so raw was my grief. When I returned to town this spring, I decided I must meet my niece and the lady my brother had ruined."

He smiled tenderly at her. "You will like Verity very much," he promised. "And Amity, who is five, is simply a joy to be around. With the increased funds I gave them, Verity no longer had to clean the house or wash their clothes. She was able to hire help for those tasks."

Aunt Matty clucked her tongue in disapproval, and Mirella couldn't help but agree. To think that a young lady had fallen in love with a handsome marquess and been used so badly and then abandoned by him hurt her heart.

"I have become friends with Verity. In truth, I look upon her as my sister-in-law because Amity is my niece. They will always be in my life, Mirella. I must care for them. They are an obligation I refuse to neglect."

Her hand went to cup his cheek. "I would never want you to keep you from that duty, Byron. I do want to meet them. In fact, I do not think they should be living separately from us. They should come to Bridgefield with us."

He smiled at her, the look in his eyes so tender that she almost came undone.

"You would allow that?"

"They are family," she insisted, smiling. "And you know how I value family."

"Mama had requested that she be moved to the dower house once she returns from this Season so that you might take up the rooms designated for the marchioness. I could give Mama new rooms in the house and allow Verity and Amity to live in the dower house."

"Or in the main house with us if your mother would prefer her privacy," she told him. "It is something we can work out."

Byron grew thoughtful. "Verity was very close to her mother."

"Then why didn't her mother stand up for her?" asked Mama, clearly distressed by the entire situation.

He looked out at the group. "She told me that her father is very controlling. That if it had only been her mother, the two of them might have moved to the country and led a quiet life. Instead, Lord Hall dictates what his wife is to think." He frowned. "Verity has seen bruises on her mother before. She fears her father abuses her mother."

"Then we must bring Lady Hall with us," Mirella determined.

James spoke up. "I know this Viscount Hall. He is a heavy gambler and a braggart. A most unpleasant fellow to be around."

"I have wanted to confront him about this issue," Byron revealed. "I have been reluctant to do so because I did not want him to retaliate against Lady Hall more than he already does."

Her brother smiled grimly, and a chill ran through Mirella as he did so.

"I am a duke," James stated. "You are a marquess. Together, we can bring down Lord Hall for his sins."

"Would you reveal that he lied about his daughter's death?" asked Sophie.

"It would not be to Verity's benefit to do so," Byron said. "She goes by Mrs. Smithson now and has no visitors other than myself. For Polite Society to learn what happened to her would shame her terribly. And it would affect little Amity, as well. I cannot embroil her in any scandal here in town simply to punish her father. In the long run, it would be Verity who paid the highest price."

"When Verity comes to Bridgefield, we can put out the word that Mrs. Smithson is your widowed cousin, and Amity is like a niece to you," Mirella suggested. "That way, there is the possibility that some country gentleman in the neighborhood might wish to offer for her someday."

"Then you will need to get word to Lady Hall," Mama said. "That she is to leave her husband and come to Bridgefield with her daughter and granddaughter. I know who she is and can speak to her at tonight's ball about this if you would like."

"That would mean a great deal to Verity," Byron said. "Even if Lady Hall only leaves with the clothes on her back, I will make certain to provide for her."

"You and I can see to Lord Hall's markers being bought up," James said to Byron. "We will then call in those markers. The viscount will be ruined financially. After that, no one will receive him socially. His wife, daughter, and granddaughter will be safely away from the fray."

Byron nodded. "Then see to it, Your Grace. I will reimburse you for my share of these markers."

James smiled. "You are about to be a member of this family, my lord. Surely, you should start referring to me as James."

Her fiancé grinned at her brother. "I would be more than happy to do so, James."

Mirella said, "We need to go now and see Verity and Amity. Let them know of the plans in motion."

"Do you feel up to it?" he questioned.

"I feel fine, Byron. Besides, I am eager to meet them. They must also come to Shadowcrest for our wedding."

He beamed at her. "So, the wedding is back on? And you will rescind the order given to Powell which banned me from this house? I had to fight my way into the house and drawing room, you know."

She brushed her lips against his. "I can think of no one else to wed. It is you—or no one, Byron. I love you too much to give you up."

He kissed her in front of her family, and she heard everyone chuckling.

The captain said, "Welcome to the family, Byron. You will find we are a kissing lot." He snagged his wife about the waist and gave her a quick kiss. "It seems we never can get enough of those sweet kisses from our women."

Byron stood, setting Mirella on her feet, and she asked, "Do I look a fright?"

"A few pins have come askew," Aunt Matty told her. "Nothing you and I cannot remedy. Let us go make you presentable."

A quarter-hour later, she and Byron were on their way to St. John's Wood.

"I have yet to ask how you even wound up in this part of town," he remarked.

She smiled wryly. "I was dropping off blueberry scones at your house when I saw you leave in your carriage." She shrugged. "I thought to surprise you with them when you reached your destination, so I followed you."

He took her hand. "Again, I apologize, my love. I came straight from Verity's to see you and ask you to accompany me to meet her and Amity."

"I know that now. Shall we make a pact never to be angry with one another again?"

He laughed. "Even as much as we love one another, we are not perfect, Mirella. There will be times when we are put out with one another. How about our pact consisting of always communicating with the other when we are upset or angry? That way, we will never get the wrong impression and leap to false conclusions."

"Agreed," she said. "Since we have no way to write up this agreement, it will be an orally binding contract." Smiling mischievously at him, she added, "And instead of signatures, we should seal the deal with a kiss."

One kiss turned into many, and they did not cease until the carriage came to a halt.

"I hope they will like me," she said.

"Mirella, they are going to adore you," he assured her.

Byron handed her down, and they knocked on the door, being admitted by a butler.

"It is good to see you again, my lord. Mrs. Smithson said you might be returning with a guest. She is in the parlor with Miss Amity. Follow me."

Mirella saw that the house was small and sparsely furnished. The same was true of the parlor they entered. Immediately, her eyes went to the woman sitting with a small child in her lap as she read to her. It was obvious the two were related. Both possessed the same golden blond ringlets and pale blue eyes.

Byron escorted Mirella across the room as Mrs. Smithson rose, setting her daughter down and eyeing Mirella eagerly.

"Mrs. Smithson, I would like you to meet Lady Mirella Strong, my betrothed."

Both women curtseyed to one another, and Mirella chuckled when the child also curtseyed.

"Since we are to be family, I would like to suggest that you call me Mirella."

Mrs. Smithson's eyes widened. "Truly? Has Byron told you my story, my lady?"

"Not only does Mirella know the truth, her idea is for you to leave town permanently."

"Yes," she said quickly, seeing the panic flash in the other woman's eyes. "I wish for you to come and live with us at Bridgefield."

"Please call me Verity." Tears cascaded down her cheeks as she wrapped an arm about her daughter's shoulders. "This is Amity. My pride and joy."

Mirella knelt. "Hello, Amity. How are you?"

"I am good, Aunt Mirella."

She warmed at the familiar address and suspected that Byron had already told the girl to call her aunt.

"Would you like to come and live in the country with us and your mama?"

"Uncle Byron told me I could come visit. And ride a horse," the girl said brightly.

"It will not be a visit, Amity. You will live with us there. I hope you will like that."

The child nodded, smiling sweetly.

A maid appeared, saying, "It is time for Miss Amity's milk and bread."

"Do I have to go, Mama?"

Verity nodded. "Yes, you do. You will be seeing Uncle Byron and Aunt Mirella again very soon."

"Promise?" Amity asked.

"You will be coming to our wedding next Tuesday," Mirella told the girl. "You can even help decorate the chapel with flowers if you'd like."

Amity clapped her hands gleefully. "I want to do that. I like flowers." She skipped to the maid. "I am going to a wedding."

Once her daughter had left, Verity asked them to sit, saying, "I cannot thank you enough for what you are doing for me and my girl. To take us into your own home. It is more than generous."

"You are family," Byron said. "Family looks out for one another. Mirella has taught me that. She would also like your mother to come, as well."

"Mama? What . . . how . . ."

"Leave that to us," Mirella said firmly. "Byron has explained that your mother is in a very difficult situation and we would like to extricate her from it."

New tears brimmed in Verity's eyes. "Oh, if you could save Mama, that would be so wonderful. She has never seen Amity. She always longed for grandchildren." Verity paused. "And her freedom from Papa."

"We will close up this house for good," Byron said. "It is rented, and my solicitor will take care of doing so. If you ever wish to come to town again, you will stay with us in the family townhouse."

"What of my staff?" Verity asked. "They have been so loyal to me. I cannot abandon them."

"We will find them positions," Mirella promised. "Whether that is in town at Byron's residence here, at Bridgefield, or even at Shadowcrest where I grew up, no one will be left behind."

"I cannot believe this is happening," Verity said. "We have been alone for so long. Family is the most important thing to me," she said. "We will be family—and I hope you and I will also be friends."

They briefly explained to Verity that she would be Mrs. Smithson when she arrived in Kent, a widow with a young child, and a distant cousin to Byron. She was also told to pack her things immediately because it had been arranged for James to send a carriage for her and Amity in the morning.

"Your mother will hopefully be in the carriage," Byron explained. "We will speak with her at tonight's ball. It will be up to her, though, whether she chooses to leave Lord Hall or not." He paused. "Things are about to become very difficult for your father."

"Good," Verity said. "He is a terrible person."

"We must take our leave now," Mirella said. "Byron is sending word to Bridgefield to notify them of your arrival. He will also see that you and Amity are brought to Shadowcrest to witness our wedding."

Verity threw her arms about Mirella. "You are both so good to me. I will never be able to repay you."

"There is no need to think in those terms," she replied. "You are with those who love you and will always stand by you."

Verity walked out to the carriage with them, and they waved goodbye to her.

"A lot still has to happen," Byron said once they were inside the vehicle. "Hopefully, your brother will see to the markers being bought up from the gambling dens Lord Hall has frequented. When we meet to sign the marriage settlements tomorrow, I will give Pilsbury instructions regarding Verity's house. I think it best if I also provide a dowry for Verity and Amity. He can draw up those papers, as well."

Mirella snuggled against his shoulder. "That is thoughtful of you. I only hope Lady Hall will be willing to break away from her husband and come to Kent."

"We will see tonight," he said. "Hopefully, by this time tomorrow, the three of them will be safe at Bridgefield."

CHAPTER TWENTY-EIGHT

"I SEE HER," Mama said. "She is speaking with Lady Pance."

Mirella and Aunt Matty turned slowly so as not to be obvious.

"Lady Pance is a talkative creature," her aunt said. "I will sacrifice myself in the interest of helping Lady Hall to escape not only her husband but the countess. If I am still engaged in conversation with her after an hour, I expect to be rescued."

She giggled. "We will not leave you stranded, Aunt Matty."

They moved to where Lady Hall stood with Lady Pance and greeted the pair. Slowly, Aunt Matty skillfully turned her body and that of Lady Hall's over a few minutes of conversation, allowing Mirella and Mama to free Lady Hall.

"We must speak of urgent matters," Mama told the viscountess. "Come with us."

Her mother did not give Lady Hall a chance to protest. She slipped her arm through the other woman's and guided her away from those gathered in the ballroom.

Mirella followed, saying, "Do not leave the ballroom, Mama. We mustn't cause anyone to be suspicious."

"Suspicious?" Lady Hall said, a worried look on her face. "Oh, is this a test? Did my husband send you?" True fear was visible on this woman's face.

"No, my lady," Mama assured her. "We are going to save you."

They stopped in a corner of the room, next to a large, potted plant which partially obscured them. Mama maneuvered the viscountess so her back was to the room. Mirella knew why her mother did so because Lady Hall's face would give away the scheme.

"Why have you brought me here, Your Grace?" Lady Hall asked, visibly trembling.

Mama slipped her arm through the other woman's. "It is Mrs. Andrews now. I am a widow, now married to a former sea captain."

Mirella kept her expression bland since she faced the crowded ballroom and said, "We wish to reunite you with your daughter."

Lady Hall started. "You know Verity? How? How is she?" Tears misted in the woman's eyes.

"I am betrothed to Lord Bridgewater," she explained. "The younger brother of the man who took advantage of your daughter. My fiancé has been paying for the house Verity and Amity stay in and—"

"Amity?" the viscountess interrupted. "The babe was a girl?"

She realized Verity had had no contact at all with her mother since being forced from her father's house.

"Yes. Amity is five now, and I assume exactly how your daughter looked at that age."

Lady Hall's mouth trembled. "They are well?"

"We do not have much time," Mama cautioned. "You never know who might see us and get word back to Lord Hall."

Mirella nodded. "Listen carefully, my lady. You are being given a choice. I am to wed the marquess next Tuesday in Kent at my childhood home. Lord Bridgewater's country estate is also in Kent. The two of us wish to have Verity and Amity come to live with us in the country. They have been here in town since you last saw your daughter. They are traveling tomorrow. More than anything, Verity wishes you would leave Lord Hall and join her at Bridgewater."

Lady Hall sadly shook her head. "He would never allow it, Lady Mirella. Hall is cruel. He would hunt me down and force me to return. Not that he wants me. He never did. I was merely a hefty dowry to him. A worthless woman who could never provide him with a son."

"Lord Hall will not have the resources to locate you, my lady," she assured her. "My betrothed and brother—the Duke of Seaton—are very angry at how your husband cast Verity from her home and declared her dead. Verity has told us how you love her and would have supported her, despite the terrible mistake she made."

Mirella paused. "Amity is certainly no mistake. Your grand-daughter is bright and beautiful. And she needs you. Just as your daughter does. Because of your husband's cruelty, His Grace and Lord Bridgewater are going to make Lord Hall pay."

Lady Hall gasped. "How? Why?"

"The how is unimportant," Mama said. "The why is because we believe in family. Amity is Lord Bridgewater's niece, and he wants her close to him and my daughter. Verity, too." Mama paused. "I am a mother, the same as you, Lady Hall. If it were me, I would accept the help being offered and escape town and the vicious gossip to come. My stepson and Lord Bridgewater will ruin Lord Hall. They possess all his markers and will call them in. He will be left penniless."

"And he won't have a clue where you have gone," Mirella added. "Or who helped you. The question is, are you willing to break away from him?"

Lady Hall bit her lip. "If what you say is true, I would be a fool not to accept your help. Hall is already an angry man who beats me regularly. If he is broken financially, he will probably kill me." She smiled weakly. "Besides, I would do anything to be with Verity and Amity."

"Then you must say nothing to him," Mama cautioned. "Go home and pack. Do it yourself. Not even the servants should know."

"Only take what is absolutely necessary," Mirella warned. "Lord Bridgewater will replace anything you leave behind."

"May I bring my lady's maid?" Lady Hall asked. "She has been with me for years. I cannot allow her to suffer Hall's wrath. He very well could beat her to death, trying to get out of her where I have gone."

She and Mama exchanged glances, and Mama nodded. "Yes. You may bring her. Tell only her what is going on when you return from the ball. Have her undress you from your finery and then dress you again in a day gown. While your husband goes to bed at dawn, slip out, through the kitchens, and you and your maid will be met."

Mirella had learned that James would have three sailors from Strong Shipping meet Lady Hall and take her to Verity's. The captain was sending another three men from the Neptune Shipping warehouse to Verity's, and they would accompany the women to Bridgefield in an unmarked carriage.

"By the time your husband awakens tomorrow, you will already be in Kent," she assured the viscountess. "With your daughter and granddaughter."

A sob escaped from Lady Hall, and Mama quickly led the woman from the ballroom, skirting the crowd and exiting out a door leading to the terrace. Mirella chose not to follow and draw unnecessary attention.

The plan was in motion now. All that remained was to ruin Viscount Hall.

BYRON AND JAMES finished signing the marriage settlements at Mr. Pilsbury's office. They had requested that their appointment be moved up to this morning. Already, James' men had reported to the duke that they had retrieved Lady Hall and her maid and driven them to her daughter's house in St. John's Wood. From there, the captain's men had loaded the two women into the waiting carriage containing Verity and Amity. A separate carriage with their things and two of Verity's servants had already left for Bridgefield.

The documents now official, James received his copy, while Pilsbury provided Byron with a copy for himself and one for Mirella. He had wanted her to have one of her own. By now, his fiancée should also be packed and ready to leave for Shadowcrest with the duke and duchess. Her mother and the captain would journey to Kent tomorrow, while Byron, Mama, and his aunt and uncle would leave for Bridgefield.

Byron had asked that all servants be cleared from the breakfast room this morning, and it was then that he had broken the news to his relatives of the child Dawson had fathered. His mother had wept, but she said she was eager to meet her granddaughter. He explained how Verity would continue to be known as Mrs. Smithson to all the servants, both here in town and at Bridgefield, and that they would claim she was a distant, widowed cousin. He shared how he hoped one of their neighbors might recognize Verity's goodness and offer marriage to her, allowing her to find happiness and remain in the neighborhood so they might see her often.

He empathized how they must address Lady Hall as Mrs. Hall. Without going into any detail, he said he and the Duke of Seaton were assisting Lady Hall to be reunited with her daughter. He could tell from Mama's face that she had read the announcement of Verity's supposed death and why Lord Hall had disowned his daughter. Mama even mentioned how divorce would be out of the question since the process was quite expensive. Byron revealed that Lord Hall would be an impoverished man by the end of the day.

No one asked him how he knew this, but Uncle Hugh had given Byron a nod of approval.

"Anything else, Pilsbury?" he asked his solicitor.

"No, my lord. I will see that the lease on Mrs. Smithson's house is not renewed. In fact, I will notify its owner that the house has already been vacated. While I am not expecting him to refund the remaining portion of the rent for the rest of this year, he will be free to lease it again."

Byron and Mirella had discussed where Verity's servants would go, and arrangements had been made regarding them.

"I suppose that is it," he said. "I will be at Bridgefield until next Season. Write if you have need of me."

He left the offices, climbing into the grand ducal carriage, sitting opposite James.

As the carriage took them to Lord Hall's townhouse, Byron said, "Thank you. You have involved yourself in my affairs. Without your help, I doubt I would have thought of this plan, much less been able to pull it off with such speed."

James smiled, and Byron could see more of the sea captain than duke in him.

"You are family," the duke said. "You love my sister. That is more than enough."

They arrived at the viscount's townhouse, and his butler told them, "Lord Hall just left for White's, Your Grace. My lord."

"Then we will speak with him there," James said easily before adding, "If I were you? I would pack my things and tell all the servants to do the same. Your employer will not have two farthings to rub together by the end of this day. I will be happy to write references for any servants who request one. Spread the word amongst your staff to report to the Strong Shipping offices next Wednesday if those references are needed. I will take time to write them personally myself. I would do it earlier, but I have been called out of town for the next several days."

The butler's eyes widened in surprise. Recovering, he said, "That is most generous of you Your Grace. I will inform the staff." He paused. "Thank you."

They returned to the carriage, and Byron said, "That was most generous of you, James."

"No reason for hardworking servants to be caught up in the scandal, much less have a hard time finding employment. Lord Hall does not strike me as a man who would bother to write references in a time of crisis. It would be unfair to punish the servants for their employer's sins."

When they arrived at White's, Byron saw his future brother-in-law smile. He was glad he was on the good side of this powerful duke.

They entered the club, one which Byron had never visited, and were greeted profusely.

"Ah, Your Grace. It is good to see you," said a nattily dressed man who was obviously in charge of the establishment.

"This is the Marquess of Bridgewater," the duke said easily. "We are looking to speak with Lord Hall. Might he be here?"

"Yes, Your Grace. He is in the second Morning Room. Might I bring you coffee? Tea?"

"No. We will not be here long, I am afraid, but thank you kindly."

The servant must have understood that the duke had business. Byron watched him nod politely and scurry off. He accompanied James into a room filled with gentlemen who perused the newspapers or sat chatting idly, drinking coffee or tea.

"Where is he?" James asked quietly, scanning the room.

Byron located the viscount. "At the second table near the windows. Sitting by himself." Not quite certain what the duke had in mind, he added, "I will follow your lead."

James strode toward Lord Hall, and Byron noticed the duke's commanding presence had drawn the eye of every man in the room. He glanced over his shoulder and saw other gentlemen gathering at the doorway to the room, ready to relish the verbal blood they anticipated being shed.

Approaching the table, James asked, "Lord Hall?"

The viscount glanced up from his newspaper, his eyes going wide. Springing to his feet, he said, "Your Grace. It is an honor."

James indicated his companion. "This is the Marquess of Bridgewater."

Turning to look at Byron, Lord Hall said, "Ah, yes. I knew your brother well."

"I suppose you knew him from the gaming hells, my lord?" he inquired.

Hall smirked. "Why, yes, I did. Bridgewater was quite charming and enjoyed the turn of a card."

"As do you, my lord?" James asked, and Byron sensed his soon-to-be brother-in-law moving in for the kill.

The viscount chuckled. "I do enjoy card play, Your Grace. Perhaps we might spend a night together in the gaming hells. I have never seen you in the establishments I frequent."

"You won't be frequenting them ever again," James said flatly. He paused, and Byron knew it was time for him to step up and take the lead.

"You are finished, Lord Hall," he told the viscount. "His Grace and I have purchased all your markers."

The man blanched. "*All* of them?"

"Yes," Byron said. "It took a bit of doing because I do not think there is a gaming hell you have not frequented, running up large debts at each of them. His Grace and I are now in possession of every marker." He paused, staring at Hall. "Every. Single. One."

The viscount visibly trembled. "Is . . is there a reason? Why you would purchase these?"

"You have behaved very poorly," Byron said, not wanting to mention Verity or Lady Hall by name. "*Very* badly. You have put a blight on your family's name. Your dead daughter is mostly likely rolling in her grave, seeing what her father has done."

Understanding slowly dawned in the viscount's eyes. Byron knew this man comprehended why they were here.

"Bridgewater?" he croaked. "This is because of . . . that . . . business?"

"Yes. I am now Lord Bridgewater. And I take care of my

family. *All* my family."

He hoped he conveyed—without naming Verity and Amity—exactly whom he meant. Byron glared at the man a moment, watching him squirm under the scrutiny. He turned, nodding as James dealt the final blow.

"Bridgewater and I will be calling in your markers, Hall. Today. Every last one of them."

"But . . but . . . they number . . . I owe . . . in the thousands," the viscount protested weakly.

"You are correct," James said, glaring at the man who was now breaking apart before their very eyes.

"I cannot pay the full amount, Your Grace," Hall said hoarsely.

"Then sell anything that isn't entailed. Property. Furniture. Artwork. Immediately. Lord Bridgewater and I will not be kept waiting. Is that understood?"

"Yes, Your Grace," the viscount whispered.

James looked to Byron. "I could use a strong cup of coffee, Bridgewater. And one of my cook's scones."

"That sounds heavenly, Your Grace," he replied, doing his best to keep a straight face as dozens of eyes peered at them.

The duke glanced about the room, as if only now noticing all the gentlemen eavesdropping on the conversation.

"Bridgewater is to wed my sister, Lady Mirella, in a few days' time," he announced. "Our family is most pleased with the match."

Murmurs filled the room and as he and James left White's, dozens of men shook Byron's hand or gave him a friendly pat on the back, offering him congratulations.

Only when they were inside the carriage and it pulled away from White's did both men burst into laughter.

EPILOGUE

Shadowcrest—1 September 1811

MIRELLA WOKE FIRST, savoring her husband's warm front against her back. Even in sleep, he held her close, his arm possessively around her waist.

Her expanding waist.

Already, she could note the changes in her body. Her waist thickening. Her breasts growing tender and becoming slightly larger. She was craving any kind of bread with jam spread across it, the more, the better. For the first two months, she had awakened feeling nauseous. Thank goodness she had never vomited. They had found if she kept a piece of fruit by the bed and nibbled on it when she awoke—even before leaving the bed—the nausea subsided. That was gone now, as was the fatigue of those early weeks.

She estimated she was three months along now. They had yet to say anything to anyone, keeping the sweet secret to themselves, relishing it for a bit. Today, though, was Byron's birthday. Mirella had told him with the house party ending in two days, now was the time to announce the coming child and celebrate his birthday.

It had surprised her when he told her that he had never truly celebrated his birthday. She supposed it was because he had been ignored by his parents, who had favored their firstborn son.

She could wait no longer and began stroking his muscular forearm. Soon, he was nibbling her neck, his hand stroking her belly, going lower. He slid a finger into her, and she arched against him, moaning as the deep strokes brought her to orgasm. She started to muffle her cries of ecstasy, knowing she had Pippa and Seth on one side of their bedchamber and Georgie and August on the other. Across the hall were Lyric and Silas, while next to them were Allegra and Sterling. Then again, all her sisters and cousins were in love with their spouses, so Mirella didn't bother to keep quiet. Let them all know she was in love with the most perfect man in the world.

That is, he was perfect for her.

Byron turned her now onto her back, his hands roaming her body, his kisses hard and demanding. This husband of hers had taught her so much about physical pleasure since their wedding. He could be wildly exciting one moment in bed and then tender the next. All Mirella knew was that she would always love one man for the rest of her life.

He kissed his way down her body, feasting on her full breasts, bringing her to another orgasm. She panted, out of breath.

With a wicked grin, he teased, "Oh, you are so easy to arouse, love. I think I could merely look at your breast, and you would come for me."

She sighed. "I know it. And I love that."

Byron kneaded her breasts as he kissed his way further down her body, finding her core and slipping his tongue inside. His hands moved to her hips as his tongue toyed with her. Mirella writhed beneath him.

"I need you in me. Now," she commanded.

He grinned. "I never knew how tyrannical you were. You order me about in bed as if you were Wellington himself."

Smiling lazily, she said, "Wellington never did this to you."

Mirella encircled his swollen cock, stroking it, seeing the

satisfied smile appear on his face. Soon, she had him panting and eager for her. He pushed her hand away and thrust into her, burying himself to the hilt.

"Ah," she whispered. "That feels so good."

"Then this will feel even better."

He began their dance of love, moving in and out of her, kissing her, touching her, branding her as his. When he spilled his seed inside her, collapsing atop her, she wrapped her arms about him, holding him to her.

Byron kissed her again, a long, drugging kiss that made her want to make love all over again. She told him so and he laughed, pulling her along with him as he turned so that they lay on their sides, facing one another.

"Happy birthday, Husband," she said, touching her lips lightly to his. "Just think—we met for the first time this day last year. At Grasmere. I recall your aunt had a cake baked, and we ate it at dinner."

He brushed his lips against her brow. "And then we went to the drawing room and you played for us." He looked at her in wonder. "I had never heard music played the way you performed that night, Mirella. I believe that is when I fell in love with you."

Kissing her again, he broke the kiss, holding her cheek to his chest, stroking her back. "Who knew a year later, we would be wed, and you would be carrying our babe."

"I do want to tell the others today," she said. "With my entire family here, it is the right time. That way, I do not have to write a dozen letters and repeat the news over and over." She paused. "I do hope that Amity will be happy about the babe."

"Oh, do you think her nose will be out of joint, not being the center of attention?" he teased.

"Perhaps a bit," she said. "After all, she gets quite a bit of attention being the only child at Bridgefield."

"For now. I am certain more will follow this one. And think how good she has been around the other babes during this family house party. Why, she and Adam almost seem like best friends.

And she has been very good with Alexandra. I haven't really seen her with the smaller ones, though."

She laughed. "That is because Allegra and Lyric's babes are infants, Byron. They were only six weeks old when they arrived at the house party. Amity has not been interested in them because all they do is sleep and eat and fuss a bit."

"Is that what infants do?" he asked, kissing her again, long and slow.

"They do. And look adorable," she said saucily.

"Oh, so the babe will take after you?"

"If you think I am adorable, then yes. He—or she—will be incredibly adorable."

They both laughed, and then Byron rang for her maid and his valet. After they dressed, they went down to breakfast. It was served buffet style since there were so many of them coming and going.

All through the day, she looked for the perfect time to share her news with her family, wanting everyone to be present. Yet there was always someone gone. Even at dinner, both Georgie and Lyric excused themselves for a time, having to go to the nursery to check on their little ones.

Finally, they all gathered in the drawing room. Mirella could tell Mama was tired. She would give birth in a couple of weeks, and everyone had praised her for putting together such a wonderful party to welcome Pippa and Seth home and allow the entire family to come together.

"Play something for us, Mirella," her mother asked.

Going to the pianoforte, she didn't think she would play in total silence. There were too many people talking and laughing. When she struck the first few notes, however, conversations ceased. Mirella put heart and soul into the composition, finishing minutes later, the last chord sounding.

Knowing she had everyone's attention, she said, "This is the only time I think everyone has been quiet, so I will tell you now that Byron and I will be welcoming a new little Balfour come next

February."

Cheers erupted throughout the room. Byron's brothers-in-law pumped his hand enthusiastically as the women in the family gathered around Mirella, giving her hugs and kisses.

Aunt Matty said, "I knew he was for you from the moment I saw the two of you together at Benbrook."

Effie said, "I agree. It was obvious you were both smitten with one another."

She placed her hands on her belly, rubbing it. "It is hard to believe this next generation of Strongs is growing. Well, the babe will be half-Strong, half-Balfour."

Mama framed Mirella's face with her hands. "Oh, my darling girl. I am so thrilled for you. You will make for a wonderful mother, and Byron will be an excellent father."

The captain joined them, saying, "What Byron doesn't know, he can learn from me. After I learn about babes myself, that is."

Everyone laughed, and her stepfather encircled her with his strong arms. He kissed the top of her head. "You will be a good mother, Mirella. Just as your own mother is."

"I will certainly look to Mama for guidance."

Verity took Mirella's hand. "I am so happy for you and Byron. It is nice that our family is growing."

She smiled at Verity, who in a short time had become like another sister to her. Mirella looked out at all her family, happiness radiating from them all.

It was good being a Strong—and finding her soulmate as so many of them already had. She looked across the room and caught her husband's eye.

"I love you," Byron mouthed, breaking away from those gathered around him.

He came to her, his arms going around her, his warm mouth touching hers in a sweet, gentle kiss.

Mirella told him, "I have all I could ever wish for in you."

Smiling down at her, her husband said, "You are the one I was looking for. Waiting for—even when I did not know that was what I did. And in that quest for love, Mirella, I have found you. I am complete, my love. And utterly content."

Byron kissed her again, the kiss full of their shared love, one which promised her that he would be there for all their tomorrows.

About the Author

USA Today and Amazon Top 10 bestselling author Alexa Aston lives with her husband in a Dallas suburb, where she eats her fair share of dark chocolate and plots while she walks every morning. She enjoys travel and sports—and can't get enough of *Survivor* or *The Crown*.

Her Regency and Medieval historical romances bring to life loveable rogues and dashing knights. Her series include: *The Strongs of Shadowcrest, Suddenly a Duke, Second Sons of London, Dukes Done Wrong, Dukes of Distinction, Soldiers and Soulmates, The St. Clairs, The de Wolfes of Esterley Castle, The King's Cousins, Medieval Runaway Wives,* and *The Knights of Honor.*